CAPTIVE

By the Author

Healing Hearts

No Boundaries

Love's Redemption

Unbroken

Captive

Visit us at www.boldstrokesbooks.com

CAPTIVE

by

Donna K. Ford

2018

CREDITS

EDITOR: RUTH STERNGLANTZ
PRODUCTION DESIGN: STACIA SEAMAN
COVER DESIGN BY MELODY POND

Acknowledgments

In the past few years, human trafficking has gained much-needed public attention, but we are far from where we need to be. According to FBI.org, human trafficking/involuntary servitude is believed to be the third largest criminal activity in the world. It includes forced labor, domestic servitude, and commercial sex trafficking. This trade does not discriminate; it includes US citizens and foreigners alike and has no demographic restrictions. The individuals held captive in these organizations are often held in unsanitary and inhumane conditions and forced to work for little or no pay. They are coerced into captivity through the promise of a paying job that will support a starving family, threatened with the lives of those they love, and stripped of their identities and all ties that give them hope of freedom. But the problem goes even further. There are laws in the United States that allow businesses to "employ" those with physical and mental disabilities for less than minimum wage. Daily, migrant workers are required to work long hours doing demanding physical labor only to be underpaid, and they are often the victims of assault and robbery, stripped of their hard-earned wages. We have a long way to go as a society before we can rid the world of these crimes against humanity.

Writing *Captive* was my way of shedding light on the underworld where human beings continue to be bought and sold for the pleasure and financial gain of others. It is my hope that we will all be a little more attentive to the things around us and alert authorities when we see evidence of these crimes.

Each character I created in this book represented a real person, not someone I know, but those I know exist out there in the underworld. In a romance we are given the certainty of a happy ending, but for the real victims there is little hope. We are heading in the right direction, but there is much left to do if we are going to put an end to these crimes.

If you or someone you know is the victim of human trafficking or if you have information about a potential trafficking situation, please call the National Human Trafficking Resource Center (NHTRC) at 1-888-373-7888.

I want to offer a special thank you to all those engaged in the war against human trafficking. Please join us in this fight. To quote John F. Kennedy, "One person can make a difference, and everyone should try."

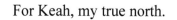

For Keah, my true north.

Chapter One

Breaking News
Authorities have just confirmed the discovery of the remains of at least four unidentified women in an abandoned strip mine in Tennessee. Reports indicate the sheriff has requested assistance from the FBI as the deaths are now suspected to be the work of a serial killer.

The Recruiter watched the woman from the safety of his car as she passed on her third circuit around the park. He chewed his lip trying to separate one problem from the other. The dump site had been compromised, and he didn't want to think about the shit that could open up for him. At least he had time to figure out a new dump site and a way to clean up so there would be no leaks. It would be months, maybe even years, if ever, before the authorities figured out what they were really dealing with was way more important than some pathetic little serial killer.

He sighed, bringing his focus back to his target. He was lucky he had stumbled upon her when he did. He had received the order from the Employer weeks ago and resorted to searching area gyms looking for just the right woman to fill the order. This wasn't his usual hunting ground, it was risky, but he hadn't had any luck in his usual territory. He didn't like hunting in the general population, but this order was special. He studied the woman as she stopped in the middle of her run to do push-ups. She wouldn't have been his personal choice, but he had to admit the package was nice. The moment he saw her he knew she was the one.

He sucked his teeth as he glanced at the list and back to the woman. He guessed her to be just under six feet tall, so the height was right. Her black hair and dark features were a nice touch too, although not his personal preference. He got out of the car and began a casual stroll around the track to get a closer look at the goods. The woman stopped at a pavilion, where she used the rafters to do pull-ups. Her bare shoulder muscles bulged and rippled beneath the thin straps of her tank top as she pumped her body up and down in a controlled motion. She crossed her legs at the ankles and lifted her feet in front of her body each time her chin was even with her hands.

He stopped a few feet away, pretending to tie his shoe. He didn't want to draw attention to himself, but he needed to be sure of his choice before he contacted the Employer.

She barely glanced at him as he passed, and he nodded hello. As expected she continued her workout seemingly unaware of him. His heart raced with excitement. She was the *one*. She fit the profile perfectly. He had found his prey and he could taste the anticipation of the chase coating his tongue like chilled whiskey.

He smirked and reveled in his good fortune. The Employer would be pleased with his choice, and he liked it when his clients were pleased. If he could get the woman on board and ready before the big event, he would have a hefty bonus in his pocket. He slid back into his car with a troubled sigh. There was only one catch. This one was not his usual prey. She wasn't just a girl off the streets or an immigrant looking for work. He would have to come up with a plan to snare this one without drawing too much attention. With the discovery of the dump site, he couldn't risk any more mistakes that could jeopardize the operation. He rubbed his finger and thumb across the stubble on his chin. This was the part he liked the most, playing the game. He raised his camera and snapped off a few frames. He would give the Employer a little taste to sweeten the deal. He would worry about the details later.

He watched the woman gather her bag and toss her towel over her left shoulder. When she reached her car, he noted the make and model of the old Jeep Scrambler and scratched down the license plate before pulling out of his space to circle the park. She would be easy to follow in such an uncommon vehicle, and she wouldn't notice him if he casually pulled in behind her on the way out. He grinned, pleased with himself.

He could make a call to a trusted friend to trace her car and have her address before morning, or he could simply follow her home. He decided to follow her—the fewer people who knew about her, the better. As planned, she drove past him as he circled the picnic area. He licked his lips and pulled out behind her. He ran his hand over his crotch, the excitement of the chase making him hard.

He smiled. "I'll find a way. You'll see. I always find a way. Soon you'll be mine."

❖

Greyson settled back into her seat with a smug grin as her cell began to ring. It was barely noon and she had only been out of the office for a day and a half, and the boys were already calling. She tried to guess which one of her office buddies had caved first. Would it be Scott, the one she lovingly referred to as her shadow, or would it be Daren, the constant voice of doom? Privately she referred to the two of them as Piss and Moan, although she couldn't decide which one was which.

At the last minute, she answered on the chance it could actually be her boss calling. "Hello, Greyson Cooper speaking."

"Oh, thank God, Greyson, please tell me you've reconsidered this ridiculous vacation."

Greyson rolled her eyes. "What is it, Daren?"

"You can't just leave us hanging like this. There's too much to do on this project. We'll never get the new trails in on time without you. It'll be a complete disaster if we don't manage to save that wetland and those beavers are not going to be easy to deal with and…well, Scott is already freaking out. He's been walking around all morning muttering to himself, *What would Cooper do?*"

Greyson chuckled. "Calm down. It can't be that bad. I've only been gone a day and my vacation doesn't even start until tomorrow. Stop panicking. The plans are all there—all you have to do is implement them. Land management and conservation is what we do. We've worked together on this for months. This is nothing new. Trust yourself. You know what to do."

She heard him whine. Oh God, he wasn't going to cry, was he?

"Come on, Greyson. Can't you just shorten your trip by a couple of weeks, or postpone it until after the project is finished?"

"No. Absolutely not. I'm hiking the leg of the Appalachian Trail from Damascus to Georgia this summer, and I'm not going to let anything get in my way. You won't even notice I'm gone."

"Yeah, right. I can't believe we won't even be able to call you. That's abandonment, you know."

"You're a big boy. I trust you to handle it."

"Cooper," Daren whined.

"Got to go, Daren. See you when I get back." Greyson disconnected, laughing. She finished her glass of tea and dropped a tip on the table. Two whole months of no phones, no office walls, and no bickering coworkers. She couldn't wait to be surrounded by trees and birds and all things wild. She could almost imagine the smell of damp earth, trees, and honeysuckle. She looked up at the sound of a mockingbird as she stood to leave.

"*Oomph.*"

Someone grunted as Greyson registered a soft body slam into her. Instinctively she wrapped her arm around the woman who had just bounced off her, pulling her close reflexively to prevent the woman's fall.

The woman shrieked as ice-cold liquid soaked them both. The front of the woman's dress was covered with a wet brown stain, and the cold liquid was slowly seeping into her shoes. She pushed away from Greyson and held her hands out in front of her as she stared down at the disaster.

"I'm so sorry," Greyson said. "I guess I wasn't watching where I was going."

"Obviously," the woman snapped.

Greyson already felt terrible about ruining the woman's dress, and the admonishment stung. Her instinct was to quip back, but her retort died on her tongue the moment the woman looked up at her. Greyson expected her eyes to be blue, but they were brown, the color of rich chocolate and honey. They were the perfect complement to her golden blond hair. Something warm began to grow in Greyson's belly, and the heat was beginning to spread through her like a wildfire across a summer field.

Greyson smiled. "I really am sorry."

"Well, you should be. I was on my way to an interview and now I'm going to be late, thanks to you."

Greyson had no idea what to do next, so she dropped her bag and rifled through it until she found her gym towel. "Here, let me help you," she said as she began cleaning the woman's hands and forearms.

The woman pulled back and smacked at Greyson's hands. "No. Stop. I can do it," she said, snatching the towel from Greyson.

Greyson fumbled for words. "Don't worry, it's clean. I was just on my way to the gym."

"I'm sure it is, but you could use it yourself." She pointed to Greyson's shirt.

Greyson looked down at her chocolate-stained shirt and laughed. "I guess we should both be happy that was iced coffee."

"So you think this is funny. You've ruined everything," the woman said, raising her voice. People turned to look at them, making Greyson feel even worse.

Greyson felt terrible, but what could she do? It wasn't like she had meant for this to happen. "Look, you're the one who ran into me, and I said I'm sorry. What do I have to do, buy you another coffee or maybe a new dress?"

The woman scoffed. "I hardly think that would change anything. I need this job. I can't show up like this. Who wants to hire someone that can't even show up for an interview on time?"

"I'm sure they'll understand…"

The woman groaned and stomped her foot, her frustration escalating. Greyson wasn't sure if she was about to cry or scream.

"This isn't helping at all." The woman pushed the towel into

Greyson's hand. She turned away from Greyson and went back inside the coffee shop. Greyson watched her through the windows as she pushed her way into the bathroom.

"Some people," Greyson muttered, shaking her head. She understood the woman was upset, but there was no reason to be so rude.

❖

Olivia closed the bathroom door, pressed her back against it, and let out a deep breath. Her head was spinning and her skin tingled as if she had been standing near an electrical current. She closed her eyes and took a deep breath to steady herself. How could this be happening? She had to land this job. She couldn't bear the thought of moving back home with her parents. This was her big break and now everything was ruined.

She rushed to the sink to get some of the sticky mixture of chocolate, sugar, and coffee off her skin and try to make herself as presentable as possible. She grabbed a handful of towels and wiped at her neck and cheeks and even washed the mess off her feet, but her dress was a total disaster and couldn't be salvaged. There was no way to get the ugly brown stain out of the pale yellow fabric. She groaned in frustration and threw the paper towels in the trash.

She fumed as she took one last look at the mess that was her dress. At least that clumsy woman was in the same mess—her shirt had been ruined too, although Olivia doubted it bothered her much. How could she have been so careless? Some people thought they were the only ones in the world who mattered.

Olivia cringed. This was pointless. There was no way she could get the stain out, and it was too late to go back to her apartment and still make it to the interview. She sighed. She would just have to go like this. Getting this job was the only way she would be able to stay in Knoxville. She needed a rescue if she was going to salvage this day.

Olivia came to a halt a few feet away from the table where the woman responsible for this terrible mess sat waiting on the patio. Oh no, not her again. Why was this woman still here? The woman stood and smiled as she approached. There was no way to avoid her. "What do you want now?"

"Look, I know you're in a hurry, but I thought this might make things a little better for you." She handed Olivia a small paper bag.

Olivia frowned. "What's this?"

The woman shrugged. "Good luck with your interview. I hope you aren't as rude to them as you were with me."

Olivia's mouth fell open. She didn't know what to say. Olivia looked into the bag and was shocked to see she had bought her a new dress from the boutique next door.

"Well, are you going to try it on?"

Olivia was suddenly embarrassed. Perhaps she had been a little harsh. She nodded. "Yes. Thank you." She hesitated. "Look, I know I've been terrible to you. I shouldn't have. This wasn't all your fault. After I get through with this interview, would you like to meet me back here? I feel like I need to make things up to you. I promise to be nice this time."

The woman smiled. "I'd like that."

Olivia smiled back, feeling heat warm her cheeks. "Good. I shouldn't be more than an hour. Is that okay?"

"I'll be here."

Olivia lifted the bag. "I better try this." She went back into the bathroom to try on the dress. She might just make the interview if she'd hurry.

She slipped into the dress, delighting at the feel of silk gliding across her skin. It was a knee-length sundress. The burnt-red shoulder straps draped across her shoulders allowing the fabric to lie naturally against the curves of her body as the color slowly blended into a rich blue at the bottom. The dress was beautiful and the fit was perfect. At least the woman had good taste. Maybe this wasn't the disaster she had thought it was.

❖

The Recruiter followed the target to the café. He moved through the crowd toward a table behind her. As he passed, he jabbed his camera bag into her back.

"Sorry," he muttered as she moved her chair to let him pass. As expected she paid little notice of him. He smirked. He loved having power over others, even if they had no idea what was happening to them.

He shifted his chair so the target's back was to him. It was the perfect position to listen to her phone conversation without being noticed.

He pulled a notebook from his bag and took notes. To those around him he would look like any other businessman or student working on a project. People only saw what they wanted to see.

Today had been a huge success. Not only had he learned the target's name, but he had a pretty good idea how he was going to catch his prey without any notice.

He prepared to leave when Greyson pulled out her wallet and tossed a couple of bills onto the table. As she stood she crashed into another woman passing by. He watched the exchange between the two women with amusement. He hadn't considered that the woman might be gay, but that didn't matter to him. He needed her to do a job—who she slept with didn't matter. But the blonde she had ran into was a different story. She was perfect for his personal collection. His cock twitched as he studied her. Maybe he would get more out of this deal than a bonus.

It was time to regroup. He had enough information on the target that he could find her when he was ready. But the blonde was a mystery. If he was going to claim her, he at least needed to know her name. He would let the target go for today. He had new prey to stalk, and this time the prize would be all his.

He picked up his bag and followed the blonde through Market Square. She looked behind her more than once, and he wondered if she could feel his presence, somehow sense that she was being followed. The thought sent a thrill up his spine. He wanted her to feel him, anticipate him. It was a sign that they were meant to be together.

He followed her to the Museum of East Tennessee History, casually walking by as she pushed through the door. He was having fun. Things were working out better than he could have hoped. He circled back to the café to wait. She had made this too easy for him. He would have to think of a way to spice up the chase a little. He wanted to have a little fun before taking his prize. He laughed. She'd give him everything he needed and wouldn't even know it. Greyson had turned out to be worth his trouble. She was going to give him a hefty paycheck and a toy to play with. This was his lucky day.

As expected Greyson was back at the café within the hour. He waited patiently for her to get her drink and sit down at a table before going into the café himself. He'd have to be more careful this time. He had two targets to keep up with and couldn't afford any mistakes.

He managed a seat just inside the café, where an open window separated him from Greyson. It was the perfect spot to sit and listen to her conversation. He didn't have to wait long before the blonde walked through the door.

He listened intently. The bits of information they shared would be the map that would lead to their capture. He smiled. This was going to be fun.

❖

Olivia ran over the details of the interview in her mind. She couldn't put her finger on any one point that had gone wrong, but she had a bad feeling about the outcome. Maybe she was just overreacting because she really needed the job. She had to practice some patience.

Her palms were sweating, and she was sure her heart had sunk into her stomach. She ran her hands down her sides to wipe away the perspiration. The cool silk brushed against her skin, reminding her of her morning encounter. She took a deep breath to calm the sudden racing of her heart. Her hands were sweating again, but this time it had nothing to do with the interview, and everything to do with the beautifully handsome woman responsible for the dress she was wearing.

She was suddenly more nervous about having a cup of coffee than she was about the interview. She looked at her watch. Had it really only been forty-five minutes? She frowned. *I was so rude to her. What if she isn't even there?* She sighed. There was only one way to find out.

Olivia stopped at the curb, looking across the street at the café. As promised, the woman sat at a small table waiting for her. She had her head tilted upward to the sun, her eyes closed, soaking up the rays of sunshine. The light made her skin glow like warm caramel. Olivia licked her lips. She sure hoped this meeting went better than the last one.

Olivia got her coffee. She walked up to the table and gently cleared her throat. The woman looked up at her with eyes as blue as the sky. Olivia stopped breathing. Her focus locked on the azure pools gazing up at her.

The woman smiled. "Hi."

"Hello again." Olivia held out her hand. "I'm Olivia, Olivia Danner."

The woman took her hand. "I'm Greyson Cooper."

Olivia smiled. "Do you mind?" she asked, motioning to the empty chair.

Greyson stood and pulled out the chair for Olivia. "The dress looks amazing. Do you like it?"

Olivia smiled. "I do. Thank you. And thank you for waiting for me. I'm sorry I was so rude to you before. I just had a lot on my mind and I lost it a little."

Greyson raised her eyebrows. "A little?"

Olivia wrinkled her nose. "Was I really that bad?"

Greyson laughed. "Not too bad. I'm here, aren't I?"

Olivia nodded.

Greyson leaned forward, giving Olivia her full attention. "So, tell me about the interview. How did it go? Did you get the job?"

Olivia sighed. "I don't know. They said they would make their decision in the next week. It seemed to go okay, but I have a bad feeling about it."

"What's the job for?" Greyson asked.

Olivia smiled. "I would be teaching science classes through some special learning courses at Ijams Nature Center this summer."

"Wow, that sounds like fun."

Olivia nodded. "Yeah, it's just the kind of thing that can really get young minds interested in science. And it would be so much more fun than working in a regular classroom. Although I'm looking for a more permanent teaching job too. I just thought this would be a great way to bridge the gap this summer."

Olivia realized she'd been going on about herself since she sat down. To her credit, Greyson had been the perfect listener. "So tell me about you. What do you do?"

Greyson smiled. "I'm an environmental engineer. I work over there in the TVA building." She pointed to a tall gray building at the end of Market Square.

Olivia was surprised. "Wow. That's exciting. I thought you were going to say you were some kind of fitness coach or athlete or something."

Greyson frowned. "Why?"

Olivia shrugged. "Well, earlier you said you were on the way to the gym and you are obviously in really good shape." Olivia glanced at Greyson's arms and quickly ran her eyes across Greyson's body.

She felt heat gather in her cheeks when she met Greyson's eyes again. Greyson smiled at her with a half grin, half smirk. She had obviously enjoyed watching Olivia check her out.

Olivia cleared her throat. "Well, you can see it was an easy mistake."

Greyson reached across the table, placing her hand over Olivia's. "No worries. I'm glad you noticed me. I was afraid our little run-in had tainted your impression of me."

Olivia's smile widened. "Well, the dress did have something to do with it. I decided I liked your taste. Everyone deserves a second chance."

"I agree," Greyson said, sitting back in her chair and looking around at the people around them.

"Do you have to get back to work?" Olivia asked, feeling that their time was almost up.

Greyson looked into her eyes, as if understanding her thoughts. "No. I'm officially on vacation. As a matter of fact, I leave tomorrow for a trip I've been planning all year."

"Really? Where are you going?" Olivia asked.

"I'm hiking the Appalachian Trail from Damascus, Virginia, to Springer Mountain in Georgia." Greyson's eyes lit up with excitement the moment she began describing her plans. "It is four hundred and sixty-three miles."

Greyson's enthusiasm was contagious and Olivia soon found herself lost in the idea of the adventure. "Wow, that's a long way. How long will it take you to hike that far?"

Greyson smiled. "I've given myself sixty days to get it done. I think I can do it in less, but I wanted to give myself extra time in case something happens to slow me down."

Olivia felt a bit of panic. "Like what?"

Greyson shrugged. "Anything really. A sprained ankle would add a couple of days' rest, and weather could be a problem."

"Oh," Olivia said with some relief. "I guess I hadn't thought of all that. How many people are going?"

Greyson shook her head. "It's just me on this one. I want to test myself. See what I can really do when I put my mind to it. I want to get away from all the computers, cell phones, and on-demand living."

"So you're going to be gone for the next two months?"

Greyson nodded. "I know it seems like a long time, but I would do more if I could."

"Wow." She admired Greyson's determination and her sense of adventure.

Greyson looked at her watch. "Maybe when I get back we could see each other again. I'd like to hear how things turn out with the job. I'd like to hear more about you."

Olivia smiled. "I'd like that too."

"So it's okay if I call you?" Greyson asked.

Olivia nodded. She gave Greyson her number. "Are you sure you'll remember to call? Two months is a long time."

Greyson placed her hand over Olivia's again. "I won't forget. If I wasn't leaving tomorrow, I wouldn't let a day pass without calling you and asking you to dinner."

Olivia's heart skipped a beat. Greyson looked at her with such intensity that she swore she could feel a connection form between them. Maybe that was silly, but after a rotten day, it was nice to dream. "In that case, I'll be waiting."

Greyson checked her watch again. "I'm sorry, but I have to go. I have some things I have to do before I leave tomorrow."

"Oh. Okay," Olivia answered, trying to hide her disappointment.

Greyson gathered her things to go but hesitated before leaving. "I'm glad I bumped into you today. This feels—important. I wish I had more time."

Olivia nodded. "I know what you mean."

Greyson leaned down and kissed Olivia's cheek. "Good luck with the job. I'm sure you'll do great."

Olivia smiled. "See you in two months, Greyson Cooper."

Greyson smiled back. "See you."

CHAPTER TWO

Olivia jumped when her phone rang, and winced when she recognized her parents' number on the screen.

"Hi, Mom."

Olivia had been putting her parents off for days, not wanting to have to explain why she wanted to stay in the city instead of coming home. She had hoped to have a job by now so she would at least have a solid argument for staying after her temporary teaching position had ended.

"Hi, sweetie, you're not driving, are you? You know I don't want you talking on the phone when you're driving."

"No, Mom, I'm not driving."

"Oh, good. I have your room ready for you this weekend. I know it's a long drive, so you should get on the road early. Your father and I want to go to the auction on Saturday. Oh, and I ran into Larry Wallace the other day—he's in town visiting too. Wouldn't it be nice to catch up with him? You two haven't seen each other in ages."

Olivia rolled her eyes and sighed. "Mom, I don't want to see Larry Wallace. There's a reason we haven't seen each other. Besides, I thought he got married."

"Oh, that's such an unfortunate story, poor boy. I'm sure he could use a friend right now. He was sweet enough to agree to have dinner with us Saturday night. Isn't that nice?"

"Mom, please do not set me up with Larry Wallace. Don't set

me up with anyone. I don't want to meet a boy and settle down in the middle of nowhere. That's not my life. I have other dreams."

"We're having dinner Saturday night," Olivia's mother continued as if she hadn't spoken, "and I expect you to be there. When you meet the right boy, you'll see."

"I'm never going to meet the right boy, Mom. I know you don't like it, but I'm gay, and nothing can change that."

"Olivia June, that's enough. I won't hear any more of this. We will see you Saturday."

Olivia stared at her phone in disbelief. Her mother had hung up on her. Olivia wanted to scream. What would it take to get through to her mother that she was a lesbian? It had been the same thing for years. Her mother just couldn't let it go. She had been trying to fix Olivia up with every single man her age ever since she came out to the family.

She took a deep breath. She would get to her parents on Friday, spend the day Saturday, and make some excuse to leave early Sunday morning. They might make her sit through dinner with Larry Wallace, but there was no way she was going to church with them. They could pray all they wanted, but she was having none of it.

She missed the days when she was close with her family. When they laughed and enjoyed spending time together. Everything had been forced between them since she had quit her job and moved to the city. Her mother seemed obsessed with the thought that she was living a life of sin.

She sighed and started the computer. She really needed a job. It was the only way she could get her mother off her back. Today, if there were no teaching leads, she would have to look at daycare centers, the Boys & Girls Club—maybe the YMCA would have something. She had to start thinking outside the box. Something would come up sooner or later. She had to believe that.

"Come on, give me something," she muttered.

Her mood brightened when she saw an email regarding her online résumé. Maybe this would be the break she needed.

She read carefully. This wasn't the position she had expected or hoped for. It was a private individual needing someone to homeschool a child in their home three days a week through the summer, with the potential for a full-time position during the school year.

Olivia sighed. This wasn't what she was looking for at all, but she didn't have any other options at the moment. But this job would have to be a last resort. She didn't like the idea of going into someone's home alone. That was never a good idea, but desperate times called for desperate measures. She would have to figure something out.

Olivia rubbed her temples. The last thing she wanted was to go back to her hometown with her tail between her legs. She had to make this work. She had some savings to get her over the rough spots if she had to, but it wouldn't last long without a steady income.

"Two steps forward, three steps back."

Frustrated, she turned off the computer. Why was this so hard?

Her phone rang again, making her jump. She stared at it as if it could bite her. She did not want to talk to her mother again. She picked up the phone, checking the screen this time. *Greyson.*

"Hello," Olivia said into the phone, not wanting to get her hopes up.

"Hi," Greyson said, her voice raspy and deep. Chills skimmed across Olivia's skin at the sound of Greyson's voice. "I know I'm a little early, but I couldn't wait two months to see you again. I have a little time this evening and was wondering if you'd have dinner with me."

Olivia bit her lip, not wanting to sound too excited. "Sure. Dinner sounds good. What do you have in mind?"

"I could meet you in the square. How does Craft and Barrel sound? This will be my last chance to have a good burger for a while."

"Okay. That's just around the corner from me. What time?"

There was a pause on the line. Olivia imagined Greyson checking her watch.

"How does seven o'clock sound? It will take me a little more than half an hour to get there."

"Perfect," Olivia replied. "I'll see you in about an hour."

"Great. See you there."

Olivia smiled as she hung up the phone. Greyson was turning out to be the perfect distraction to her otherwise stressed-out life.

❖

As Olivia expected the restaurant was busy, but she'd arrived early to make sure they could get a table. She was excited to see Greyson again.

"Hi," a raspy voice said close behind Olivia.

Olivia turned to see Greyson smiling down at her. She wore an aqua-blue shirt that matched her eyes perfectly in the evening light. Her tailored black slacks hugged her slender hips, hinting at the curve of her muscled frame. Olivia didn't even try to hide her perusal of Greyson's physique. "I swear if Superman had a sister, she'd look just like you."

Greyson laughed. "Well, thank you. But most women usually like me for my mind."

Olivia laughed. "That too."

Greyson leaned down and kissed Olivia's cheek. "Thank you for seeing me. You look beautiful."

The pager in Olivia's hand began to vibrate, signaling their table was ready. A young woman led them to the back of the room. The restaurant was small and there wasn't a lot of space. Most of the tables were for couples and there was a small bar in the middle. Their table allowed them to be out of the busy traffic and allowed them a little more intimacy.

Greyson pulled out a chair for Olivia, then sighed as she took her own seat.

"So, what changed your mind?" Olivia asked.

"What do you mean?"

Olivia shrugged. "Earlier you made it sound like you were all out of time. I really didn't expect to hear from you."

Greyson grinned. "To be honest, I'm not sure. I just knew I had to see you again, and I didn't want to have to wait two months."

Olivia smiled. "Well, I'm glad you called."

The waiter appeared and they placed their orders. After their drinks came, they fell into easy conversation as if they'd known each other for years, although they were just beginning to explore each other.

"You sounded a bit stressed when I called earlier. Is everything okay?" Greyson asked.

Olivia sat her glass down. "I have a lead on another job."

"Yay, that's great," Greyson encouraged. "Isn't it?"

"Maybe," Olivia said, "but I'm not sure about it. It's for a private family who wants me to homeschool their son this summer and maybe through the school year. It could be enough if I don't hear back about the other job."

Greyson took a drink. "Okay, so it's not a school. At least it's a teaching job."

"Yeah, but it's in their home, and that creeps me out a little."

Greyson frowned. "Why?"

"I don't know, it just seems weird. I don't like it. There's been all that talk about those dead girls they found. The whole thing has me paranoid."

"Well, I can't argue with that. How many bodies have they said it is now? I think it was something like ten the last I heard."

Olivia nodded. "And they're still looking for more."

"Any identifications yet?"

"They released the names of three women so far. All three were immigrants who went missing shortly after coming into the country. Each woman was reported by a family member who managed to gain legal status. They think more of the women may have been immigrants as well, but they haven't been reported missing because the families haven't come forward, probably fearing deportation."

"That's terrible."

"I know, right," Olivia said in disbelief. "I can't imagine someone I love going missing and not being able to go to the authorities to try to find them."

Greyson leaned back in her chair. "As awful as that story is, it doesn't sound like this sicko is looking for people who are easily missed or likely to be reported. Doesn't sound like someone who would hire you to look after their kid."

"I know, but just because it might not be the person who killed those women doesn't mean it isn't some other sicko."

Greyson nodded. "True."

Olivia slumped. "I don't know what to do."

"Maybe you could meet with the kid at a community center or library or something, and not have to go to the house," Greyson offered.

Olivia brightened. "Yeah, maybe. That would work." She considered her options and what this could mean for her long-term goals. "I guess it wouldn't hurt to check it out. If I don't like it, I can always wait tables for the summer."

"That's an option," Greyson agreed.

"I want to wait and see what comes of my interview today, but I don't know how long I should wait. Something has to pay the bills, and I don't want to have to leave Knoxville."

Greyson frowned. "Why would you leave?"

Olivia shook her head. "My parents are giving me a hard time about living in the city. They want me to move back to the farm, teach at the local high school, and settle down with a nice farm boy."

Greyson's eyes widened. "Oh."

"Yeah," Olivia agreed. "*Oh* is right." Olivia pushed aside her drink. "Enough about all that. When do you leave tomorrow? Are you excited?"

Greyson smiled. "First thing tomorrow morning, and yes, I'm very excited. I've been planning this trip so long, it doesn't seem real now that it's finally happening. I can't wait to get on the trail and put the rest of the world behind me for a while. I can't wait to be outside, surrounded by fresh air, endless stars, and everything wild. I hate being cooped up inside. My job allows me to be outside a lot, but it's not the same. I want to feel free."

"You make it sound so romantic. I've done a lot of camping, but nothing like what you're going to do. I can't imagine being alone all that time, not to mention the work."

Greyson laughed. The waiter came and Greyson paid the check. "Can I walk you to your car?"

Olivia shook her head. "No need. I just live around the corner in one of the lofts. It's a small space, but I love living downtown."

"Okay. Can I walk you home then?" Greyson asked.

Olivia smiled. "Yeah, I'd like that."

❖

The Recruiter pulled his motorcycle into one of the small spaces the city had created just for bikes along the narrow streets of downtown. The target was on the move. If something had changed, he didn't want to be left in the dark. He wasn't about to let this one get away. He was anxious to get started on his personal prize, but right now he had to secure the order for the Employer.

The blonde, Olivia, would present her own set of challenges, but he was a pro. She wouldn't be a problem. This hunt would be different for him. He enjoyed bringing in a paying prize, but this girl was special. He would claim her himself. And when it came to his collection, he was patient. Only the right girl would do.

He secured the helmet to the bike and made his way to Market Square. Why was Greyson back here? She was easy to follow, but he wanted to stay close. He'd make contact if he had to, but that was only in extreme cases. She was out of her pattern and he didn't like it. Most people never realized the patterns they created in their daily lives. The smallest clue would often lead him right to the one he wanted. Things like having lunch at the same place at the same time on Tuesdays, going to the gym every evening, having a regular girls' night, or getting a haircut on a schedule. Everything made it easier for a man like him to find what he was looking for.

He followed Greyson to a restaurant. He spotted Olivia just as she turned to face Greyson. Ah, that's why she came back to town. *She likes the girl. Hmm. I do too.* What a treat.

He took a seat at the bar, close enough to watch but not close enough to listen. He'd have to settle for being the voyeur. He couldn't risk trying to get any closer.

The Recruiter paid his check and followed the women out.

He wanted to make sure he could follow the target without being noticed, so he crossed the street and followed at a distance. With any luck he would have her in his den in no time at all.

He smiled when the women stopped outside the entrance to a set of studio apartments. He laughed. Greyson was doing all his work for him. She had led him right to the girl's door. He would have to thank Greyson for that later.

He stood in the shadows as Greyson kissed the girl good night. The stab of jealousy filled him with rage. He wanted to beat Greyson. He wanted to make her hurt. He pulled back into the shadows, willing his fists to open. He'd teach Greyson a lesson. Soon enough she'd learn her place. The girl was his.

❖

Greyson inventoried her gear for the last time and closed her pack.

"Well, that's it," she said tossing her keys to her best friend. "Thanks for looking after the place while I'm gone."

Dawn Sawyer grinned. "Yeah, like that's going to be such a hardship for me. I can't believe you're going to give this place up during the best part of summer. This place is a certified love shack, and I plan to take full advantage."

Greyson shook her head. Dawn always talked big about her charm with the ladies, but Greyson knew Dawn was more the romantic fall-in-love-forever type. She just hadn't found the right woman yet.

"Right, just make sure she stays afloat. I have to live here, you know."

Dawn picked up a box Greyson had addressed to herself. "What's this?"

Greyson glanced at the box as she pulled her pack over her shoulder. "Supplies. I'm mailing them to myself so I don't have to carry everything. I'll pick them up at my first stop and send more on ahead of me."

"Man, that's smart."

"Pretty standard procedure. You might know that if you ever ventured out of the air-conditioning."

Dawn's eyes widened. "Now you're just talking crazy."

Greyson laughed. "Come on, let's get going. I'll call to check in at each town, so you'll know where I am on the route. That way if you don't hear from me, you can send out the cavalry."

Dawn nodded. "That's good. I'm going to be bugging nuts with worry. I still think this is a crazy idea. I don't like the thought of you being off in the woods alone with a serial killer on the loose."

Greyson clasped her friend's shoulder. "There's no need to worry. I'll be fine. That's a couple of counties away from here, and where I'm going is even farther away. I'll be back here cramping your style in no time."

Dawn gave Greyson a playful shove. "There's enough for both of us." She paused. "Are you sure there's nothing that will change your mind?"

Greyson thought for a moment, and the memory of Olivia flooded her mind. That was one thing that could change everything. She pursed her lips and shrugged. "Nope. Nothing."

Dawn squinted at her as if seeing something Greyson couldn't. "Are you sure you don't have someone going with you and you just don't want to tell or something? I'd actually feel better if there was someone going with you."

"No one is going with me."

Dawn picked a shirt up off the floor. "Good grief, what happened to this?"

Greyson took the shirt and tossed it into the trash. "Nothing. Just me being clumsy."

"What does that mean?"

"It's nothing. I just bumped into this woman yesterday and wore her iced coffee home as a result."

Dawn grinned. "Was she cute?"

Greyson frowned, suddenly recalling the rich chocolate color of Olivia's eyes. She shrugged. "I don't know. I guess. I wasn't thinking about that at the time. I was too busy dodging her insults. She was pretty pissed that I'd ruined her dress and she was late for some meeting or interview or something. Like I said, I just ran into her—I mean, I literally ran into her."

"And?" Dawn pushed. "Is that your new way to meet girls?"

Greyson laughed. "I don't recommend it. She wasn't very nice."

Greyson cringed inside. She was being truthful, kind of, but Olivia had turned out to be more than just nice. And she was stunning. But Greyson knew if she gave Dawn the slightest hint that she was interested in someone, she'd never stop hounding her about it.

"I bet she won't forget you, though. Way to make yourself memorable."

Greyson squinted at her friend. "And you wonder why you're single."

Dawn grinned. "I have special charm."

"Yeah, you could call it that."

Dawn spread her arms and turned in a circle. "Now that I'll be staying here, I have all the charm I need. The girls will be crawling all over this place."

"Whatever, Casanova. Grab that box and let's go. I don't want to miss my flight."

Dawn slid the box under her arm. "You promise you'll call? I don't want to have search and rescue looking for your ass and have them find you shacked up with some girl in your tent."

"I promise I'll call. Seriously, I'll call. I know you're going to miss me."

"Sometimes you're a real pain in the ass, you know that?"

Greyson patted Dawn on the back. "That's what you're going to miss the most."

Dawn grinned. "I might not miss you as much when the girls get here."

Greyson got serious for a minute. "Why is it so important to you to meet someone? If you ask me, relationships are overrated."

Dawn shrugged. "One of these days you're going to meet a woman who makes you want to stick around in the morning and find out what she likes for breakfast. When that happens, you'll see things different."

Greyson laughed. "I'm not that bad."

"Yeah?" Dawn countered. "When was the last time you actually woke up in bed with a woman and saw her for a second date?"

Greyson stopped laughing. "That doesn't mean I'm some kind of womanizer."

Dawn put her hands up. "Hey, I didn't say that. I'm just saying that you don't usually want to stick around and get to know the women you...see."

"There's nothing wrong with sharing a little love," Greyson argued. "I just don't want all the headaches that come with that second date."

"Hey, I'm not saying you have to get married and get a dog, but I'd bet most women would at least like breakfast."

Greyson scowled. "I think this conversation just got offensive. I always remember their names and our arrangement is always mutual."

Dawn shook her head. "Whatever you say."

Greyson smacked Dawn's shoulder again. "Ass. Get in the Jeep already. I have to be at the airport early."

Dawn grinned and threw the box in the back seat.

Greyson would never admit it to Dawn, but the conversation bothered her. If her best friend thought she cared so little about the women she dated, how did she make them feel? Greyson stuffed her pack into the Jeep and sighed. "Breakfast is overrated."

Greyson continued to ponder the conversation as they drove. It wasn't that she was opposed to relationships, but she just hadn't found anyone she connected with on that level. Maybe she was too picky. Maybe she had commitment issues. Maybe she was just waiting for the right woman to come along and sweep her off her feet.

She thought of Olivia. Olivia had come at her with fire and vinegar, but there had been something about her that had stirred her up. Once they got past the fear and frustration, Olivia had been smart, funny, and captivating. Greyson definitely wanted to see Olivia again. But they hadn't slept together. Was that why? If she slept with Olivia, would the spark die out? Greyson frowned. She didn't like where this thinking was taking her.

"What's up with you?" Dawn asked. "You haven't said a word the whole drive."

Greyson shrugged. "Just a lot on my mind. I guess I was daydreaming."

Dawn laughed. "Get used to it, buddy. You've got sixty days of sleeping alone and living in your head in front of you."

Greyson decided she was right not to tell Dawn about Olivia. She had two months to clear her head before exploring anything with Olivia. Maybe they'd be good friends. Maybe they'd have good sex. And maybe, just maybe, they could even have breakfast.

CHAPTER THREE

G reyson departed the airport terminal with a satisfied sigh. She was one step closer to the start of her journey. She slid into the back seat of the first cab waiting at the curb. From here it wasn't far to Damascus, Virginia, where she would finally take her first steps on the Appalachian Trail. Then she would have eight glorious weeks of complete isolation from civilization—no computers, no television, no traffic, no phones, no distractions.

She let out a long slow breath, expelling the weight of her stress, and gave the driver the address as she settled into her seat. She allowed the gentle sway of the car to lull her into a peaceful reverie. She thought of all the months of planning it took to make this trip happen, and various friends who thought she was crazy to go out on the trail alone. She replayed her conversation with Dawn that morning. Greyson knew why Dawn was skeptical about her intentions with women, but she didn't like it that Dawn thought she cared so little about the women in her life. She had always been respectful and honest with women about her feelings. She had tried the relationship thing and it hadn't worked out. She didn't want to be tied down. She liked her life the way it was. She liked her job, she had good friends, and she had plenty of adventure to look forward to, to keep things fresh. But something was missing. She thought of Olivia. They had shared one good-night kiss. And now that one kiss was all she could think about. Olivia kept popping into her mind like a craving.

"Welcome to Damascus," the cabbie said, slowing for the now twenty-five miles per hour speed limit.

Greyson looked out the window at the sprawling little town. It didn't seem much different than the old towns she frequented in Tennessee. Places like this were special to her. It was like taking a step back in history to a time when life was so much simpler, and people moved at a different pace, ruled more by the rising and setting of the sun than a twenty-four-hour clock.

She spotted Quincey's Pizza to her right and her stomach growled. It wouldn't hurt to have one last indulgence before she set out on the trail.

"You can let me out here," she said to the cabbie.

He pulled to the curb and waited as she fumbled with her wallet, handing him the fare and a generous tip.

"Thanks, man," Greyson said.

He waved the bills in the air. "Thank you. And good luck out there."

Greyson smiled and patted the back of the seat as she stepped onto the curb. She drew in a deep breath, filling her lungs with the smell of fresh-baked pizza. Her stomach rumbled.

Greyson settled her pack and slid into a booth along the wall. She ran a finger along the fake brick panel. The room was bigger than she had expected from the outside, but the place was clean and inviting.

A waitress appeared at her table with a smile and the usual ticket pad.

"Hey, sweetie, what can I get you to drink?"

Greyson smiled. "I'll have a water with no ice and no lemon."

The waitress eyed Greyson's pack. "Let me guess. You're heading out on the trail, right?"

"How'd you know I wasn't just coming in?"

The girl smiled. "You're too clean and you don't look hungry enough. The ones who've been on the trail a week or so come in here looking wild-eyed and are barely able to hold the drool in their mouths. You still have that fresh look about you."

Greyson held her hands up, as if in surrender. "Guilty. But thanks for letting me know what to expect in a few days."

The waitress smiled. "Do you know what you want to eat?"

Greyson laughed. "I was going to have a small veggie pizza, but based on what you said, I think I'll have the supreme."

"Good choice. I'll get that right in." She smiled again before sauntering off as if she didn't have anywhere to be and wasn't in any hurry to get there.

Greyson pulled out her cell phone and dialed Dawn.

A couple of rings later, Dawn's chipper voice chimed on the line with, "Hey, did you make it to Damascus?"

"You should be a detective," Greyson teased.

"Smart-ass. How was the trip?"

"Good. I'm grabbing something to eat before I hit the trail. I'd like to put in at least six to ten miles before I make camp. It isn't much, but enough for the first day since I'm getting a late start."

She heard a rustling through the phone and Dawn cleared her throat.

"Dawn?"

"Yeah, I'm here. Are you *sure* you want to do this alone? I mean, you know I don't go for that outdoor shit, but I'll come with you if you want me to."

Greyson smiled, and her heart warmed that her friend would even suggest such a thing. "Thanks. But I love you too much to put you through something like that. Besides, you'd drive me bat-shit crazy."

"Seriously, Greyson, I mean it. I don't like this."

Greyson ran her hand through her hair. "Come on, I told you there's nothing to worry about. Just think of it as a work trip. You never bug out about me being in the woods then."

"You have people with you then. At least someone close by if you get into any trouble or get hurt or something. That's different."

The waitress approached the table and placed the pizza on a small stand in front of Greyson. Greyson nodded her thanks and went back to her conversation.

"Don't worry. I'll call as soon as I get into Hot Springs. You'll always have a good idea where I am, and if something happens you can be my hero."

Greyson took a bite of the pizza. She closed her eyes in bliss as the smooth, rich cheese filled her mouth. "Mm-mmm."

"What?"

"Sorry. Pizza. Really good pizza," Greyson said with her mouth full. "I'll call you in a few days."

"All right, be safe out there."

Greyson grinned. "I will," she said, ending the call.

"Can I get you anything else?" the waitress asked, placing the check on the table in front of Greyson.

Greyson shook her head. "I'm good. Time to get this show on the road." She wiped her mouth and pulled a ten and a couple of ones from her wallet. "What's your name?" Greyson asked.

"Margaret."

"Well, thanks for everything, Margaret. You have great pizza here. I'll be sure to spread the word." Greyson handed Margaret the money and the check.

Margaret smiled. "Thanks. What's your name?"

"Greyson Cooper."

"It was nice to meet you, Greyson Cooper. Enjoy your trip."

Greyson shoved her wallet back in her pocket. "I plan to."

She stepped onto the sidewalk and let out a long slow breath. From this moment onward, she would have peace. She tightened the straps of her pack a little tighter at her shoulders and tugged at the weight resting on her hips. Satisfied, she set off along the street following the signs down Main Street directing her to the AT.

Greyson stopped at the post office to register her hiking name so there would be a record of her being on the trail. Just inside the door was a stand of postcards featuring local monuments and pictures of the mountains along the AT. She picked up a couple, deciding it was a good idea to send one to Dawn so she wouldn't be so freaked out, and it would be a good cheap souvenir of her own travels. She paused for a moment before picking out a third card. She'd drop a line to Olivia to let her know she was thinking of her. That couldn't hurt. Greyson jotted down a quick note and dropped the cards into the mail. At last, she was ready.

Not much farther down the road Greyson stopped under the rough wooden arch marking the Appalachian Trail, and welcoming hikers to Damascus.

She took her first step through the arch. The adventure had begun.

❖

Greyson skirted the edge of a rock cliff making her way to the precipice of a massive boulder. Her heart swelled. Stepping to the edge of the cliff was like walking onto heaven's front porch. This was what she came to see—the world as it should be, peaceful, natural, wild. Thunder rumbled across the mountains like a long cascading drumroll making her skin prickle. It was her third day on the trail and she had only hiked ten or so miles today. She was still eight miles away from the Watauga Lake Shelter, but dark clouds were closing in fast. If she was going to have any shelter at all, she needed to make camp quick. She studied the storm clouds heading her way. She sighed in acceptance. It was about time Mother Nature flexed her muscles a little.

Greyson decided to use the rocks to her advantage, setting up her camp with a slanting rock wall to her back, like a lean-to. She took a moment to watch the curtain of rain push across the mountains below her. Based on the movement of the clouds and rain, the rocks would act as a break against the force that was headed her way.

She unpacked her tent and rainfly, making swift work of setting up camp. She wouldn't have time for a fire, so dinner would have to be packaged tuna, wheat crackers, and a cup of blackberries she had picked along the trail. She spread out her sleeping bag and secured her pack inside. She pulled out a dry pack she had been using to secure her trash and got her dinner. She went to the edge of the rock and watched the rain roll in as she ate. Just as she scraped the last bits of tuna out of the package, a raindrop landed on her arm. That was her signal—it was time to clean up and head for shelter.

Greyson snapped the carabiner onto the dry pack and tossed it over a tree limb, tying off the rope to prevent bears or other critters from getting to the trash. She had only brought sealed packaged foods, so she wasn't worried about attracting animals to her tent. Greyson lay on top of her sleeping bag listening to the *pat, pat, pat* of raindrops on her tent turn to a thundering deluge pounding on the thin fabric separating her from the cleansing going on outside. The tent was small and didn't offer much in the way of comfort, but it was doing the job. She was dry and safe. What little light had been left in the day had been snuffed out by clouds and rain. She folded her arms behind her head, letting the thrum of the rain lull her to sleep.

She woke to the fresh smells of earth, pine, and honeysuckle. Greyson stepped from her tent and stretched, soaking in the crisp morning air. The rain had cooled the temperature, and the valley below was blanketed by fluffy white fog. Despite the full night of rain, the trail was remarkably clean. The ground was damp, but not muddy. Some of the rocks along the path were easily dislodged making the path a little tricky to maneuver. She would have to pay even more attention to each step as she walked along the cliff, or she could take a tumble over the edge. She took time to heat water for coffee and some instant oatmeal with some nuts and a few of the blackberries she'd saved from dinner.

If she read the map right she would cross a stream sometime around noon. She was eager to wash off the sweat and grime from the past few days. If she was lucky she might even get a swim to work out some of the stiffness in her muscles.

Greyson watched a couple of squirrels play tag, running circles around a giant oak, pausing from time to time to chatter and fuss before launching into another round. A chipmunk peeked at her around a rock and made his hesitant way closer to where she was sitting. She placed half a walnut on the rock a couple of feet in front of her.

At first the chipmunk was cautious, stretching his head into the air to sniff the tempting morsel. He scurried around the rocks, peeking out at her, testing her. At last he stepped into the clearing within a foot of the nut before running for his life back to the rocks. Greyson didn't move. He tried again, this time reaching his reward. He gave it a sniff before stuffing the nut into his jowl and sprinting away.

Amused, Greyson tried again, this time placing a small pile of mixed nuts for him. The chipmunk was braver this time. He stopped at the nuts and inspected the treasure. He twitched nervously and turned his head, studying Greyson. He picked up another walnut and chewed at the edges before stuffing it into his mouth. Greyson stifled a laugh as he stuffed the entire pile of nuts into his cheeks. By the time he had them all in place, his head was twice its original size. He scratched at his side with his back foot, his leg moving so fast he looked like a cartoon on fast-forward.

The chipmunk ran to the top of a rock almost as tall as Greyson, where he unloaded his treasure and sat down to breakfast. His meal complete, he stretched out on his belly on the rock and yawned, his legs stretched out in front and behind him in the perfect sunbathing pose, without a care in the world.

Greyson did laugh this time. She knew how he felt. She couldn't imagine a more perfect way to start her day. She was tempted to lie there in the sun with him, but the trail was waiting.

The chipmunk twitched and jumped up when Greyson moved. "Sorry, buddy, I've got to go. Thanks for the company." He scratched again. He looked up at her with his beady black eyes and smacked his mouth. She took that as thanks for breakfast. She nodded and smiled.

Greyson packed her tent and gear back in her pack and set off in search of the stream. She heard the water long before she could see it. She spotted a small overgrown trail that snaked off the main path leading toward the sound that beckoned her. The air grew cool and damp as Greyson drew closer to the water. The earth was scattered with ferns and covered in a thick blanket of green moss. Each step was like walking on a sponge. She pushed through the branches of a grouping of spruce trees and stepped into an oasis.

Water cascaded down the steep mountain, battering against rocks that buffered the wild water into control as it dropped the final twelve feet or so into a rippling pool. The pool was deep and alive at the base of the waterfall but settled into faint ripples at the other end before slowly making its way farther down the mountain. Greyson dipped her hand into the icy cool water. Periwinkles littered the pebbled floor like tiny conch shells from a fairy world. She was tempted to wade into the water and submerge her face and head to wash off the sweat and grime coating her skin, but she was patient. She knew how destructive this simple act could be to the life in the stream. The chemicals still trapped in her clothes and on her skin would contaminate the water for the wildlife as well as any hikers downstream.

She filled her camp shower bag with water and set it in the sun to heat. She then put a dirty pair of socks and a pair of shorts in a gallon size freezer bag, added some baking soda, and topped it off with water. She shook the bag vigorously for several minutes. She walked about two hundred yards away from the pool before emptying the soiled water on the ground and wringing out her clothes. She repeated this with all her laundry until she had most of the stink out of her clothes. When she was done, tree limbs around the area were decorated with socks, underwear, a pair of pants with zip-off leggings, her base layer, and a bra. She fastened her rainfly around a tree branch, making a privacy screen against a large tree, before she set up her camp shower, which was now toasty warm from the sun.

Greyson stepped behind the rainfly, then stripped off her clothes and tossed them on the ground outside her makeshift shower. The water was warm and soothing against her skin. The biodegradable soap didn't have any scent so it wouldn't attract insects, but at least she would be clean. She opened the valve to the shower bag and let the warm water cascade over her until she was damp all over. She closed the valve again, saving the rest of the water. She lathered soap into her hair and scrubbed her skin thoroughly before rinsing off. She used a small micro towel to dry herself before slipping into clean clothes.

It was getting late. She might as well camp here for the night.

She checked the clothes hanging from branches around her—her shorts, shirt, and underwear were almost dry, but it would take a while for the socks and her base layer, and by the time she washed the rest it would be getting dark. There was no sign of a fire ring, indicating this spot hadn't been used as a camp before. She decided against a fire. There was no point marking this spot. She wanted to make as little impact on the trail as possible. She pitched her tent, folded the dry clothes, put them in her pack, and prepared dinner. Tonight, dinner would consist of fresh water, a tube of peanut butter and jelly, some dried fruit, and a pack of beef jerky. She was beginning to understand what the waitress in Damascus had meant about the hikers having a hungry look about them. She would be more than ready for a real meal by the time she made it to Hot Springs. She would have to reconsider her food options for the next part of the trail so she wouldn't get too burned-out on the prepackaged food.

As night fell, she slipped inside her tent and snuggled into her sleeping bag. She was tired but not ready to sleep. She lay on her back staring up through the screen in the roof of her tent. The stars were so bright she could see them through the tops of the trees.

She thought about what Dawn had said about her sharing her tent with a woman and wondered what it would be like to share this with someone else. It was strange for her to want to share experiences like this with anyone. Usually she talked to Dawn, but she knew Dawn didn't get her need to be in the woods. It would be nice to have someone in her life who really got her. But she had learned it was best to keep to herself. She wouldn't want someone chattering on all the time, complaining about this and that. At least Olivia had seemed excited about her plans to do this hike. She wondered if this was the kind of thing Olivia could get into. She'd admitted she'd been camping before. Maybe they could do a hike together sometime. Greyson shook her head. What was she thinking? No, she was happy keeping this for herself.

❖

Olivia ground her teeth to keep from screaming at her mother. She wasn't even sure why she bothered to come home at all anymore. Her mother never listened and she was tired of trying to defend who she was.

"He's such a nice boy. I expect you to show your manners when he gets here."

"Don't you even want to know why I stopped being friends with him in the first place? He's not as nice as you think he is."

"Kids always argue. I'm sure it was all a misunderstanding—besides, that was so long ago, and you've both grown up since then. People change."

Olivia sighed in frustration. She knew what her mother meant by *people change*. Her mother just would not give up on the idea of her settling down with a man and having babies. What was that all about anyway, like she couldn't possibly have any other purpose in life than being a baby factory. But really it wasn't about kids. Olivia loved kids—hello, that was her job. She just didn't want it to be all anyone expected of her. If she ever found the right woman, she wouldn't mind settling down and making a family of her own.

"I don't want to change, Momma. I like who I am. I like my life. I don't want the same things you want. Why can't you just let me be?"

They were interrupted by the sound of heavy footsteps on the porch and her father's deep voice talking to someone.

Her mother wiped her hands on her apron and pushed back the loose strands of her hair. You would have thought she was the one Larry was there to see.

Larry walked through the door, and Olivia hoped her surprise didn't show on her face. He had gained about twenty pounds of muscle since she last saw him and his hairline was already receding. He certainly wasn't the wiry boy she'd remembered.

"Hello, Mrs. Danner." He nodded toward Olivia's mother, then to her. "Olivia, it's good to see you. It's been a long time."

"Hello, Larry."

"Dinner's almost ready," Olivia's mother said in a rush. "Why don't you all go ahead and have a seat at the table. Olivia and I will bring everything out in a moment."

Olivia took the bowl of mashed potatoes and the plate of chicken her mother handed her. She reminded herself all she had to do was get though dinner. She took a deep breath and followed her mother to the table.

"Everything looks delicious, Mrs. Danner. I appreciate you inviting me over."

"Think nothing of it. We're glad you could make it, and it's nice it worked out that Olivia could be here too."

Olivia stifled a groan but was certain her mother saw her roll her eyes.

Larry smiled at Olivia. "That is very nice."

Olivia swallowed the piece of bread she had been chewing and cleared her throat. "So, Larry, what have you been doing with yourself all these years?"

"I joined the military after high school. I'm a helicopter pilot in the army."

"Wow, that sounds exciting," Olivia said with genuine enthusiasm. This was a big switch from the pigheaded boy who skipped school more often than he showed up. By the looks of things Larry really had turned his life around. Maybe her mother was at least right about that, she admitted. There had been a time when she'd considered Larry a good friend. But sometime in high school, everything changed. She hoped the changes Larry had made had brought him back to the friend she remembered growing up.

"It is," Larry agreed.

"What brings you back home then?" she asked.

Larry looked down at his plate. "Well, after Alice left me, I guess I needed to come back to my roots and find myself again. I'll only be here for a few more days before I fly out. When I ran into your momma, I'd hoped maybe you and I could spend some time together, catch up on life."

Olivia glanced at her mother. "I'm sure Momma explained that I don't live here anymore. I'm just visiting for the weekend."

Olivia's mother pushed back her chair, scraping the legs across the old wood floor. "Oh, but you don't have to be in any hurry to get back. Since you don't have work, you can stay as long as you like."

"I'll be leaving in the morning," Olivia snapped.

Olivia's mother huffed. "We need more tea." She stomped out of the room.

"Pass me the cornbread and that bowl of onions," Olivia's father said, seemingly unaware of the drama playing out in front of him.

Olivia passed the bread and Larry handed over the onions.

Olivia's mother returned with the tea and a fresh bowl of banana pudding. "I hope everyone saved room for dessert," her mother announced cheerfully.

Larry put his napkin on the table. "I'm sorry to hear that, Olivia. I'd hoped I could take you out to dinner tomorrow."

"How nice," Olivia's mother said before she could answer.

Olivia glared at her mother. "That is very nice, but like I said, I need to be getting home."

"Oh, nonsense," her mother huffed.

Olivia snapped. "Stop it, Momma. Stop trying to run my life."

"Well, someone's got to. You've already made a fine mess of things on your own."

Olivia's father put down his fork. "Settle down, Jewel. The girl's got a right to a life of her own."

"Well, someone's got to do something. I won't have a daughter of mine living like that."

Larry looked thoroughly confused. "I'm sorry. Am I missing something?"

Olivia turned to Larry, feeling the heat of anger burning her face. "I'm a lesbian, Larry. I don't date men."

Larry's eyes widened. "Oh." He seemed to take the information in for a moment. He shrugged. "Cool."

Olivia's mother slammed her napkin down on the table as she stood. "Olivia June, that's enough. I won't have that talk in my house."

"Fine, Momma." Olivia turned back to Larry. "I'm sorry, Larry. It was good seeing you." Olivia pushed away from the table and stormed out.

❖

Greyson made it to the Watauga Lake Shelter a little past twelve the next day, only to find a sign tacked to the lean-to noting that the shelter was closed due to bear activity. The hairs at the back of her neck bristled. She would have to be a lot more careful from here on out. She had been aware of bears, of course, but this made things real. She had heard of hikers having their food stolen and their gear ripped to shreds by bears who were getting too used to hikers and the easy access to a free meal. The last thing she needed was to lose all her supplies and risk getting hurt. She would start staggering her hiking to camp a few miles away from the shelters for a while. If she was lucky, the bears would gravitate to the shelters and be less likely to stumble across her. She could stop at the shelters during the day and fill up with water and maybe visit with some other hikers and get news about any other trail activity she needed to know.

She looked around long enough to find the water source. Her water supply was more important than food, as the days were hot and humid. She had just filled her bottles and her CamelBak when she heard footsteps along the trail behind her. She looked up to see a man and a woman headed her way. The man had shaved his hair close to the scalp and wore a multicolored bandana around his neck. He was thin and his boots were well worn from the miles he had trekked. The woman had white dreadlocks pulled back at the neck. She wore large white-rimmed plastic sunglasses that were too big for her face, and a line of tattoos peeked out at the neck and sleeves of her T-shirt in stark contrast to her pale skin.

The woman waved as they approached. "I hope you left some there for us."

Greyson secured her water in her pack and smiled. "More than enough."

The man dropped his pack on the ground and went straight for the water, scooping up big handfuls and splashing his face. He dipped the bandanna in the water and washed his face and neck.

"Man, that feels good," he said as he rose and faced Greyson. He extended his hand. "I'm Green Man and this is Summer Rain. But Green and Summer will do."

Greyson took his hand. "Good to meet you, I'm Mountain Troll. It's good to see you guys. You're the first hikers I've seen out here so far."

"How long have you been out?" Summer asked.

"Just a week. I thought for sure I'd see someone long before now," Greyson answered.

Green shrugged. "It's like that sometimes. Then sometimes you'll run into someone every day or so. We stopped in Erwin for a few days and got in some solid playtime. We met a lot of folks there heading south, but they're a good week ahead of you."

"Have you seen any bears?" Greyson asked, curious just how intrusive the bears had become.

Summer had joined them by the water and was filling her water bottle. "We had a close call a couple of nights ago. We were setting up camp when a bear wandered into the area. We had no choice but to pick up and keep moving. There was no way we wanted to risk losing all our gear. The guys in Erwin warned us about the bears this far down. They said some dude had been feeding the bears and they got used to the free grub. Some people just don't have a clue how much harm they cause when they mess with nature."

Greyson shook her head. She was sure the guy probably meant well without a notion of the harm he was doing, but it was hard to believe people were still so reckless. Feeding the bears not only put people at risk, but it inevitably meant harm or even death for the bear.

"Any news if anyone's been hurt?"

Green shook his head. "None that we know of, just trashing camps so far. We hope the bears will move on as the food source dries up."

Greyson noticed the muscle at his jaw jump as he clenched his teeth, showing his frustration.

"Did you guys find any suitable sites to camp outside the shelters?"

Green nodded. "Yeah, there's a place about twelve miles out that hikers have started using, but there's no water source. There are a few streams near the trails along the hike, though, so it works out. Take as much water as you can from here—it might be all you get for a while."

"Same here. I found a nice stream about ten miles down. You'll see it on the map, but it's off the trail a bit. There's no established camp, though. It's still pretty pristine. I camped another few miles down at a nice rock ledge when the storm came through. The view is great."

"Thanks, man, we'll look for it."

Greyson and her new friends hiked back to the camp and sat down to lunch. Although she had been enjoying the off the grid solitude of the mountains, she had missed having human conversation. She noticed how easy it was to talk to Green and Summer. They talked like lifelong friends forged from adventure and mutual experience. She wished more of her relationships felt like this. Maybe it was because they really weren't friends and would likely never see each other again that made the connection so easy.

With lunch finished, Greyson topped off her water and picked up her pack. "Safe travels out there," Greyson said as she accepted a quick hug from Summer.

She looked back and gave a final wave. Summer was blowing her kisses in true Hollywood style. Greyson laughed. You never knew what you'd see in the mountains.

Moments later silence engulfed Greyson and her solitude was securely back in place. The brief encounter with Green and Summer had left her rejuvenated and eager to find out what other surprises the mountain had in store for her.

❖

Olivia listened to her parents' muffled voices filter up through the floor from downstairs. A few minutes later she heard footsteps on the stairs and the front door close. A gentle knock sounded at her bedroom door.

"Come in."

The door opened and her father stepped into the room. "We're heading off to church now—you sure you don't want to come?"

"I'm sure, Daddy. I think it's best if I just head on home."

Her dad rubbed his big hand across his jaw the way he did when he wasn't sure how to say something. "I don't know how to settle this thing between you and your momma. She can be stubborn as an old mule when she sets her mind to something, but she loves you. Don't you forget that."

Olivia sighed. "I know, Daddy. I just want her to love me for who I am, not for who she wants me to be."

He nodded. "Well, you be safe on the road. Don't stay gone too long."

Olivia stood and went to her dad. She wrapped her arms around his big frame and squeezed. She felt his strong arms close around her, his hand cradling her head like when she was a child.

"I love you, Daddy."

"I love you too, baby girl."

Olivia smiled up at him.

"Well, I best be getting or your momma will have my butt in the coals."

Olivia laughed. She watched her daddy walk away until the top of his head disappeared down the stairs.

The visit had been a disaster, but she loved her parents. She wondered what they would think if she ever brought a woman home. She thought of Greyson and smiled. With Greyson's good looks, maybe even her momma would have to see the light. Olivia laughed at the thought of her momma gushing over Greyson the way she had done over Larry. She shook her head. That was only a dream. Given her luck, her momma would have a stroke. Olivia would never be able to live that down. She packed up the rest of her things and said good-bye to her childhood room as she closed the door.

A clap of thunder startled her just as she tossed her bag into the car. She looked up at the dark clouds blowing in from the west. It looked like they were in for one heck of a storm. She shivered, as an ominous feeling slithered across her skin. She hurriedly got into the car, eager to get on the road and get home.

Olivia pulled onto Highway 52 just as the storm hit. Rain beat against her windshield in steady sheets, obscuring her visibility. She had slowed the car to a crawl but had no choice but to pull over to the side of the road when the hail threatened to break her windshield.

"Oh no, my poor little car. I'm sorry, Daisy." Olivia peered into the rain and hail trying to find any sign of a break in the weather. Her hopes were dashed when a flash of lightning pierced through the already deafening drum against the roof of her car, followed by another loud crack of thunder.

A knock against her driver's window made her scream and jump. This was just like the things she saw in those scary movies. At least it wasn't dark outside. Olivia tried to make out the figure through the window, but between the rain and the hooded jacket the person wore, there was no way to see who it was. She cracked the window just enough to hear what they had to say.

"You all right, ma'am?" A man's voice.

"I'm fine. I'm just waiting out the storm."

The man slid his fingers through the crack of the window and leaned down to peer in at her. "You've got a flat tire on the rear and the weather is giving a tornado warning for the area. Can I take you someplace safe? There's a café just up the road in Rugby where you could wait this out until someone can come fix that tire."

Olivia slumped into her seat. Great, all she needed was a flat on top of everything. The wind whipped the rain around and rocked the car. Maybe this guy was right. Maybe she should go somewhere else until this blew over. She looked through her rearview mirror, but all she could see was the chrome grille of a big truck, and the persistent yellow blinker signaling his turn off the road.

"Ma'am?"

Olivia nodded. "Okay. I guess you're right. I don't want to be sitting here if a tornado whips through." She reached for her phone and turned off the car's ignition. She pushed open the car door and stepped into the pouring rain.

The man shut the door behind her, and they ran to his truck. He opened the door, helping Olivia inside as quickly as she could manage. He slammed the door, and she watched him run around the front of the truck, his head down as the rain pelted down on him. He jumped up into the truck and slammed the door.

"Whew, that's some storm."

Olivia shivered. Her hair and clothes were soaked.

"Here, let me put on a little heat and knock down the chill." He reached for the knob to the heater, and a second later warm air blew across her skin.

"What do you say we get out of here?" the man said as he put the truck in gear and pulled out onto the road. The windshield wipers had little effect as they worked to push aside the waves of water, but the man didn't seem bothered by the rain or the poor visibility.

"Thanks for your help."

He smiled. "No problem." He glanced over at Olivia. "I have a blanket behind the seat that you can use to dry off if you want." He reached behind the seat and pulled out a soft cotton blanket.

Olivia wiped at her face and arms and wrapped the blanket loosely across her lap. She leaned back against the seat, relieved. She closed her eyes and let out her breath.

Olivia opened her eyes as she felt the truck slow and the tires leave the pavement. She peered out the window looking up at the storm. "Is everything okay?"

Olivia jumped as the man's hand and a wet cloth closed over her face. She panicked as a pungent smell filled her nose, coating the back of her throat. She pushed at the man's hand and tried to pull her face away, but he held on too tight. Olivia tried not to breathe, but it was too late. She felt dizzy and faint, then nothing.

CHAPTER FOUR

The Recruiter studied the map in front of him with cold intensity. Based on what he had been able to learn about the target, she should be coming through the area in a matter of days. He had scoped out several trailheads and campsites, but so far everything had been busy with too many people around. He didn't want to go too far into the trail. That would make it difficult to get in and out without being noticed. He needed a quiet, secluded area close enough to the trail and the road, but out of sight of people. He ran his fingers along a line indicating a small parking area with a connecter trail that crossed the AT. He followed the line to a small triangle indicating a campsite. It had potential.

The roads here were barely wide enough for two cars to pass and were rarely paved. The only people he passed or saw along the way were usually on foot, hikers making their way down the mountain into town. Many of the smaller sites were open to the public and didn't require registration. That was convenient. He could stay in the area for a while without notice. The people here were used to strangers hanging around, and if anyone did see him, he would just be another hiker passing through.

He pulled off the road onto a small packed-dirt parking area. The trail here appeared overgrown, indicating little traffic came through there. He checked the map again. This was the spot he had been looking for, and it was perfect. Mostly concealed from the road, his van was barely noticeable. He could park here, hike into the woods, and camp near the trail. He would have perfect access to the target when the time came.

He pushed through the thick brush that encroached on the thin line of trail. He stopped inside a thick growth of mountain laurel and smiled. The plant grew in large sprawling bushes clustered together forming the perfect cover for his gear. Positioned right, he would be hidden completely. It would be nearly impossible for a passerby to spot him if he didn't want them to.

He smiled. The hunter had found his lair. Now all he had to do was wait.

❖

Greyson let out a long slow breath. After two weeks alone in the mountains she had finally made it to Hot Springs, North Carolina, the second state she'd pass through on her journey. She was only a few days' hike away from home. She was excited about crossing the Smoky Mountains. She was tempted to call Olivia to see if she'd join her along the route for dinner. But that was a reach, and way off course. She was just getting lonely.

Although she enjoyed her solitude, it was good to see civilization again. She was looking forward to a long hot shower, the biggest steak she could get her hands on, and a real bed. She followed the familiar AT diamond symbol inlaid in the sidewalks along Bridge Street, turned onto South Andrews Avenue, and managed to get a room at the Iron Horse Station. After sleeping on the ground for two weeks, this was more than a treat. Not only was the hotel right in the heart of town, the restaurant downstairs looked like the perfect place for that steak she had been craving.

The shower was pure heaven. She would never take hot water for granted again. She washed her clothes and inventoried her gear to see what she could live without, what she needed to resupply, and what she had discovered she needed but didn't have. With the smell of days of sweat and dirt scrubbed from her body and clothes, she felt human again. Her stomach rumbled. It was time for a real meal.

Greyson took a seat at the bar and looked around the room. The restaurant was decorated with the history of the railroad that was just outside the door. The decor was very understated and comfortable, the kind of place a group of friends could gather regularly to have a drink, share old stories, and make new ones. Wow. Maybe the solitude had gotten to her more than she thought.

"Hey, stud, what are you drinking?" the bartender said as she slid a menu in front of Greyson.

"I'll have the Gaelic Ale," Greyson answered.

"You just drinking or would you like some food too?"

Greyson smiled. "Oh, I'm eating. I've been looking forward to this for the past three days."

"Ah, you just came off the trail," the waitress said with the knowing tone of someone familiar with hikers.

"Yep. I guess you're used to hikers coming through here."

"You bet. The town counts on it. Plus, it makes work more interesting. I'm sure you have your own stories to tell."

Greyson smiled. "Not really. I've had a good couple of weeks, but nothing you haven't heard before."

The bartender cocked her hip against the bar. "So, what's it going to be tonight?"

Greyson licked her lips. "Rib eye medium rare, loaded baked potato, and broccoli. Oh, and I'll have a side salad with ranch dressing too."

"Bread?"

Greyson's stomach growled as she imagined the meal. "Oh yeah, lots of bread."

The bartender laughed as she slid the beer in front of Greyson. "You've got it, champ."

Greyson lifted her glass and took a deep drink of her beer. She sighed as the cold taste of hops and barley brought her taste buds to life. The fatigue she had been carrying for the past two weeks weighed on her shoulders as if she still carried her pack on her back. She sighed to release the weariness. She rubbed her face—maybe a good meal would pick her up and give her that boost she needed to keep going. She lifted her beer for another drink, savoring the smooth taste as some of the tiredness lifted.

The bartender set a basket of rolls in front of Greyson. "Here you go, sweetheart. This will pick you up a little. Want another drink?"

Greyson snagged a roll. "Yes, please." She tore into the bread and slathered it with a pat of butter. The moment the salty tang and the fluffy yeast hit her tongue, Greyson moaned. This was better than sex. She chuckled as she chewed. Well, it was close to as good as sex at the moment.

She ripped through the salad, reminding herself to chew her food and to slow down so she wouldn't scare the other patrons.

"Easy there, champ, you better slow down if you plan to get through this steak."

Greyson slowed her pace and put her third roll back in the basket. She was back in civilization and needed to act like she had some manners.

She looked up as the still sizzling steak was placed in front of her. The smell alone was enough to make her cry. Manners were overrated.

She sighed. "Thank you, God."

Greyson took the first bite of steak and groaned. This made every handful of nuts, every cup of noodles, and every packet of tuna she had choked down in the past two weeks worth every bland bite. This was serious flavor overload. This was the kind of moment that made her realize all the things she took for granted in her life. She had a home and good friends, she liked her job, and she had every material thing she needed. She was even lucky enough to have the time to make this journey. What had taken her so long? That was something she needed to work on from now on. Work was important, but not more important than knowing what she was working for.

"Looks like you did okay with the meal. Want another drink?" the bartender asked, sweeping away the empty plate.

"What's your name?" Greyson asked.

"Laura."

"Thank you, Laura. That was the perfect meal, and yes, I'd love another drink. I have a feeling I'm going to have the best night's sleep of my life."

Laura smiled. "I bet you're right." She set a fresh beer in front of Greyson. "What name are you using?"

Greyson laughed. "I'm Mountain Troll, but you can call me Greyson."

"Okay, Greyson, what would you say has been the biggest lesson you've learned on the trail so far?"

"Is this one of those things hikers talk about?"

Laura grinned. "All the time. As I understand it, there are three reasons people do the AT. They're either running from something, looking for something, or need to prove something."

Greyson thought for a moment. "Well, I think I'm learning to appreciate my life more, especially the people in it. According to your categories I guess I'm doing the trail to challenge myself, but I think I'm also looking for something."

"What are you looking for?" Laura asked.

"Good question. I'm not sure I have the answer."

"Then how will you know if you find it?" Laura asked.

This question caught Greyson off guard. "I guess I'd like to think I'll know it when it happens."

"So you're a journey and not a destination kind of person." Someone called for Laura to pick up an order. "I'll be right back."

Greyson nodded. She took a drink of her beer as she contemplated what Laura had said. She knew the answer was too complicated to put into one category or another, but Laura had made a point. What would be the lesson of this journey? Would the trip show her things about her life, herself, that she had been too busy or too stubborn to see? Well, at least she had plenty of time left to find out.

Laura returned with the check. "Can I get you anything else?"

"No. I think I'm ready for that good night's sleep," Greyson answered.

"How long are you sticking around?"

Greyson shrugged. "I'll be here tomorrow. I think I need a couple more good meals before I head back out."

Laura laughed. "Maybe I'll see you tomorrow then."

"Maybe," Greyson said with a smile. "Oh, and to answer your question, I think it's about both the journey and the destination. The trail makes me think outside my comfort zone. I consider possibilities I never would have thought of before. But without a destination I'd just be lost."

Laura smiled. "Good luck out there, Mountain Troll. I hope the trail angels are kind to you."

"Thanks." Greyson stood to leave. "Save a steak for me tomorrow."

❖

Greyson pushed through the door of the small post office. It was just one room, lined with post office boxes and a small counter. The building was so small it was easy to miss if you weren't paying attention.

She walked to the counter and heard a bell chime in the back. She looked down to see sensors at both ends of the counter. She had broken the beam alerting anyone in the back that she was there.

"I'll be right there," someone called.

A moment later a sixtyish woman with spiked silver hair rounded the corner. She squinted one eye and surveyed Greyson. "Hmm, haven't seen you before. Are you a through-hiker? Which direction, north or south?"

Greyson smiled. "How'd you know I was a hiker?"

"You have that worn-down look, like you haven't been eating right and your skin doesn't quite fit anymore. Besides, I know everyone in town and you're a new face."

Greyson laughed. "Well, I am a hiker, but I'm just a section hiker this trip. I'm hoping you have a package for me, Greyson Cooper."

"Ah, yes, that one's been here awhile. I was wondering when you were going to show up." She disappeared around the corner again. Greyson could hear her shuffling things around. She reappeared like a mole in one of those carnival games.

"*This* trip, you say. I guess you know what you're getting yourself into out there then."

Greyson shrugged. "So far, so good. As long as these supplies keep showing up, I just might live."

The older woman laughed. "It's not the mail you need to worry about, it's the bears. They've been unusually active this year. They're either getting drawn in by the traveling snack bar or they're hurting for their usual grub. Either way, you watch yourself."

Greyson nodded. "I ran into some hikers who had a close call a little over a week ago. I've been avoiding the shelters since then. Several of them have already been closed because of the bear activity, but I haven't had any trouble myself."

"Well, that's good. I guess that means you came from the north. I don't know of any shelters closed south of here."

Greyson lifted her box, then noticed the small name tag pinned to the old woman's shirt. "Thanks for the heads-up, Pat."

Pat smiled. "I've been working in this post office for the past thirty years, and I've seen an awful lot of you kids pass through here. Most had no idea what they were getting into when they started."

"Thirty years, huh? Have you ever done the trail yourself?"

A glint sparkled in Pat's eye. She squared her shoulders as a brilliant smile lit her face. "I've been bottom to top and back three times."

Greyson extended her hand. "That's impressive. Any advice?"

Pat's expression grew pensive as she shook Greyson's hand. "You never know who you'll meet on the trail. Keep your head up. Make noise to scare the bears away. Make sure you drink enough water, and..." She paused. "Should you meet Lucile on the trail, tell her hello for me."

Greyson frowned, confused by the last part, but something told her it wasn't something she was meant to understand. "Thanks again, Pat. I appreciate your help." She turned to leave but stopped at the door. "Hey, Pat." She turned to see the old woman watching her. "Do you plan on doing the AT a fourth time?"

Pat grinned. "Does a bear shit in the woods?"

Greyson laughed. "Roger that. See you on the trail."

Greyson was eager to get back to her room, settle her gear, and grab another big dinner. She wanted to get the most out of this zero day because she planned on getting some serious miles under her feet tomorrow. She was heading into home territory and the Great Smoky Mountains were calling her name.

She decided to change things up for dinner. She took a seat at a small cast iron table on the deck at Spring Creek Tavern where she had noticed a group of hikers gathered. As expected it didn't take long for the group to commandeer most of the tables around her on the patio.

A baby-faced young man with sunburned cheeks and a buzz cut came over to her table. "Hey, man, you mind if I use these chairs?"

"No problem." Greyson nodded toward the chairs in question. "You guys just come off the trail today?"

He grinned. "Yeah, we've been out for about a month now. We're really looking forward to some beer tonight. What about you? You been out?"

"Yep, I came in yesterday. I'll be back out there tomorrow."

"Cool, man. Hey, you want to join us? We're just bullshitting and celebrating Bull's new haircut." He pointed to a petite young woman with a buzz cut.

"Bullshit and celebrating sounds like my kind of night. Thanks."

Greyson and the young man pulled her table and the remaining chairs up to the group.

"Hey, guys, we've got a new friend."

The group all seemed to look up at Greyson at once. She smiled and raised a hand in greeting.

A thin man with muddy brown hair pulled back in a bun waved back. "Good deal, man. What's your name?"

Greyson sat down. "I'm Mountain Troll."

"Cool. I saw your login in Damascus. Pretty cool shit. How did it go? Something about the trail and the journey, right?"

"Good memory."

"*My feet shall take this path, but it is my spirit that makes the journey.*" The girl they called Bull rubbed her head as if the feel was unfamiliar to her. "That's the truth of it, isn't it."

The baby-faced guy said, "That's sure true for you, Bull. I never would have imagined you cutting off all your hair before we started this. I always knew you wanted to be me."

Bull gave him the middle finger.

"Well you were a bit of a prima donna."

"Bite me, Rascal."

Greyson was enjoying the playful banter and could tell the group had known each other for a while.

"How much hair did you cut off?" Greyson asked.

Bull sighed. "We think it was sixteen inches, scalp to tip."

"Wow, that's a big change. Why'd you do it?"

Bull rubbed her head again. "I got tired of it. It was too hot on the trail, it stayed dirty and smelly all the time, and I kept getting it caught in bushes. Now that it's gone, I realize how heavy it was."

"Do you think you'll be okay with it once you're off the trail?" Greyson asked.

Bull grinned. "I really don't know. It feels so weird. All I know right now is that the next few weeks on the trail are going to be a breeze. By the time we're done, my hair should be as long as yours." Bull reached over and tugged at the hair above Greyson's ear. "If mine looks as good as yours, I just might keep it short."

While they were talking, the waitress brought the first round of beer. Greyson leaned closer to Bull and asked what she assumed was the obvious question. "So how did you get the name Bull?"

That stirred everyone at the table. It seemed this sweet young woman had a tendency to get herself into a bit of trouble.

The guy with the man-bun laughed and elaborated. "Bull is the quintessential bull in a china shop on steroids. If you only knew how many fights we've all been in because she dumped her beer over some guy's head."

"Shut up, Boone."

The group laughed.

"Here's to Bull," Rascal called out, lifting his beer.

"To Bull," the group sang out in unison.

It was a good night. The group made Greyson feel like she was a part of their little tribe. It was nice to laugh. It made her miss her own friends and their crazy outings. She thought of her last night at home, saying good night to Olivia outside her apartment. It would be nice to hear her voice, tell her about the trail, find out how things were going with her. Greyson sighed. It was strange to miss someone she hardly knew. But that was what she was feeling. Of all the people she knew, Olivia was the one her heart longed for.

She decided it was a good time to call it a night. "That's it for me, guys. See you on the trail," she said finishing her beer.

"No way, dude, you can't bail yet, it's still early." Rascal held on to her chair so she couldn't leave.

Greyson leaned close to Rascal. "You guys are about ten years younger than I am, you still have the day off tomorrow, and I plan to take advantage of a full night's sleep in a real bed. I can't afford to be hungover on the trail tomorrow."

"Yeah, man, I hear you," Rascal conceded.

"You guys are moving faster than I am. You'll probably pass me on the trail in the next few days anyway."

"All right, man. Journey on."

Greyson fell onto her bed the moment she stepped into her room. She rolled onto her back and dug her cell phone out of her pocket. She had a promise to keep.

The phone rang twice before being picked up.

"It's about time you called."

Dawn's raspy voice crackled though the phone. Greyson could hear noise in the background and knew Dawn had people over.

"Sounds like there's a party going on."

Dawn laughed. "Yeah, it's just the usual group. Man, they are so jealous of me right now."

Greyson laughed. "Did you get my postcard?"

"I did. Very clever of you. I thought for sure you'd forget all about me the moment you hit that trail. I thought you were supposed to call yesterday. One more day and I would have been calling search and rescue."

"You might want to give me a couple of days' wiggle room before you call in the troops. I don't want to be lagging behind because of weather or something and jump the gun. I really am okay. I'm having a really good time and I'm getting used to things."

"So is it everything you'd dreamed?"

Greyson yawned. It was good to talk to Dawn, but fatigue was getting to her. "It's everything and more. I don't know what took me so long to do this."

"Well, you better get your butt back here in one piece," Dawn teased.

"I will. Listen, I'm heading back out tomorrow and I'm dying for some serious sleep. I'll talk to you in a few days."

"Okay, buddy. Stay safe."

"I will. Oh yeah, one more thing," Greyson added.

"What's that?" Dawn asked.

"Don't sink my boat."

Dawn was still laughing when Greyson hung up the phone.

She stared at the screen. There was one more call she wanted to make before going to sleep. She dialed Olivia's number. She frowned when the call went straight to voicemail. She hung up without leaving a message. What would she say? She pushed aside the wave of disappointment. Maybe it was for the best. She was letting Olivia get into her head. She needed to rest and she needed to get focused on why she was here.

CHAPTER FIVE

A sharp pinch at Olivia's wrist pulled her out of her sleep. She woke from a terrible dream, the kind you know can't be real, but won't allow you to wake. The dream clung to her like cold mist, making her skin feel clammy. She shivered, then blinked. Her mouth was dry and tasted of something sweet. The persistent pinch at her wrist drew her attention. She stared at her arm in disbelief. A fresh tattoo stood out on her wrist. "What? No. This can't be real. I would *never...*"

She looked around the room for the first time, realizing something was wrong. This wasn't a hospital. What was it? There were no windows and the walls were made of cinder block. Bars blocked the only entrance. It felt like a cell or a dungeon.

A sinking feeling settled in her stomach. Her dream had been real. Olivia screamed. Her voice echoed around the sparsely furnished room, the concrete walls around her magnifying her terror. Every passing minute seemed like hours. Her mind raced, fueled by fear and adrenaline. Where was she? What was happening? Why was she here? She tried to remember. She had been at her parents'. They had fought again. She closed her eyes remembering the look of disappointment in her mother's eyes. "Oh, Momma. Where are you? I'm so sorry I yelled at you." Tears pricked her eyes. She had been driving. She remembered a storm. And a man. A man stopped to help her. A sob caught in her throat as she realized what had happened. "Oh no. Please, no."

She replayed the news reports over and over in her mind. Those poor women who had been found murdered. Had the reporters said anything about tattoos? She remembered something about signs of torture. Oh God, would she end up like them?

Was this the same man who had hurt all those women? Panic rose up in her throat again and she wanted to scream, she wanted to throw herself against the cell doors until someone came to let her out. But the thought of that someone was more terrifying than anything else. She shook with fear. All she could do was sit and wait. She tried not to imagine the horrors those women had gone through. She couldn't allow herself to believe that was her fate. Tears streamed down her cheeks. She had been so determined not to go back to her parents'. She had been desperate and had made a fatal mistake. Now she would give anything to be back on the farm listening to her mother preach at her.

She heard footsteps in the hall. She stared at the cell door, dreading what was coming. Her heart hammered against her chest with such force she thought it might burst. She held her hand over her mouth to hold back the sound of her choked sobs.

A tall, thin figure stepped in front of the door and stood for a moment watching her. The sound of a key being inserted into the lock was like thunder as the tumblers fell. The door opened and the man stepped inside. The door closed and she heard the *snick* of the lock. She wouldn't be getting out that easy.

As her eyes focused, she trained her gaze on the man who held her life in his hands.

"Who are you? What are you going to do to me?" Olivia said through sobs.

He smiled. "Don't worry, I don't want to hurt you."

"Then why are you doing this to me?" Olivia asked.

He brushed the hair away from her face, making her flinch. "You were chosen. That means you're special."

Olivia shook her head. "Why?" Her voice cracked. Her mouth was dry and her throat burned.

His smile turned wicked. "Because I always get what I want."

The blood in Olivia's veins turned cold. By the look in his eyes and the tone of his voice, she was certain she didn't want to know what he wanted with her.

He sat on the cot next to her, too close for her comfort.

"You see, Ms. Danner, I'm a collector. I collect many things, but my most prized possession is life. I knew the moment I saw you in that coffee shop that you would be special. You have a certain quality about you that speaks to me." He inhaled a deep breath, waving his hand in front of his face as if sampling the scent of her.

Olivia clenched her hands tight around her middle. The thought of this man getting anywhere near her was nauseating.

He hadn't missed her response. He leaned back with a satisfied smile. "I like the smell of your fear. I would have liked to have taunted you for a while before taking you, but I couldn't risk losing you." He ran a finger along her cheek. Olivia jerked away from him. "Don't worry, we can start slow. I have a job for you. As long as you do what I tell you, no one will touch you. If you don't do what I say, we'll have to change our arrangement. You'd be worth a lot more in the sex trade anyway. It's up to you."

Olivia wasn't sure what he was talking about or what this job might be if it wasn't sex, but she was willing to do just about anything to keep him away from her.

"How long do I have to be here?" she asked.

He smiled. "This is home now, Ms. Danner. Didn't I make myself clear? You belong to me."

Tears flowed freely down Olivia's cheeks. She was helpless. Her worst nightmare was coming true and she had no way out.

He grabbed her arm. She tried to pull away, but he was too strong. He slapped her across the face. "Be still," he commanded.

Olivia stilled. The sting in her cheek burned to the bone and she felt the flesh begin to swell.

He pulled out her arm, studying the fresh tattoo etched into her skin. He ran his thumb across the tender flesh. Olivia realized he was rubbing something onto her skin.

"What is that?" she asked.

"Just a little ointment. We don't want this to get infected."

The contrast was astounding. This man had abducted her,

drugged her, branded her, and was holding her captive. Now he was worried her arm would become infected.

"What do you care?"

"Ah, I care a great deal about all of my investments," he said with a smile.

Olivia frowned, trying to make sense of what was happening. She looked at the tattoo. The skin was raised and red, but the swelling wasn't too bad. The pattern was strange. It was some kind of shield or coat of arms or something. She looked closer at the number *33* elegantly displayed in the center. What did it mean?

"What are you going to do to me?" she asked.

"We'll see," he said with a grin. "Slow. Remember? You'll learn everything you need to know soon enough."

He stood, placing the tube of ointment on the table. "Keep that arm clean and put this on a few times a day. It will heal in a few days."

He walked back to the door. "See you soon, Ms. Danner."

As he stepped out, Olivia threw herself at the door, trying to push it open before it could be locked. But she was no match for him, and the door pulled closed an instant before she could slide her fingers into the gap.

Olivia slid to the floor, pounding her fists against the unforgiving metal until her hands were sore and bruised. Defeated, she crawled back to the bed. She repeated everything he had said to her over and over in her head. What coffee shop did he mean? She had never seen him before. She groaned. How had she been so gullible, or desperate, as to allow something like this to happen?

❖

Olivia searched the room for a way to escape, but the cell was a fortress. She studied the wall across from her. It was lined with photographs of other women who looked remarkably like her. Had they been kept in this room? Where were they now? What had happened to them?

She jumped at the sound of keys outside the door. She retreated to the corner of the room as if she could blend in with the walls and wouldn't be seen.

The door opened and in stepped a woman that could have been Olivia's mother. Her blond hair was pulled back at her neck and fell between her shoulders. The most striking difference between them was their eye color—this woman had deep blue eyes. A guard closed the door behind her once she was inside.

The woman carried a bundle of blankets and sheets in her arms. "I'm Liz," the woman said. "You don't have to be afraid of me."

Olivia studied the woman and flicked her eyes to the pictures on the wall, finding the woman's photo almost instantly.

"You're alive," Olivia said with surprise.

The woman looked to the photos and back to Olivia. "Yes, and you will be too if you do what you're told."

"What about the others?" Olivia pointed to the photographs.

Liz shrugged. "Some are still here, some have been sent away, others, I'm afraid, didn't work out."

Didn't work out? Olivia flinched at the understanding of what that meant. "Oh God, they're dead?"

Liz nodded and looked away.

Fear surged through Olivia, making her want to run, but there was nowhere to go. "What does he want with us?" Olivia's voice trembled at the mere thought of him.

Liz set the bed linens on the sink and started stripping the bed. "Different things," she answered. "You might have assignments sometimes, but mostly we are part of a group of women who fight for the enjoyment of men."

Olivia was taken aback. "Fight? What do you mean?"

"You'll see. But don't worry, he won't let the men touch you as long as he considers you his. He wants the satisfaction of having something no one else can have. If you don't work out, you can be put in general population with the other women. You don't want to go there. People get hurt there—some die. It's pretty brutal. Some of us have been sent there as punishment when we mess up, and let me tell you, it isn't a place you want to go."

"How long have you been here?"

Liz looked to the photos again. "I've lost track really. I guess you could say I've been here since the beginning."

Olivia studied the photograph. Liz was younger then, much younger. Her heart sank at the realization. "You mean you've been here for years?"

Liz nodded.

"Oh, dear God, no."

Liz finished making the bed before facing Olivia again.

"They pair the women based on size, kind of like professional boxing. You know, heavyweight, lightweight, that kind of thing. At least that way those like us aren't getting crushed every time we fight."

"You can't be serious?"

Liz shrugged. "I'm afraid so."

Something Liz said made it through the confusion clouding Olivia's brain. "What about you, do you fight?"

Liz shook her head. "At my age, I have other responsibilities."

"You mean, this will never end?"

Liz looked away. "At first he'll have you spend time with the other women. He'll want you to get a taste of why it's smart to stay on his good side. Once he feels you're ready, he'll bring you in for your audition. Get through that and you'll officially be his girl. Trust me, it's a lot better here with us."

Olivia tried to swallow, but her mouth had gone dry. How had she gotten into this? More importantly, how was she ever going to get out? She glanced to the door.

Liz shook her head, reading her intentions. "Don't bother. There are guards outside the door waiting for me. We don't go anywhere without guards. Even if you did get past them, this place is like a real prison, you'd never get out."

There was something about Liz that struck Olivia as odd. Her tone was flat, but she didn't have the look of someone who had been in captivity for years. She looked relaxed, almost as if she was at home.

"How can you live like this?" Olivia asked. She trailed her eyes over her, taking in every detail. She locked her gaze onto the faint flash of color at the woman's wrist, recognizing the tattoo. They were marked for life. Had Liz been here so long she had given up hope of her own freedom?

"You get used to it," Liz said.

"How could anyone ever get used to being a slave?"

"He's not so bad if you do what he wants. Most days he doesn't even come around. It isn't so much to ask really. He cares for us when we're sick, or hurt. He punishes us when we're bad."

Liz had a faraway look in her eyes that said she had given up a long time ago.

Olivia clenched her fists and tried to fight back tears. That could never be her. She would never give up.

"Tell me about the fights."

Liz smiled sadly. "Sometimes we just wrestle around for his amusement or if he's entertaining special guests. You know, like a show. But other times there are real fights where the men make bets or we have to punish each other while the men watch. Those things are harder. Most of the time we just spend time with him, do things for him. He needs someone to take care of him."

The last statement made Olivia's skin crawl. How far inside this woman's head had this creep infected? She talked about him as if she cared about him. Olivia felt sick. "When you say we take care of him, does that include sex?"

Liz didn't answer, but the look in her eyes filled Olivia with fear and disgust. Her brain didn't want to accept this as reality. It was just too much.

❖

Something in Olivia's brain told her it was morning. She forced her eyes open at the sound of the lock turning. She was surprised she had been able to sleep. She had been certain she would never sleep again after what she had been through. But despite her fear, exhaustion had eventually won out.

Liz stepped through the door as casually as if she was in her own home. "Good morning. I thought you would feel better after a shower," Liz said, placing a fresh set of scrubs on the chair by the bed.

"Where?" Olivia asked.

"I'll take you."

Olivia wasn't sure what to do, but the idea of a shower after days in the same soiled clothes was enough to tempt her.

"You'll be safe, I promise."

Olivia doubted there was anything that could keep her safe in a place like this. She climbed out of bed and followed Liz as she stepped out of the room. She had hoped they would be alone, but as soon as she stepped through the door, she noticed a man with cold eyes waiting for them. He didn't look right. It was as if he was trying to be two people at once. One was hard and dark, the other had the same tired look that her accountant always had.

"Don't worry about him. He won't hurt you—he's just the guard. Follow me," Liz said cheerfully.

Olivia frowned. Liz acted as if they were on a tour of some museum or something. She followed Liz down the hall to a communal bathroom that reminded her of her time in college. No one else was around, and the space was so quiet Olivia could hear her footsteps echo around the room.

Liz pulled a towel from a stack on a shelf and handed it to Olivia. Hesitantly, Olivia took it.

"I'll wait out here for you. Don't worry, you're alone."

As she went to the stall farthest from the door and turned on the water, Olivia wondered where everyone was. Why was she being kept away from everyone? And why was Liz always the one to come for her? Liz brought her clothes and food, changed her bed, and now was allowing her out of the room to shower. Liz was always nice to her, but Olivia couldn't help but think of Liz as one of her captors. The thought made her feel guilty when she thought of the amount of time Liz had spent here. Then there was the guard. She wasn't sure how to read him and didn't want to start out on anyone's bad side. For now, she would do what she was told. She would never get out if she stayed locked in her room forever.

After the shower, Liz took Olivia on a tour of the living spaces where the women worked. There were too many turns and too many stairs for her to remember where she was going or how to get back to where she'd started. Everything looked the same. The paint on the walls was old and the halls smelled faintly of mold. She had seen the kitchen, where she would most likely be given chores, and the laundry, where she hoped she would never be again after seeing the piles of bloody towels in the bin.

Olivia glanced over her shoulder to the man following them. He was staring at her. He didn't even look away when she looked right at him. A shiver ran up her spine, and she looked away. But there was something in the way he'd looked at her that made her take a second look. He was still looking at her. Was that pity on his face? Did he actually feel sorry for her?

Liz took her arm. "Don't mind him. He likes to look, but he would never touch one of the Recruiter's girls."

"The Recruiter?"

Liz nodded. "He calls himself that because it's his job to bring in the girls. It's just like a business. Someone wants someone for their team. He finds the right girl and brings her in."

"But I thought you said everyone belonged to him."

Liz shook her head. "No. You belong to him. Other girls belong to other men—they call them the Employers. That's about all I can tell you."

None of this made any sense to Olivia. Liz made this sound normal, as if these men were just trading stocks or property. Her heart sank. That was exactly what they thought she was, property. "This is human trafficking."

Liz nodded.

Before she realized where they were, Olivia was back outside her room. Liz smiled at her knowingly.

"I'll be back tomorrow. You'll see for yourself how things work." Liz nudged Olivia inside the room. "Try to get some sleep. Tomorrow will be a big day."

Olivia wanted to ask questions, but the door closed in her face and she heard the finality of the lock sliding into place. She would never sleep now, not while knowing what she did and dreading what she didn't.

Olivia fell onto the bed, hugging the pillow to her chest. Was anyone looking for her yet? Surely, they'd found her car on the road. What did her parents think? Would they ever forgive her? Tears spilled from her eyes, carrying her fear, her grief, her hope. Someone would find her. Wouldn't they? Olivia thought of the bodies of the women on the news. Would they find her or would she end up like those girls or be trapped here forever like Liz?

Olivia closed her eyes against that image. She took a shuddering breath, and for the first time in years, she prayed.

CHAPTER SIX

The Recruiter watched the target through the window of the restaurant. He sat at the bar where he had a clear view to the patio outside. She sat with a group of hikers, talking and laughing like old friends. Would they be joining her on the trail? If he had miscalculated this, his plan would be a wash. There was no way he could take her with that many people around. He studied each member of the group, evaluating their threat and their potential usefulness. He discounted the men right away, but some of the women had potential. They were a bit too thin and too disheveled for his taste. He wondered how they would react when pitted against their friends for their own survival. He smiled. That could be fun.

If this worked out, he would have to reconsider the AT as a viable hunting ground. It didn't present the usual ease of capture he was used to, but he was enjoying the chase and the risk. The only thing that could sweeten the pot was to have the prey know she was being hunted. The smell of fear was intoxicating. But he was smarter than that. He knew better than to tip his hand.

He got up and went out to the patio to smoke. He leaned over the rail watching the current of the small creek carry away the seconds as he listened to Greyson and the group, trying to glean information about Greyson's plans. He kept his back to them. He didn't want to risk Greyson recognizing him. If she drew attention to him, it could cause trouble once the search for her began.

It wasn't long before he had all the information he needed. He knew she was here, he knew her trajectory, and he knew where the interception would take place. It was time to put this plan into motion.

The Recruiter stubbed out his cigarette and stuffed it into his shirt pocket. No use risking leaving his DNA behind. He went back inside and closed his tab. There were still a couple of hours of daylight left and he wanted to set the trap.

He pulled the van onto the small recess on the side of the road where he knew the obscure trail was hidden from view. He grabbed his small pack and set out to make camp. If he was lucky, he wouldn't have to wait more than a day for his prey to walk right into his lair.

He studied the area. She would come from his left. He spotted a large red oak bearing the AT symbol. He smiled. Perfect.

He walked around the area to make sure his camp was hidden from view. The mountain laurel was thick enough to hide his camp but left plenty of room for him to access the trail when the time came. It all worked. The laurel would provide the perfect cover for him to get the target back to his van without being noticed. He had to get this right. He wouldn't have another shot like this for days, if ever. The Employer was anxious to close the deal, and he was anxious to get the game started. He had his new girl waiting for him, and he was eager to get started on her initiation.

The night passed slowly. He dozed but was awake long before dawn. He dismantled his tent and stored his gear. He didn't want the small details to slow him down later if the target did show up this morning. He hoped he wouldn't have to wait long.

Heavy fog blanketed the mountain obscuring his view. It seemed the universe was on his side this morning. The target would never see him coming.

The sound of footsteps on the trail caught his attention. He worked his way to the red oak tree and peered through the fog. He could just make out someone coming down the trail. The person was almost to the turn in the trail where it passed by him. He could see her now. She was alone. It was time. This was his lucky day.

He counted her footsteps, clicking off each pace until she stepped onto the path next to him. He struck her hard across the face and she crumpled into a pile in the middle of the path. He grabbed her by the shoulder straps of her pack and dragged her off the trail into the thicket of laurel. Moving quickly, he slid the sleeve of her jacket up her arm and deftly inserted the needle beneath her skin. "Gotcha. Welcome to the game, Greyson Cooper."

Once he was certain she was out for a long nap, he removed her pack, tied her hands, and placed tape over her mouth just in case she did wake up before he had her secure. He put her pack on his back and grabbed his gear before heading for the van. To anyone who might see him, he would just be another hiker. He would get the gear to the van to make sure it was clear before moving the target.

All clear. He tossed the gear inside and looked around the area one last time. Everything was quiet. There wasn't even any traffic on the road. Convinced the timing was right, he went back for Greyson.

He smiled down at her, gloating inwardly about the bruise forming on the side of her face. He would have liked it if she had seen the hit coming. He loved that moment of surprise in a target's eyes just before they went down. Unfortunately, that had been too much of a risk this time. He would just have to find another way to have his fun with this one.

She was heavy for a woman. All that damn muscle made her harder to handle than he had expected. Once back at the van, he didn't waste any time. He laid her on the floor, strapped her hands to the rings welded to the walls, and shut the door.

"Bagged and tagged. Time to get paid."

❖

Greyson woke to a pounding in her head as if she had spent the night drinking. She squeezed her eyes tighter against the jackhammer making mush of her brain. She tried to roll over, but pain pierced her hands and shoulders when she moved. An alarm sounded in her mind. Something was very wrong.

She opened her eyes with sudden urgency, realizing the ground beneath her was cold. Her body was stiff as if she had been lying in one position too long. Had she fallen and hit her head?

Her eyes adjusted to the dim light as she searched the area around her. She was in a room. What little light filtered in illuminated stone walls and iron bars for a door. What the hell? Why was she in jail?

She shifted, moving as little and as slowly as possible. Clammy sweat clung to her skin and mingled with tears running into her hair that was now slick with the sickening smell of fear. What happened to her? How had she gotten here? She fought through the fog of her memories. She remembered getting up early and heading out on the trail. It was early morning and the fog hadn't yet lifted. But after that, her memory was blank. She worked her jaw, confused by the pain and stiffness.

Someone hit me.

The harder she tried to remember, the more frustrated she became. Her memory was just too fragmented. The answers weren't there.

She started to panic. Someone had attacked her. She had no idea where she was or how to get out. She fought the urge to scream. She went to the door.

"Hey, is anyone there? What the hell's going on? Why am I here?" Her voice was coarse and it hurt to speak.

"Shh," someone hissed from nearby. "You have to be quiet."

"Why?"

Greyson's heart pounded against her chest as if it too were trying to escape the prison around it. She focused on her surroundings. She needed information. She had to figure a way out of this. She listened, trying to hear beyond the pounding of her own heart. She held her breath to quiet the rush of air from her lungs. In the stillness, she heard the faintest whisper of voices in the distance.

"Who's there?" Greyson said softly.

She strained to hear the whispered conversation, desperately hoping to learn who was behind this and where she was being held. But the voices were too faint and too far away for her to make out the words. She thought she heard a woman crying but couldn't be certain.

She took a deep breath and licked her lips. Her mouth was dry and her throat hurt.

"Hello, someone tell me what's going on," Greyson croaked. The words came out garbled and barely audible. She licked her lips again and swallowed.

"Hello," she tried again.

The whispers stopped.

"Hello? I know you're there."

"Be quiet," a voice said from somewhere nearby.

Greyson jerked her head in the direction of the voice, straining to see through the dim light.

"Where am I? What's going on?"

"You're in hell," another voice answered. This one was gruff and low, but definitely female.

"Just be quiet," the first voice said again. This one was also female. "He'll come for you soon enough, and you'll know more than you want to know."

"He *who*?" Greyson asked, clinging to the faint voices with the desperation of trying to breathe through a straw.

"He calls himself the Recruiter," the first voice answered.

"We call him the devil," the second voice said.

Greyson's stomach clenched at the implication in that one word. Understanding dawned. She had been abducted. "Shit." She wasn't even scheduled to check in with Dawn again for days. No one would have any idea she was missing. If anyone did look for her, they'd think she was still on the trail somewhere between Hot Springs and Mount LeConte.

Greyson closed her eyes and groaned, realizing how screwed she was. "Who are you?" she asked.

"I'm Samone," the first voice answered. "And the woman next door to you is Raquel. We'll meet soon enough. Just be quiet now and rest."

"You'll need it," Raquel said through the wall next to hers.

"Why am I here?" Greyson asked.

Silence was her only answer.

❖

Greyson woke to the smell of mold and mildew mingled with the stench of stale sweat and fear. It was impossible to tell what time it was or how long she had been in this place. She had no idea if it was night or day. The only light filtered through her cell door from industrial metal lights strung from conduits along the ceiling in the hall.

She rubbed her hands over her sore wrists. She was certain now that she had been drugged. There was no other explanation for the time she had missed.

Greyson pressed her face against the bars and peered down the hall. Several more cells lined the corridor. The cells were staggered so no room was directly across from another. She pulled at the door and worked at the lock until her fingers were sore. The echo of footsteps on the stone floor startled her and she retreated into the darkness of her cell.

The room was empty except for a small cot, a sink, and a toilet. It was a prison. There was no window and nowhere to hide. She had no way to defend herself.

The footsteps stopped at the end of the hall. She heard metal scrape against metal as if something was being slid across the metal bars.

Greyson went back to the door, cautiously peering down the hall again. She could see a man in gray coveralls carrying a tray to one of the cells. He pushed a small metal cart, and he stopped briefly by each occupied cell. The smell of food wafted through the air, making her stomach churn. It must be dinnertime. A thread of relief mingled with her terror. If they were bringing her food, at least she knew she wouldn't starve to death.

As the cart came closer to her cell, Greyson forced herself to remain at the bars, despite her overwhelming urge to hide. The cart stopped outside her cell and an older man with dark eyes peered at her beneath thick wooly eyebrows that ran from one side of his brow to the other, creating a thick ridge that shadowed his eyes. His hair was white with a hint of black hovering at the back of his head. His gaze was menacing. She imagined him as Santa's evil twin. He stared into her eyes as if measuring some quality about her. His mouth twitched, making the whiskers of his thick mustache bristle like the quills of a porcupine.

The man pulled a metal tray from the cart and slid it through a thin slot in the bars.

"Let me out of here," Greyson demanded.

"Take the food, stupid woman, and keep your mouth shut," the old man responded, his voice a deep growl.

"Why are you keeping me here?"

He smiled. "You have a job to do. Now take the food or starve, I don't care either way."

Greyson took the tray of mashed potatoes with gravy that had strange lumps in it, which she assumed were chipped beef. She wanted to throw the food in his face. She wanted to scream and demand to be set free, but something in the look in his eyes dared her, as if that was exactly what he expected her to do.

She knew there was no way she could get out on her own. This guy wasn't about to give her any help or information. But she wouldn't get anywhere making enemies.

He handed her a bottle of water.

"Thanks," she said. "Who are you?"

He grumbled nonresponsively and left.

Greyson looked at her tray of food and single bottle of water. She needed to eat, but the smell of food made her stomach revolt. She put the tray on the floor by the door. The water she would keep.

The old man returned an hour later to retrieve the trays. Two other very large men were with him.

"Put your hands through the bars," the largest man ordered.

"Why?" Greyson asked. As much as she wanted answers, she was afraid of what was going to happen next.

"Do as you're told and we won't have to kick your ass," the second man snapped.

Hesitantly, Greyson complied.

They led her down the corridor to a set of concrete stairs. They made several turns down various hallways until Greyson was thoroughly lost, besides not knowing where she was to begin with. They stepped through a set of large, heavy doors into an expansive room with concrete floors surrounding what looked like an indoor pool. All the water had been drained.

Greyson flinched when the doors opened behind her and two women were escorted into the room and led into the pit. What the hell was all of this about?

A tall, thin man stepped out of the shadows. He faced Greyson. "I understand you've been asking questions. Since you're so eager to learn, I arranged this little demonstration for you. Pay close attention—this will be your only tutorial. I'm sure you'll get the idea."

He stepped aside. Rough hands pushed Greyson to the edge of the pool until she was peering into the pit. The two women stood facing each other, their heads bowed. They were flanked by two more large men.

"Begin," the thin man ordered.

The two men pushed the women toward each other.

To Greyson's horror the stocky brunette put up her fists. The second woman with the long jet-black hair launched toward the brunette, delivering a flurry of punches.

The shorter, stockier woman blocked most of the blows, but several hit their mark. Her lip was bloody and swollen, and she guarded her left side with her elbow.

What the hell was all this about? Greyson's body shook with rage and revulsion. She tried to pull away, but the hands gripping her arms tightened, holding her firmly in place.

She watched helplessly as the taller woman delivered blow after blow. In a sudden turn of events, the stocky woman struck out, landing a fierce punch to her opponent, knocking her off balance. Before the tall woman could recover, she took two more blows to the face. She stumbled, then fell into a heap on the floor.

Greyson's breath came in gasps as she fought against the horror playing out in front of her. She wanted to run. She had to get the hell out of this place. She pushed and pulled against her captors and kicked at their shins, trying to break free.

"Let me go. You can't keep me here!"

The thin man laughed. "There's the fight we were looking for. I assume you understand your position now."

He turned to the men. "Take her back to her cell."

Greyson fought against the men every step of the way back to her prison. They threw her into her cell and shut the heavy metal doors behind her. She jumped up and grabbed the bars, shaking them with all her strength until she was exhausted. Nothing made sense. She didn't understand what was happening. She was alone and scared, and no one even knew she was in trouble.

Heavy footsteps and the rattle of the food cart signaled the return of the old man. Greyson unfolded her long frame from her cot and went to the door. The long hours of the night had crept by like grains of sand slipping through cracks in a wall of stone, threatening to bury her alive. The silence had drilled into her mind like pricks of a needle. She hadn't slept. Every time she closed her eyes, images of the two women fighting filtered into her mind. She didn't understand what this place was or who these people were, but it was painfully clear why she had been brought here.

"Hi," Greyson said when the cart stopped outside her door. "My name's Greyson. What's yours?"

The man didn't answer, just handed her a tray.

"You look like my uncle Dan. He was an electrician in the coal mines when I was a kid. He had hands the size of shovels and spent every free moment in the woods around his home." She accepted the tray. "Thanks." She set the food on the floor and reached for the bottle of water. "Uncle Dan didn't talk much either."

He stared at her unblinking. "Eat. You're going to need your strength." He handed her another bottle of water.

She smiled as he turned and pushed the cart farther down the hall. She knew she couldn't fight her way out of captivity, but maybe she could kill them with kindness.

Breakfast consisted of eggs, oatmeal, and toast. There was no coffee, which was cruel—no coffee and no flavor. But this time Greyson ate every bite of her meal. She planned to get out of this hellhole and she couldn't do that if she let herself starve.

She didn't know what was going to happen next, but she knew she didn't want to push her luck by asking more questions. She knew she would find out more than she wanted to know soon enough.

At the sound of keys rattling against a cell door, Greyson jumped to her feet, sending her tray skittering across the floor. She eased up to the bars and peered down the hall.

The big man from the day before stepped in front of her cell, making her jump. "You know the drill, princess. Let's go."

Greyson didn't argue this time. She doubted anything could get through to these blockheads. She would go along with this part, but there was no way she was going to participate in this sick game.

This time the room with the pit was bustling with people. Men surrounded the pit and others guarded the doors as the women were brought in to fight.

Greyson counted five other women besides herself.

A dark-haired woman with bronze skin, perhaps of Hispanic origin, and a blond white woman were the first two led into the pit. The blonde was fast and moved around the pit like a fox ready to pounce on its prey in a henhouse. But the other woman was crafty and patient. She waited for her opponent to come to her.

The men standing around the pit sneered and hurled insults at the two women, elevating the fevered tension in the room.

The blonde danced around and attacked in bursts of violent punches before retreating again. After the third attack, the Hispanic woman seemed to catch on to the pattern and struck with a fierce blow to the blond woman's face. The skin above her eye split open and blood poured down her face.

Greyson shut her eyes, wanting to block out the brutality playing out in front of her. A sudden burst of cheers forced her to open her eyes. The blonde had the Hispanic woman backed against the wall and was hitting her with a series of punches to the side and face. The beaten woman did her best to cover her head with her arms as blow after blow crashed into her.

At last someone blew a whistle and the fighting stopped abruptly. The women were removed from the room while the men laughed, celebrated, and made bets on the next fight.

The big man behind Greyson shoved her in the back, pushing her toward the pit. She was up next.

Greyson stumbled into the pit with the reluctance of a doe stepping into an open field. Fear blinded her reasoning as her flight or fight instincts took over. She looked around the edge of the pit at the men glaring and sneering down at her. They taunted her and spat at her like she was nothing more than a piece of trash. The noise and the stench were disorienting. She spotted the thin man grinning down at her as if daring her to defy him.

Greyson glared back.

Her attention was suddenly drawn back into the pit as her opponent was led in. She had beautiful dark skin with long black hair that had been braided down her back. Her eyes were the color of midnight and bore dark shadows as if she hadn't slept in days. Her cheeks and lips looked like they had been sculpted by an artist. Even in this terrible place, she was beautiful. The only blemish to her features was a scar below her left eye from a wound that hadn't healed properly. As she came closer, Greyson saw a bruise on her chin that hadn't had time to heal.

This woman had already seen her share of violence delivered here. As Greyson looked into those midnight eyes, she could see the damage they still bore. Greyson found her courage. She would not be a pawn in this sick game, and she refused to add to this woman's pain.

"Begin," a tall, thin man yelled.

Greyson took a step back as the other woman came toward her.

"You don't have to do this," Greyson said, dodging a punch aimed at her face. "Please stop. We have to stop this."

The woman lunged at Greyson like a hyena bringing down a rabbit.

Greyson was fast, but this woman was faster, and she caught Greyson around the middle, slamming her against the wall. She drove her forearm under Greyson's chin, pinning her.

"You must fight," the woman growled at Greyson. "They will only make things worse for you if you don't." She drove her fist into Greyson's side.

Greyson gasped as her breath exploded from her lungs. Pain seared through her side as if she had been branded.

The woman released her, and Greyson fell to the floor clutching her side.

"Get up," the men shouted at her. "Get up."

Greyson stumbled to her feet. She would have to be much faster if she was going to make it through this. She managed to stay on her feet, but there was no escaping the lightning-fast blows that came with brutal force. What her opponent lacked in size she made up for in speed and precision.

Greyson's eye was swollen, blood oozed from her nose, and her ribs hurt. She was tired and it was getting harder to resist the relentless assault. There was only one way to end this.

Greyson didn't move as the next blow came. The woman's fist crashed against Greyson's chin, spinning her on her feet. Her vision blurred. She staggered. The next blow was like a hammer crashing against her skull, and the lights went out.

CHAPTER SEVEN

Greyson woke to gentle hands pressing a cold cloth to her cheek. She groaned as the pressure intensified the pain throbbing behind her eye. She tried to pull away from the offending touch.

"Ouch."

"Oh, now you want to fight," a woman chided. The accent was foreign, India maybe.

Greyson opened her eyes. The woman she had faced in the pit sat next to her holding a bloodstained rag.

"What are you doing?" Greyson asked, pulling away.

"I am trying to help you. The swelling will be worse if you don't ice."

Greyson flinched as the woman pressed the compress against her cheek again.

"Who are you?"

"My name is Amala."

Greyson squinted up at her. "Why are you doing this?"

Amala stared down at Greyson as if she wasn't sure how to answer. Her expression hardened. "There are many things you do not understand. I didn't want to hurt you, but I had no choice. The people here will make things very bad for us if we don't fight."

"How many women are there?"

Amala shook her head. "I don't know for sure." She looked around. "They move some of us around sometimes. Some of the women never come back once they leave. Sometimes women are brought in from other places when a fight is scheduled and the men can bet and buy the girls."

Greyson reached for the compress and tried to sit up. She was shocked by what she had heard. How could anyone buy other people? "That's barbaric."

Amala nodded. "Yes, it is."

Greyson looked around the room. It was large enough to have several beds scattered around. There were a sink and a toilet at the back, and a shower nozzle protruded from the wall. "What is this place?"

"We call it the infirmary. They put us here after fights to let us help each other heal."

"This is insane. I don't belong here."

Amala's shoulders stiffened, and a muscle jumped at the side of her jaw. "No one belongs here. You were taken just like we were all taken. No one chooses to be here. We fight for our families, our children, those we love."

Greyson shifted her feet to the floor. "What do you mean you were taken? Where are your families?"

Amala sighed. "My husband was a doctor working in Colombia when he was killed by drug smugglers. My mother and daughters and I had nowhere to go. We were trying to get back to India, but the smugglers were everywhere. We paid a guide to bring us to America, but when we crossed the border into the desert, men were waiting for us. They took us. They told me I must do this or my mother would be killed and my daughters would be sold to the drug dealers as sex slaves. They cannot go back there. There is nothing for them there but death. They told me if I worked for them, my family will be safe. So, I agreed to go with the men. I have no choice. I fight for my family."

Greyson's heart went out to Amala. "How long have you been here?"

Amala shrugged. "Two years, maybe longer. I don't know for sure."

"Jesus." Greyson tried to wrap her mind around what Amala

had told her. How was she going to get out of this? She swallowed the lump growing in her throat. "What do you have to do to get out?"

Amala pinned her with her midnight eyes. "You die," she said, her words flat but definitive.

Greyson clenched her jaw. "I don't accept that. I can't. We have to find a way."

Amala shook her head. "No, my friend. We cannot do anything. The women here are all the same. The Recruiter will hurt our families. We must do as he says. We must fight or he will harm them."

Greyson leaned closer. "Maybe it's time for a different fight."

Amala looked at her with understanding, but slowly shook her head again. "I wish that was possible, but I am afraid for you. If you keep up this thinking, you will only bring bad things to us all."

"I have to find a way. Your Recruiter has nothing on me. There has to be something I can do to stop this. I won't fight for him."

Amala sighed. "I have seen this before. Those women who refused to work for him all died, or were sold for sex. I don't know about you, but I'd rather fight than have any of those pigs touch me."

Greyson was sick. It was as if she was in the middle of the twilight zone. She squinted, trying to see through the pain in her head and the pressure in her eye. "Are we the only ones staying in this room?"

Amala looked around. "For now, there are four of us including you. But others will come and go depending on the fights."

"Where are the others?" Greyson asked, not certain she wanted to know the answer.

Amala shrugged. "Some have duties assigned by the Recruiter. Some are training. The cells are separated by floors and sometimes we don't see each other for days or weeks."

Greyson cringed. "Are you telling me the women here are slaves?"

"Ah, yes. That is what we are. To the world, we do not exist. No one knows where we are, and our families are too afraid to go to the authorities. There is no one looking for us. We can do nothing. Our lives have been sold for the freedom of our children."

"I don't accept that. I'm no one's slave."

Amala smiled sadly. "You will learn."

❖

On schedule, Olivia heard the key turn to unlock her door. She had been awake for hours waiting. Liz stepped into the room, handing her a bundle of clothes and a pair of thin-soled shoes like her grandmother used to buy from the local Dollar Store.

"Put these on. You have a work assignment today."

"What kind of assignment?" Olivia asked, even though she was afraid of what the answer might be.

Liz shrugged. "They just told me to get you ready and take you to the kitchen."

Olivia was relieved. Maybe she could get some kind of weapon there. She would at least be around other people. The silence of her room was beginning to close in on her, and Liz wasn't exactly company. Maybe some of the other girls could help.

Olivia dressed quickly, eager to be doing something.

There were already three other girls in the kitchen when Olivia arrived. She noticed their stares as she followed Liz around the room, each girl stopping what she was doing, as if caught in a trance. Olivia glanced from one girl to the next, their eyes telegraphing their pity and knowing.

Liz stopped in front of the women. "This is our new girl, Olivia. Olivia, this is Mary," Liz said gesturing to a woman who looked to be around thirty, her hair cut shorter than Olivia's with a hint of red peeking through.

"This is Sherry." Olivia nodded to a woman slightly shorter than her with a round face. Olivia guessed her to be in her early twenties. She had a bruise on her right cheek that looked very much like the one on her own face, where the Recruiter had struck her that first day.

"And this is Dana." Liz smiled primly as if she had just introduced her best friends in middle school.

Dana looked at Olivia, her jaw set, and her gaze hard. "Welcome to hell."

"Dana," Liz scolded. "That's no way to welcome our new sister."

"Whatever, superfreak. You may think that bastard is a prince, but the rest of us know he's just a monster."

Liz glared at Dana, her face turning red with anger. "You can be in charge of showing Olivia what to do today," Liz said through gritted teeth. "I have better things to do than waste my time with you."

"Fine with me," Dana replied dryly.

Olivia stared after Liz as she stomped out of the room like a little girl running off to tell Daddy someone had been mean to her.

Olivia turned back to the women. "What's with her?"

Dana laughed. "She's been here so long, she's nuts. She's convinced herself that the Recruiter actually cares about her."

Sherry moved a stack of bowls and shuffled a stack of plates onto a rack. "I think she's been here so long, she doesn't know any other way to live."

"Ha," Mary scoffed. "None of us had it very good on the outside either. You don't see any of us buying into that crap."

Olivia noticed raised scars running across Mary's wrist, distorting the tattoo and disfiguring her arm. Mary caught her staring.

"Yeah, I did that. I'd rather have bled to death than have that bastard's mark on me."

Olivia absently rubbed her own arm, feeling scales of skin still flaking away as the tattoo healed.

"Come on," Dana said. "You might as well get started. If we want to eat, we better get this done."

As they worked, Olivia scoured the room for something she could use as a weapon, any weakness she could use to her advantage. She leaned close to Mary. "How did you do it? How did you cut yourself?"

Mary shifted her gaze at Olivia, sizing her up. "Why? You planning to check out early?"

Olivia shook her head. "Something sharp might be useful."

Mary grinned. "I managed to pick a piece of concrete loose from a crack in the wall in my cell. I used the shard to cut through my arm. They don't allow us to take knives out of the kitchen. They're counted every day and we're searched before we leave."

"How many guards are there? If we worked together maybe—"

"Maybe nothing," Mary admonished. "This isn't a day care, sweetheart. It's a real prison. Even if you got by the guard, you'd never get past the bars or the rest of the men. We're locked in here like pigs."

Disappointment soured in Olivia's stomach. Today wasn't turning out anything like she had hoped.

The day seemed to go on for an eternity. Olivia flinched at every sound that might signal danger. She was actually relieved when Liz came to take her back to her room. She didn't even notice how quiet Liz was on their walk. It wasn't until they were back at her cell that she noticed something was different.

A small table had been placed in the center of the room, draped with a white tablecloth. Two place settings had been set, and a small serving cart had been pushed into the room. The aroma of food filled the small space. The Recruiter sat at the table waiting for her, his hands folded in his lap, a faint smile on his lips. He had sandy blond hair and brown eyes, and dressed as if he'd just come home from the office. He wore dark slacks and a white button-down shirt. His shoes were polished and clean. To the average person he would look like any other guy. There were no obvious signs of the monster he really was.

Dread flooded Olivia like boiling water being pushed through her veins. She hesitated and was nudged inside by the guard at her back.

"Come in, Ms. Danner. I've prepared something special for us. I had a very successful outing and I feel like celebrating." He gestured to the empty chair. "Please, sit."

Olivia sat. She stared at him as if he were a snake. She never took her eyes off him in case he might strike. She loathed him.

"I hope you enjoyed your day," he said as if she had spent the day out shopping. "Liz tells me you've been getting along very well." He smiled. "I'm glad."

Olivia swallowed, holding back her anger. What was this guy up to? He acted like they were friends or on a date or something.

He reached across the table, lifting the plate cover. "I hope you like Italian. It seems so festive, so I thought it would be perfect for tonight."

Olivia frowned. "What are you doing?"

"*Tsk, tsk, tsk.*" He pressed his finger to her lips. "I see you're still angry. Haven't I provided everything you need? Food, water, clothing, shelter? In return, all I've asked for is your company."

"You're keeping me here against my will. I don't want to be here."

He poured a glass of wine and sat back in his chair, his glass held aloft. He looked at her knowingly. "This takes time. I have such high hopes for us. I know you'll like it here if you'll just give it a chance. I'll take care of you forever."

Olivia felt sick, her revulsion rising like a volcano. She picked up the plate and threw it at him, lunging across the table, her fingers curled like talons poised to claw out his eyes.

He grabbed her wrist and struck her across the face before throwing her to the ground. In an instant, he was on top of her, holding her down, his hand clasped around her throat at the base of her jaw. She gasped and struggled against him. He leaned down until his face was only inches from hers.

"That wasn't nice. Now look what you made me do," he growled. He reached for the lasagna that had splattered onto the floor, scooping it into his fist. His fingers and thumb bored into her jaw, prying her mouth open. He shoved the food into her mouth, forcing her mouth shut.

She seethed and gagged but he wouldn't let her spit it out. "Swallow it," he yelled.

After long minutes, she couldn't help but swallow. Then he forced her mouth open and poured the wine down her throat. She gasped and sputtered as the acidic liquid spilled into her nose, burning its way through her sinuses. She fought and cried and begged him to stop.

He sat back, the weight of him still holding her down. "Waste not, want not."

He stood, wiping his hands and shirt with a napkin as if he had only just spilled something.

Olivia lay on the floor crying. She curled into herself still gagging and spitting from the assault.

He sat back down at the table and poured himself another glass of wine. "I'll have to see to it that you are punished. I can't have you behaving like an animal in front of guests. Perhaps that should be your last meal for a while. We'll see how you feel when you've been hungry for a few days."

Olivia looked up at him, new fear growing in her mind. What else would he do to her? She stayed on the floor crying, afraid to move, as he ate his dinner.

❖

Greyson drifted in and out of sleep, only occasionally aware of gentle hands tending to her wounds. As night fell, cold seeped into her bones, making her shiver. She woke reaching for her sleeping bag, still caught in the memory of the life stolen from her. She looked around the dimly lit room trying to make out the number of occupied bunks.

A faint whisper and the creek of a cot drew her attention to a row of bunks at her feet. She could barely make out the silhouette of two figures huddled together beneath the covers. She strained to hear their muffled conversation. Any information she could gain might help her figure her way out of this hell.

"We'll be separated tomorrow. I can't stand it when I can't see you."

Greyson frowned. She didn't recognize the speaker. The voice seemed small but pure and clear. It reminded Greyson of a wren.

"Don't worry. I'll be close, even when we can't see each other. The others will watch out for you."

Greyson stilled her breath. This was a voice she recognized. It was Amala.

"Nothing will happen to you. I promise," Amala said firmly.

Hmm. It seemed Amala might have more reason to fight the system than she let Greyson know. Greyson turned her head away as the sound of wet kisses and a faint moan drifted through the silence. Yep, she could use this. And if Amala had something to fight for, maybe the others did too.

Greyson pulled the thick wool blanket up over her head and thought about how she could use this information to make a plan. The women here had all been taken against their will. The captors used blackmail to force the women into slavery and supplication, but there was more. Something else was going on here. The women had secrets, and perhaps they could help her find the weak link that would lead her to a way out.

Greyson frowned. She was the new girl. These women wouldn't trust her easily. She would have to work on changing that. She needed to show them she was not just one of them, but she would champion them. She needed to learn the system, fast. Greyson's mind raced as she grasped for the thinnest thread of hope.

The familiar sound of a metal cot being wheeled down the corridor drew Greyson's attention. Several women got up and made their way to the door. Some limped, others held arms close to their sides to hold back their pain. She must have been asleep when the others were brought in.

Amala patted her cot. "Come on, newbie, if you want to eat, you have to get up. No one gets a tray if they don't get it themselves. They won't let us get it for you."

Greyson leaned up on her arms as much as she could and slowly slid her legs off the bed. Her ribs screamed in protest. It wasn't any better when her feet hit the floor and she pushed herself up. She lifted her shirt, wincing at the mottled bruises along her side.

"Hey, new girl."

Greyson looked up to see a tall black woman with close cut hair and eyes as black as coal.

"Get a move on, we don't have all day."

Greyson heard the command in the woman's voice. She looked like she had the right to tell anyone what to do. In another life, Greyson imagined this woman as an African queen. She was beautiful, strong, elegant, graceful, and in command.

Greyson picked up the pace and got in line. She watched as one by one the women took a tray from the man she had nicknamed Uncle Dan. No one spoke as he handed them their food.

Greyson watched the African queen reach for her tray. She froze. There was something in the woman's hand. She was certain she saw the queen slip a small piece of paper to the man. In return, he placed a package of Grandma's vanilla cookies on her tray. No words were exchanged. Not even a smile.

When it was her turn, Greyson stepped up. The man met her gaze as if assessing something about her. She watched his eyes flicker over the array of bruises decorating her face. She thought she saw a flicker of pain or maybe disappointment in his eyes before he looked away.

"How's it going, Uncle Dan? Anything good on your cart today?" Greyson asked casually as if they were friends.

He grumbled something she couldn't hear as he handed her a tray.

She hesitated before taking it. "Got any cookies in there?" She nodded toward his cart.

"Got any fight in there?" he replied.

Greyson was surprised by the comment and wasn't sure how to respond. She shook her head.

He grumbled again. "That's too bad." He pushed the tray into her hands, turned his back on her, and walked away.

Greyson was perplexed by the whole ordeal. She was certain he was sending her a message, but what?

She turned back to the room to find the women staring at her. She had the feeling she had just done something wrong. Well, hell. How was she supposed to know the freaking rules if no one was going to share?

Greyson sat down across from the African queen. She seemed to be the one in charge, and Greyson was determined to get some answers.

She looked into the darkest eyes she had ever seen, so dark she couldn't tell where the pupil ended and the iris began.

"What?" Greyson challenged.

"Why were you talking to him?" The queen nodded toward the door.

Greyson shrugged. "How else am I supposed to learn anything around here? You guys all walk around like I'm the enemy. He was the first person I saw in here. He has answers I need."

The woman studied her. No one spoke a word as if waiting for a verdict.

Greyson decided to push her luck. "What's your name, anyway? I can't keep referring to you as the African queen in my head."

A faint smiled grew at the corner of the woman's mouth. "My name is Yoruba. But they just call me Ruby here."

"Okay, Ruby, will you please tell me what's going on and what I have to do to survive this until I can find a way out?"

Ruby's eyes narrowed. "What makes you think there is a way out? Do you think we haven't tried everything to be free of this place?"

Greyson shrugged. "Hell if I know. Every time I ask, people just tell me to follow the rules and do as I'm told."

"We make many sacrifices for what little we have here. Many have died trying to escape this place. Many more have suffered a fate worse than death. Be careful what you do. Everything you do in here comes back on us. If you get punished, we get punished." Ruby shook her head. "We can't help you if you won't fight."

Greyson stopped chewing the piece of roll she had stuffed into her mouth.

Ruby leaned forward and grasped Greyson's forearm in a

viselike grip. "Listen to me, stubborn woman. If you really want to know how to survive, you have to do exactly what I say." She let go of Greyson's arm. "Look around you. There is no malice in the faces of these women. We harbor no ill will toward each other. Think about it. The first to come to your aid was the very woman who delivered your wounds. No one here wants to fight. We do not inflict pain upon one another because we want to hurt each other."

Ruby nodded to Amala. "My girl Amala has been here a long time and she's very good at surviving. She could have killed you if she wished. The Recruiter was trying to send you a message. Amala had no choice but to deliver it."

Greyson flinched at the memory of the beating.

"She did only as much damage as was necessary to keep you both safe." Ruby took a bite of her mashed potatoes. Ruby studied her as if she was waiting for the message to sink in.

Greyson thought she understood. "Are you saying the fights are fake?" she asked. "Because that seemed very real to me."

Ruby smiled. "No, not fake, but controlled. It has to be real or the men would know and we would all be in trouble. But we train together. We know each other. And we put on a good show."

Greyson looked down the table to the other women watching her. She couldn't fathom how they could face each other fight after fight and keep going. She had heard Amala and the petite woman at her side this morning. She knew these women cared for one another. But how could they live this way?

Greyson shook her head. "I don't think I can do this."

Ruby sighed. "Then we can't help you."

CHAPTER EIGHT

Greyson watched the women spar. The whole situation was barbaric. What kind of person found pleasure in watching two people inflict pain upon each other? At least in practice they wore protective pads and face guards.

She ran her fingers down her side, feeling the tenderness in her bruised ribs. They actually felt better than they looked. The swelling in her eye had gone down, but the bruises were mottled greens and yellows that had seeped into her cheek, making her look sick. She hoped she wouldn't have to be anyone's punching bag anytime soon.

Ruby stepped away from the heavy bag she had been hammering away at for the past ten minutes. "Hey, new girl, let's go."

Greyson groaned. Could her luck get any worse? She walked over to Ruby. "What?"

"You need to learn to read punches. Watch Vinny over there. Notice how she drops her shoulder a fraction of a second before she swings?"

Greyson watched Vinny dance around an area of the floor designated by painted lines on the concrete. After a few minutes, she was able to see the slight movement in Vinny's shoulder before she threw a punch.

"Whoa, I see it."

"Good. Now watch Mandy." Ruby nodded toward Vinny's opponent. "What do you see?"

Greyson watched, trying to see something in the woman's

movements that could offer a clue as to what she would do next. Greyson sighed in resignation. "I don't know."

"You're overthinking it. Amala said you did a pretty good job of dodging her in the ring. How did you do it? How did you know when she was going to swing?"

Greyson thought back to that horrific night. "By the look of my face and the pain in my side, I obviously didn't do a very good job." She was certain she recalled every detail of the fight as if it was tattooed like a map on her skin. She focused on the look in Amala's eyes as she came after her. She flinched at the memory of each damaging blow.

"Think harder," Ruby said. "Think about her, not you. What did her body tell you?"

Greyson sighed. "All I remember was the flare of her nostrils an instant before she came at me. She was so fast I couldn't get away."

Ruby slapped Greyson on the back. "There you go. That's something. I hadn't even noticed that one. Trust your instincts, Greyson—you'll live longer."

Greyson noted this was the first time Ruby had called her by her name. It wasn't much, but it gave her hope. "I doubt I can make it here just by dodging punches."

Ruby turned to her. "No. You have to fight."

"What if I don't?" Greyson asked.

Ruby shook her head, but didn't answer.

"Ruby, what will happen?"

Ruby clenched her jaw. "If you don't fight they will either kill you or find another use for you. I've seen women sold as sex slaves. Others were beaten to death in the ring. One thing is certain—they will never let you go."

This was pretty much the same story she had heard from the others. Defiance rose up in Greyson. There was no way she would allow these men to destroy her moral fiber. They'd have to kill her. She wouldn't live this way.

Greyson looked at Ruby. "Have you ever tried?"

Ruby nodded. "I was a lot like you when I first came here.

My pride wouldn't let me see what I had to do. I wouldn't fight the others. I put all my energy into defying the Recruiter." She paused, her gaze fading as her mind traveled into her memories.

"What happened?" Greyson asked.

Ruby sighed. "At first, they beat me, but that didn't break me. They put me in solitary until I thought I'd lose my mind. Just when I was beginning to believe I was already dead, they brought me to the pit. I was forced to watch three women enter the pit, one by one, where they were beaten to death by one of the men."

Greyson's stomach flipped. "Jesus," she said through gritted teeth.

"That isn't all," Ruby continued. "They watch our families on the outside. They know where they live, where our children go to school or church. They show us what they will do to them if we disobey. There was a woman here once. A woman from the streets. The drugs had done something to her brain. They had her daughter. She wouldn't fight. She shut down and was of no use to them, so they brought her daughter here. That was the worst thing they could possibly do to any one of us. The woman hanged herself. The child simply took her place. Never underestimate them."

Greyson stared at her in disbelief.

Ruby clapped her hands together once. "Samone," Ruby called to a tall woman across the room. Without hesitation, the woman turned and walked toward them. She was beautiful with skin like honey. Her eyes were almost yellow, and her hair was a mane of wild red curls. She was softer than Ruby but matched her in height.

Samone. When had she heard that name?

Samone smiled at Greyson as she approached, stopping only feet in front of Ruby.

"Take Greyson and show her some blocks. Watch her ribs."

Samone nodded.

Ruby looked at Greyson, her gaze boring into her. "Remember one thing, Greyson—you aren't the only one they can hurt."

Ruby walked away leaving Greyson staring after her.

"Glad to see you're feeling better," Samone said, pulling Greyson's attention back to the present.

Samone's voice awakened a memory in the back of Greyson's mind. "You were there that first night. I remember your voice."

Samone nodded. "Yeah, me and Raquel. We were in solitary when they brought you in."

"Why?" Greyson asked.

Samone shrugged. "It doesn't matter. Come on, let's get to work."

Greyson followed Samone to a locker. Samone handed her a pair of gloves and a face guard.

"Put these on."

Greyson was reluctant. She wasn't looking forward to what was coming, but she complied.

"You should trust Ruby. I know all of this is crazy, but you can't do anything if you don't get with the program. These guys aren't playing around."

"Jeez, you sound just like her. Doesn't anyone want to get out of here?"

Samone frowned. "Of course we do. We all do. We just haven't figured that part out yet."

"Is anyone even trying?"

"Look, princess. The way I see it, we're the ones trying to keep your ass alive. Where do you get off riding up in here acting like everyone's savior? You need to get your head out of your ass and get with the program. Everyone wants out. We just want out *alive*."

Greyson's thoughts vanished as the first blow flew past her face like a lightning bolt, narrowly missing her chin as she snapped her head back.

❖

Greyson rolled over in her sleeping bag. Her hip hurt and her back was stiff. She pulled the edge of her sleeping bag up around her face and tucked her hands under her chin. Why was she so cold? Coffee. Coffee would be good. That would warm her up. It was a good idea, but she didn't want to get up. She wanted to stay tucked in her little cocoon. The day could wait.

She drifted in and out of sleep, chasing dreams that faded like smoke in the wind. A new thought gathered at the edges of her mind, following a new scent riding on the forest breeze. The smell grew stronger and worked its way into her consciousness, pulling her from her stupor. Coffee? Greyson frowned. Hadn't she just been thinking of coffee?

She opened her eyes, trying to separate the dream from her waking mind. She sat up. She shouldn't be able to smell coffee in the wilderness alone, unless this meant she was no longer alone. She pulled the puffy jacket she had been using as a pillow out of her bag and slipped it on. She slid her feet into her boots, not bothering with the laces. She paused before reaching for the zipper to the door flap. Faint sounds drifted among the chatter of birds and squirrels. There was the distinct sound of something metal scraping across a hard surface, the scruff of a boot across the ground. She wasn't imagining things. Someone was outside.

Greyson unzipped the tent fly and stepped outside into dense fog that attached itself to her skin and clothing, forming a layer of moisture that deepened her chill. She zipped her jacket to hold in what little warmth she still held between the layers. She peered into the thick mist at a thin figure huddled over a small camp stove. Steam rose from a tin mug as hot liquid poured from an ancient coffeepot.

"Hello," Greyson said, stepping closer.

"Good morning, did I wake you?"

"Yes, or rather the coffee did," Greyson said, nodding to the small pot over the fire.

"Hmm, that'll do it. Would you like a cup?"

Greyson stared at the old woman sitting in front of her. She was lean to the point of being too thin. Her hair was white and was pulled back in a loose ponytail. She wore sneakers and a pair of old blue jeans, and a rain poncho was draped across her shoulders. Her skin had more wrinkles than an old tortoise. Her nose was too big for her face and crooked downward like a bird's beak. Everything about her was out of place. But her eyes were kind and twinkled when she smiled.

"Sure, I'd love some coffee," Greyson answered, remembering the old children's stories about witches living in the woods. "What are you doing here?"

"Well, that's a silly question. Try again." The old woman smirked as if enjoying toying with Greyson.

"Who are you?"

The woman looked up and grinned. "That's a little better. I'm Lucile. I've been hiking this trail or at least parts of it for almost forty years. You never know who you'll meet out here, but I find a hot cup of coffee is a good place to start something new."

Greyson whistled. "Forty years is a long time. How many times have you done the AT?"

Lucile ticked off trips on her fingers. "I'd reckon I've been from one end to the other around four times. The rest of it was weekend trips, summer vacations, things like that. I can't count all those." She held up her hand. "Not enough fingers."

Greyson laughed.

Lucile handed Greyson a cup. The coffee smelled amazing.

"I didn't hear you come into camp last night."

"Nope. You wouldn't have."

Greyson frowned.

Lucile pulled a small bag from a worn green backpack that looked like something Greyson had seen in old war movies. Lucile dumped a handful of oats into a cup of hot water and stirred.

"It's no matter," Lucile continued as she prepared her breakfast, humming a tune Greyson didn't recognize. Lucile pointed a crooked old finger at Greyson. "That's a nasty bruise you've got there."

Greyson lifted her hand to her face and prodded her cheek with her finger. The area around her eye and cheek were tender and puffy.

"You need to watch yourself. You never know what can happen out here. You need to be smart and watch what you're doing, especially if you are going it alone."

Greyson was trying to remember what happened to her face. "Well, I am alone, come to think of it."

"Maybe." Lucile nodded. "If a bear wanders into your camp looking for food, is he the enemy?" She shook her head. "No, he too is on a journey along the trail. If a person you meet along the trail offers you coffee, is she a friend?"

Greyson frowned and looked down into the now empty mug in her hand.

Lucile reached for the cup, pulling it from Greyson's fingers. She wiped it out with a dingy old cloth before stowing it back in her pack. She scraped out her breakfast mug, rinsed it, gave it a swipe with the rag, and it too went into the bag. She stood, stretching her old bones before lifting her pack onto her back.

"You have a long way to go, kid. Just remember, things aren't always what they seem." Lucile waved over her shoulder as she walked away, disappearing into the mist.

Greyson opened her eyes, startled by the sound of the metal food cart trundling down the stone corridor. The smell of coffee filled the air as murmured voices began to resonate through the room. Greyson rubbed her eyes. She was in her cot in her prison. Her blanket was tucked tightly under her chin. Had she just been dreaming, or was this the dream?

Greyson tossed aside her blanket and got in line. If she had a chance to get a real cup of coffee in this hellhole, she wasn't going to miss it, even if it wasn't real.

❖

Greyson jumped when a deep male voice called out her name. She looked to the door to see Uncle Dan waiting for her. She looked to Ruby for some hint of what this could mean, but Ruby just stared at her as if Greyson had just kissed her girlfriend. The women all stopped what they were doing and stared at her too. They seemed as confused as she was.

Ruby's expression had shifted and was now unreadable. Greyson was on her own. A knot formed in her stomach. She knew she was about to be tested and she had no idea what to do.

Greyson did her best to appear unconcerned as she approached the gruff-looking man. "What's up, Uncle Dan? It's not like you to make social calls."

"Shut up, foolish girl. If you keep your mouth shut, you might learn something."

Greyson's confusion grew. "Why is everything a riddle with you? Why can't anyone in this godforsaken place just answer a question?"

"Put out your hands," he ordered.

Greyson obeyed. It wouldn't do any good to protest at this point and she was anxious to learn something, anything that might help her.

She stood still as the old man clasped handcuffs made of zip ties around her wrists. He took her arm and led her through the door. His grip was firm and steady, letting Greyson know he was much stronger than he looked.

"Where are we going?" Greyson asked.

"The boss wants to see you."

The knot in Greyson's stomach tightened. She couldn't imagine there was anything good coming her way.

"Does this boss have a name?" she asked, keeping her tone casual.

The man glared at her. "You can call him the Recruiter."

"That sounds more like a job title than a name," Greyson replied, trying to keep the fear out of her voice.

As they traveled through the corridors, Greyson noticed a change. The walls and floors in this section of the building were newer. They didn't have the old smell of decay like her cell or the training rooms. They climbed a set of large stone stairs that came to a landing where two long hallways intersected. He pulled her to the left just as a man in a black suit carrying a briefcase stepped out of one of the many doors, closing it gently behind him. He looked like any other businessman leaving the office.

"What the hell are you doing up here, Polk?" The man took an aggressive step toward them, his eyes like daggers as he stared the older man down. Greyson took an involuntary step back, expecting to be struck.

"Boss's orders," Uncle Dan growled, holding his ground.

The man in the suit glared down at them, his pockmarked face making him look like a villain in a horror story. But of course, that was exactly who he was.

"Since when do you retrieve the girls? And since when are they brought to the executive level? You wouldn't be trying to pull a fast one now, would you, Polk? Have you gone soft?"

Greyson didn't miss the animosity between the two men and wondered how she could use that to her advantage. At least she had a name for the old man besides Uncle Dan, but was Polk really his name?

Polk's grip on Greyson's arm grew uncomfortable as fingers squeezed her bicep.

"Last I heard you weren't on the need-to-know list," Polk sneered. "Climb a little higher out of the shit hole, Marty, and I'll bother answering your questions."

The bigger man towered over Polk. "Don't use my name."

Polk laughed. "Get out of my way, bean counter."

The big man straightened. "You best watch yourself, Polk. Your days are numbered here."

"Unless you'd like to explain to the boss what's taking us so long, you need to move. I won't tell you again."

Marty laughed. "You going to make me, Grandpa?"

A door at the end of the hall opened. Both men straightened and stepped aside as a third man stepped into the hall. By their deference, Greyson assumed this was the Recruiter. "Is there a problem, gentlemen?"

Polk pulled Greyson down the hall. He glared at Marty as they passed.

Marty nodded. "Just making sure the old man could handle the girl."

"Stop dicking around, both of you. I've got shit to do."

Marty glared at Polk. "Later, old man," he grumbled as he walked away.

Greyson shifted her focus to the Recruiter, assessing the new threat. He was up to something, and she knew she wasn't going to like it.

"Ah, our star pupil has arrived at last," the Recruiter said as if she was some kind of kid on his debate team. He lifted a glass of amber liquid toward Greyson. "Have a seat, Greyson. I have something very special for you today."

The room looked a lot like the conference room at her office. A long mahogany table stood in the middle of the room with plush leather chairs along both sides. Greyson studied the man. There was something vaguely familiar about him, but she couldn't remember ever meeting him. He was well dressed and looked like he had recently had a haircut. His eyes lingered on her as if he was appraising her.

Uncle Dan removed the bonds from her hands.

Greyson rubbed her wrists as she glanced around the room, trying to figure out her own strategy for the meeting. She casually moved across the room to the wet bar, picked up a glass, and filled it with amber liquid. She lifted the glass in the direction of the men in mock salute. "You look like I could use a drink. Do you know that song?" Greyson downed the drink. "I hope you don't mind," she said as she refilled the glass.

Uncle Dan, or Polk, or whatever his name was, made a move toward her but the Recruiter waved him off.

"In this case, I'll allow it."

Greyson was shocked. She had been trying to unsettle him, but she was beginning to wonder if that was possible. So far, she had only succeeded in deepening her own sense of foreboding. She decided to bring the bottle with her to the table. She had a feeling she would need it.

The Recruiter waited for Greyson to take her seat before taking the chair across from her at the table. "To your health," he said, raising his glass to Greyson. "And a long partnership." He smiled over the rim of his glass, his eyes glinting with evil.

Greyson took a gulp of her drink, trying not to choke as the liquid fire burned through her like gasoline. She wanted to throw her glass at him to shatter his smug face but held back, allowing the whiskey to act like a painkiller as it spread through her. She hoped it would numb the sting of what was coming.

"My Employer has very high expectations of you. He's eager to see what you can deliver."

"Your *Employer*?" She made air quotes. "Who would that be? What does that even mean? And what's up with these stupid titles?"

He sat back in his chair, wrapping his fingers behind his head, showing her who was in charge. "It's simple really. It's a matter of supply and demand. An Employer places an order and I recruit the girl to fill it." He smiled. "You were a very special order. Not the usual fare, not easy to find. But I thoroughly enjoyed the hunt."

Greyson swallowed. "So you kidnap women for a living." A statement, not a question.

He nodded. "Among other things. An Employer will be visiting us soon for a demonstration. I know these things can be difficult in the beginning, and up to this point you've chosen not to cooperate with the system. But I can assure you, there's no point continuing this pathetic resistance. To prevent any further delay in your progress, I've brought you a present. It's something I believe will give you the incentive you need to succeed in this program."

The Recruiter nodded to Uncle Dan. The old man opened a small door to an adjoining area, and Olivia was led into the room. Greyson took a gulp of her drink trying to burn away the shock and rage and uncertainty and confusion filling her, but the alcohol soured on her tongue and made her want to puke.

Olivia glanced nervously around the room, her gaze falling on Greyson.

"Greyson Cooper, I'd like you to meet Ms. Olivia Danner. Oh, but I believe you've already met. Thank you for joining us, Ms. Danner, you can have a seat."

Olivia sat on the end of her chair as if she was ready to spring up at any moment. Her hands were bound and Greyson could see fear in her eyes as sweat glistened on her cheeks and neck. She looked frail, as if she had missed too many meals. Bruises decorated her face and neck. Greyson was certain she could make out the imprint of a hand on Olivia's throat.

"I have to thank you for leading me to this beauty, Greyson," the

Recruiter boasted. "It was brilliant, really, a clumsy act of chance, but thanks to you, I got the girl."

Greyson frowned. "What are you talking about?"

"You remember," he said in a playful tone as if they were old friends. "It was that day in Market Square—you weren't paying attention and Ms. Danner ended up wearing her coffee."

Greyson stifled a groan. Of course she remembered. She had thought of Olivia every day since. She had counted the days until she could see her again. But not like this. What did Olivia have to do with anything?

He smiled a wicked smile. "Thanks to you, Ms. Danner has been added to my personal collection."

Olivia turned her attention to Greyson. "You? This is your fault? You did this to me?"

Greyson could feel the hatred across the room. "No. I have nothing to do with this. This asswipe kidnapped me. I have nothing to do with any of this."

Olivia eyed the class of Scotch sitting in front of Greyson. "Right. I can see how hard up you are."

"No, you've got this all wrong," Greyson protested.

"That's enough," the Recruiter said with command. He nodded to the old man who took Olivia's arm and led her out of the room.

"I'm sure you're wondering about my little demonstration," he continued. "Let me explain. My Employer is planning to make a little visit here to see what his money bought. He'll expect to see the fighter he ordered. That means the next time you step into the pit, you will fight, or I'm afraid I'm going to have to get to know Ms. Danner on a much more *personal* level."

"You son of a bitch," Greyson yelled as she lunged across the table. Before she could reach him, he grabbed her by the hair and slammed her face against the table.

"That's better," he growled through gritted teeth. "I'm glad to see we understand each other. But I'd save the fight for the pit if I were you."

He let go. Greyson shot back in her chair, almost knocking it over.

He leaned forward, taking his glass in his hand. "I want you to think of yourself and Ms. Danner as a pair. I've decided not to bother trying to break you. I've come up with a much better plan. I might not be able to break you, but I can break her. Every time you step out of line, she's going to pay for it, and I'll make sure she knows it's a special gift from you. It's one of my special talents. I know just the right way to treat a woman. I can do things that will have her begging to die, a mercy I will leave up to you."

Greyson's heart sank. What was she going to do now? It was more important than ever for her to find a way out. She knew she wasn't responsible for Olivia, but she couldn't let this be her fate. Somehow, she had unknowingly brought Olivia into this mess. She couldn't imagine Olivia going into the pit to be mutilated, and whatever this guy had planned for her sounded far worse. Her stomach churned, the Scotch in her belly turning to acid.

When Greyson didn't respond, the Recruiter laughed. "Good. I'm glad we understand each other." He nodded to the old man. "Take her back to the dormitory. I want her fit and ready to fight this weekend."

Greyson didn't say anything as her hands were cuffed. She followed the old man out. As the door closed behind her she noticed Marty standing at the end of the hall, waiting for them, his gaze shifting between her and Polk.

"What was that about?" Marty asked when they were almost beside him.

Greyson leaned close when she spoke, so he wouldn't miss the smell of alcohol on her breath. The Recruiter wasn't the only one who could play mind games. "What's wrong, Marty? Sad because you didn't get invited to the party?"

He shoved Greyson, pushing her into Polk, causing him to stumble against the wall. Greyson grabbed his arm to steady him, as if she was trying to help.

"You okay, Uncle Dan?"

He shoved Greyson's hands away and glared at Marty. "Watch yourself, bean counter."

"Or what?" Marty growled.

The old man glanced at Greyson, then back to Marty as if considering his options. "Come on, girl, stop wasting time."

Greyson smiled at Marty. "See you soon."

Marty flinched. It was almost imperceptible, but it was a flinch, Greyson was sure of it. She had hit a nerve. She wasn't sure what to do with it yet, but even this small victory gave her something to hang on to. If she was inside this guy's head, she would play it for all it was worth.

Polk had her by the arm again, leading her away.

"Oh yeah, haven't you heard?" Greyson said back to Marty. "There's something special planned." Greyson laughed as she walked away. She could feel his eyes boring into her back as they descended the stairs.

Greyson turned to the old man, who was showing a slight limp. "Are you okay?"

The old man replied through clenched teeth, "Keep moving."

Greyson slowed her pace. He was definitely favoring his left leg. "So, do I call you Polk now, or are you still Uncle Dan?"

He glared at her.

Greyson shrugged. "I think I like Uncle Dan better." She took a few steps when he nudged her onward with a push to her arm. "Why do you let that big lug talk to you like that? He's clearly got jealousy issues. I mean, come on, could he be more obvious? It was like he was mad because you got more attention from Daddy or something."

A muscle jumped at the side of the old man's jaw. "You need to worry about your own problems. It's none of your business," he growled.

"I'm just saying you need to watch yourself. You know what happened with Cain and Abel. You don't want to end up like Abel, do you?"

They stopped outside the door to the dormitory. "Your mouth is going to end up getting you killed."

Greyson shrugged and held out her hands so he could remove the cuffs. "Yeah, you could be right, if someone's fist doesn't get me first."

Greyson glanced around the room. Everyone was staring at her as he released the cuffs. Greyson rubbed her sore wrists. "Thanks. See you at dinner."

He closed the door without a word.

Greyson turned to face the women anxiously waiting. She had held her calm as long as she could. "Who wants to teach me how to fight?"

❖

Olivia was still seething when she was let back into her room. She cursed the day she had run into Greyson Cooper. Everything in her life had gone to hell since the moment that woman had spilled coffee on her. And what was that stupid trick with the dress? Greyson had been so sly about it. Olivia should have seen right through her fake apologies, her romantic dinner. She'd even kissed her good night, for crying out loud. For weeks she'd had fantasies about Greyson's return from her trip. What a fool she had been. How could she have fallen for it? She couldn't imagine hating anyone as much as she hated Greyson. How could she betray another woman this way, knowing what this life would be?

She threw herself onto the bed and punched the pillow. *I hate you, Greyson Cooper, I hate you, I hate you, I hate you.* She was certain Greyson was getting quite the laugh at her expense. Well, she hoped Greyson choked on her filthy whiskey.

Olivia stopped her tantrum when she heard someone at her door. Liz peeped her head inside.

"Are you okay?"

Olivia sat up and let out a frustrated huff. "No."

"What happened?"

"I just got to meet the woman who set me up."

Liz frowned. "What do you mean?"

"I mean I just met the woman responsible for me being here. I ran into her a few weeks ago and she played some stunt to trick me."

"She told you that?"

"No. That man…I mean, the Recruiter did."

"Oh."

Olivia held up her hands in frustration. "Well, it doesn't matter—there's no way it's not true. She was just sitting there drinking her whiskey or whatever it was as the Recruiter told the story. I'm sure they're both getting a big laugh."

"Huh," Liz said noncommittally.

Olivia stopped and stared at Liz, realizing she hadn't expected to see her. "Why are you here?"

Liz jumped as if she had been caught at something. "Oh, I almost forgot. I have bad news, I'm afraid. They're going to take you down to general population today."

Olivia flinched. "What? No. Please, no, don't let them take me there."

Liz shook her head. "There's nothing I can do." She took Olivia's hand. "I'm really sorry. But don't worry—I'm sure it's just to show you what it's like down there. He never leaves his girls there for very long."

Olivia felt a lump form in her throat. "General population? Am I going to have to fight?"

"I don't know. There's some big event coming. I'm sure this is just part of your initiation training."

The whole thing made Olivia feel sick. She wasn't a fighter. The most athletic thing she did was milk cows…and a little yoga. How was she ever going to get through this?

"What do I do?" she said, panicking.

For once, Liz looked lost. "I have no idea."

"Great, I thought you were supposed to be my mentor or something."

Liz shrugged. "I am, but this is a new one for me. I have no idea what's going on or what they're up to. But there's another girl down there, one of us. Her name is Audrey. She might be able to help you. I'm not sure how much longer she'll be in general pop, but she's your best bet."

"Okay." Olivia sighed. "At least that's something. Thank you."

Liz hugged her. There was a harsh knock at the door, and they pulled apart.

"Time to go," Liz said. She squeezed Olivia's hand. "Good luck."

As usual, the guard was waiting for them at the door. Olivia glanced at him nervously as she passed. His expression was pinched as if he had just eaten something sour. Maybe he wasn't too keen on her going into general population either. Or maybe that was just her own wishful thinking.

Olivia heard the women before she saw them. Someone was yelling, and she could hear muffled sounds beating out a rhythmic pattern: *Pat-pat-pat, pat, pat.* Pause. *Pat-pat-pat, pat, pat.* With each step her anticipation grew to a panic. As they approached the door, Olivia saw a group of women clustered around two women facing off in the center of the room.

The door swung open and the man urged Olivia inside with a push to her back. Olivia stumbled in as the door closed behind her.

As she approached the group, several women stepped aside to give her room when they realized someone new had arrived. Olivia couldn't hide her shock the moment she recognized Greyson in the center of the room. Greyson blocked several blows before throwing a punch of her own. Olivia gasped when Greyson's punch landed, sending the other woman to the floor.

Cheers erupted as Greyson stepped forward and extended her hand to the woman on the floor. The woman took her hand and pulled herself up, smacking Greyson on the shoulder as she rose. Greyson looked like she had just conquered the world.

The woman next to Olivia moved just as Greyson looked her way. Greyson's expression fell.

"Oh, shit," Olivia groaned.

Several women had taken notice of her and were closing in. They circled her as if they were sizing up their prey. Olivia's heart pounded so hard, she wondered if she was having a heart attack.

A tall, beautiful woman with coal-black eyes circled her, looking her up and down.

"I see the Recruiter has sent us another one of his girls to play with." She sniffed Olivia's hair. "You haven't been here long. I can still smell the fear on you."

Olivia stepped away, trying to put some distance between them, but when she did, she bumped into another woman standing close behind her. She looked around the room, desperate for someplace to run, anything to get away from the stalking. She felt like she had just walked into the lion's den.

The tall woman took a strand of her hair into her hand and twirled it between her fingers. "I like this one."

"Ruby," Greyson said in warning.

Ruby smiled at her.

"What the hell are you doing?" Greyson asked. "Don't we have enough problems in here without having to worry about each other?" Greyson walked toward Olivia.

Olivia shook her head. "Stay away from me."

Greyson held up her hands to show she meant no harm, but she realized too late the boxing gloves made her look even more dangerous. "Look, we need to talk," Greyson said more calmly than she felt. "This isn't what you think."

Olivia scoffed. "Yeah, right, like I'm going to believe you. It looks like you're having a good time to me. I suppose you had me brought here just so you could gloat."

Greyson shook her head, but before she could argue, Ruby stepped between them.

"Do you two know each other?"

"No," Greyson said.

"Yes," Olivia answered.

Ruby looked back and forth between them, an angry scowl on her face. "Which is it then, yes or no."

"Yes. I ran into her one time not long before I was brought here," Greyson answered.

Olivia seethed. "Ran into me? Ran into me! You probably did that on purpose. The Recruiter said it himself—you're the reason I'm here."

Ruby and Greyson both frowned.

Olivia pointed her finger at Greyson. "They had me brought into some kind of meeting this morning so they could gloat about it."

Greyson's anger sparked. "I wasn't gloating, and I told you, I'm a prisoner here too."

"Do you really expect me to believe that? You look like you're having a pretty good time to me."

Greyson took a step forward, her anger getting the best of her.

Ruby took Olivia's arm. "Come with me." She put up a hand when Greyson took another step closer. "Not you. You stay here."

Greyson clenched her teeth. "That sick fuck has put these ideas into her head. I had nothing to do with any of this."

Ruby glared at Greyson. "We'll see."

Greyson swallowed the lump in her throat. She didn't know how she was going to convince Olivia that she wasn't part of this sick game, that she hadn't been the one to have her ripped from her life. She watched Ruby walk Olivia to the far side of the room, their backs turned away from her. She had a sick feeling in the pit of her stomach. Any chance she might have thought she'd had to earn any trust in the group had just been thrown out the window.

CHAPTER NINE

Greyson watched the women huddled around a table talking to Olivia. She wondered what they were planning. If they really thought she was in on this with their captors, she was as good as dead. She wouldn't have to wait for someone to take her out in the pit—they'd do it right here.

Olivia rubbed her wrist nervously as the women talked. When Audrey reached across the table to take Olivia's hand, Greyson noticed a tattoo on the inside of Audrey's wrist. She frowned and looked closer at Olivia's arm where she continued to rub her fingers across her skin. Was that the same tattoo? Great, something else she had to figure out. Wait a minute, there was something else. She continued to look back and forth between Audrey and Olivia. The similarities in appearance were striking. They looked like they could be related, but there were differences that made the resemblance difficult to see at first. Audrey's face was round and her eyes seemed set a little too close together. Or was it just the roundness of her face and the narrow bridge of her nose? Greyson studied Olivia. Her features were softer, as if her skin had been bathed in milk, and her mouth lifted up naturally at the corners in a hint of a smile. Greyson shook her head. Olivia didn't have anything to smile about now. What had Ruby said about Olivia? Something about the Recruiter sending them another one of his girls to play with. And he'd said something that morning about his personal collection.

Greyson rubbed her temples. It looked like his personal collection had a type. He'd said she led him to Olivia. That meant he had been following *her* all along and just stumbled onto Olivia, just like she had done. Her head hurt. There were too many layers to this to keep track. The one thing she knew for certain was that this guy was really sick in the head.

Greyson stiffened when Samone got up from the table and walked toward her. She had some explaining to do, and she wasn't sure whose side Samone would be on when she was done.

"You want to tell me what's going on here?" Samone said, taking the seat next to Greyson.

Greyson let out a deep breath. "Hell if I know."

"Well, you need to come up with some answers pretty fast, because it's looking like you're a mole."

Greyson snorted. "Some mole. If I was a mole and responsible for her being here, like she says I am, why the hell would they put her in here with me? That sick bastard is playing with everyone's heads and you're all falling for it."

"True. But you've got to give me more to work with than that. How do you know Olivia?"

Greyson shook her head. "Like I said, I don't know her. I literally ran into her and spilled coffee all over us both. I apologized. We had dinner together, I kissed her good night. Hell, I wanted to date her, not hurt her. End of story. At least I thought so. Then this morning that dick brought me into some conference room and paraded me around like I was one of his friends."

"Why? Why would he do that?" Samone asked.

Greyson shrugged. "He said I needed to get with the program. He told me he only discovered Olivia after our little incident. He decided I'm somehow responsible for her. If I get out of line again, if I don't follow the rules..."

"What?" Samone asked.

Greyson swallowed. "He'll punish her to get to me."

Samone hissed. "Sounds about right. He likes to play those kinds of games with us."

"What do you mean?" Greyson asked.

Samone sighed. "We live together day in and day out. Our very survival depends on every other woman in the room. You can't live with someone, care for their wounds, learn about their families without getting close. In here, we become family. What hurts one of us hurts us all. They use those relationships against us when they can. That's what Ruby was trying to tell you. If we pull some stunt and fail, they will hurt those we love. It is a price that is too high to pay."

Greyson chewed at the skin on the side of her thumb, nervously wanting to take her frustrations out on something. She put her hand down and looked straight into Samone's eyes, needing to see the truth in her answer. "Will he do it? Will he take it out on her if I don't fight?"

Samone closed her eyes a moment. When she met Greyson's gaze, hers had hardened and her eyes were filled with hatred. "He will destroy her if he has to in order to get what he wants. She is his plaything, but you are a moneymaker. He doesn't care what happens to her. He only cares about the money."

"Son of a bitch," Greyson hissed through clenched teeth. What was she going to do now? She glanced to Olivia, who continued to talk with the rest of the group. "What do you know about that tattoo on her wrist? She didn't have that when we met. And it looks an awful lot like Audrey's."

Samone's face reddened and her jaw twitched. "That's his mark. All his girls have the tattoo, each with their own number in the center. They are like trophies to him. He parades them around the men as if they are a special breed of dog."

"How can he put them in the pit? They'll get slaughtered."

"Ah, he uses them for other entertainment."

Greyson flinched.

"No. Not that," Samone said quickly to reassure Greyson. "Don't worry—as long as they do what he wants, it's a look-only business. There are women who have been sold to other men, so we don't know what happens to them, but as far as I know he keeps sex out of the business."

Greyson couldn't figure out the connection. Why was Olivia here? "What if she's the mole? What if she's been brought here to upset the group?"

Samone looked toward Olivia and shrugged. "Maybe. Maybe you two are in this together, and maybe you are both victims. We don't know. But I promise you, everyone will be watching you both."

Greyson saw Ruby staring at her. "What about Ruby? What was she going to do to Olivia?"

Samone sighed. "She doesn't trust the Recruiter's girls. She was close to one of them once, an older woman who betrayed Ruby. The girls are sometimes asked to spy on us, to get us to do things. They can be manipulative."

"Did Audrey tell you all of this?"

Samone glanced to Audrey. "Some of it. The truth is, no one can trust anyone here. Audrey and I are friends, but she is closest to Amala. We try to protect her when she's here with us, but we can't protect her against him. He always knows everything. We don't know how he knows, he just does. Ruby thinks it's the girls."

"What do I do?" Greyson asked.

Samone sighed. "Looks like you have to decide what's important to you. If you want to save the girl, you will fight."

Greyson pressed her thumbnail into her palm, letting the pain center her thoughts. "I already know that, but then what? If I give in to what he wants, he will own me."

Samone clasped her hand over Greyson's shoulder and squeezed. "He already does."

Olivia watched the women spar. She couldn't imagine having to fight any of them. They were so fast and strong, she doubted she would last a minute. This must be what Liz was trying to tell her.

"How are you doing?" Audrey said as she took a seat next to Olivia.

"I don't even know how to answer that question."

"I know it's a lot to take in, but the girls aren't as bad as they seem. You have to remember, they're prisoners here too. They're just trying to survive."

Olivia scoffed. "I don't know. Some of them seem to enjoy this."

Audrey shook her head. "No, they've just been here a long time and know each other very well. They know what they have to do. They know who's to blame. They don't want to hurt each other."

Olivia watched Ruby land a series of punches to her opponent before sweeping her foot behind the woman's legs, taking her to the floor. The instant the woman was down, Ruby came down hard on the woman's back with her elbow.

Olivia winced. "I'm not so sure about that. Ruby seems to be having a good time."

Audrey chewed her lip. "If there is a leader here, it's Ruby. She can be a bit intimidating, but she keeps everyone together and makes the system work."

"What system?" Olivia asked.

Audrey pointed to the sparring floor. "She helps everyone learn how to fight, she makes the plan for the fights, and she's the one who keeps the girls from going at each other when they are about to lose it."

"Are you saying the fights are fixed?" Olivia asked.

Audrey laughed. "No. Not exactly. No one really knows who will go into the pit together until it actually happens. But she tries to teach the girls how to put on a good show without killing each other."

"Have you ever had to fight?"

Audrey's face paled. "You mean in the pit? Yeah, once."

"What happened?"

Audrey shook her head. Her eyes were wide as if she was facing a fight in that very moment.

"Audrey?"

"I kept refusing to follow the rules. I was still on the upper level with the rest of the Recruiter's girls. I didn't even know about the big fights. Liz tried to tell me, but I wouldn't listen. They brought me to the pit one night. I didn't know what was happening until they put me down there."

"Who did you fight?"

Audrey swallowed and trailed her gaze across the room. "Her." Her eyes were sad when she identified the woman who had delivered her fate. "Samone."

Olivia gasped. "But she's so much bigger than you! And you guys seem so close."

Audrey looked at Olivia. "We are close. I can't imagine my life without her. She's been a good friend."

"What did you do? What happened?"

"I couldn't fight her. She was too strong and too fast. The men were yelling at her to kill me."

Olivia's heart raced. She couldn't imagine. How had Audrey possibly survived?

"Samone knew what she could do to me. She had no choice but to follow orders, but instead of beating me to a pulp, she took me down as mercifully as she could and delivered a blow that knocked me out pretty quickly."

"Oh my God." Panic rushed through Olivia and she gasped trying to catch her breath. "How could she do that to you?"

Audrey shook her head. "She didn't have a choice. You don't get it. It's so much worse if you don't fight. She was trying to protect me. But the men didn't like it very much. They made her fight every fight that night until she was beaten so bad she couldn't get up. They brought her to the room where I had been taken after the fight. Her face was so bruised and swollen, I barely recognized her."

Olivia watched the women across the room, wondering what hell each of them had endured in this prison. Her gaze drifted to Greyson. "What about Greyson?"

"She's a tough one to figure out. She's new. They kept her in solitary for a while before taking her to the pit for her initiation."

At the mention of Greyson's fight, Olivia's curiosity got the better of her. "Who did she fight?"

Audrey nodded to a woman across the room. "They put her in the pit with Amala."

Olivia shook her head. "I bet she enjoyed that. Who won?"

Audrey frowned. "It wasn't like that. Greyson wouldn't fight. She did her best to get away from Amala, begged her not to do it. She tried to protect herself, but she never threw a single punch. Amala did a number on her. She couldn't make the mistake of going too easy on Greyson—they would have killed her if she had. Greyson has been nursing sore ribs since."

Olivia frowned. "It looked like she was enjoying the fight when I walked in earlier."

Audrey shrugged. "Whatever happened this morning got Greyson riled up. She came back here asking us to teach her how to fight. That was the first time she's been willing to fight anyone."

Olivia wasn't convinced. "I don't know. When I saw her this morning, she was kicked back in a chair drinking whiskey with that bastard who brought me here. I'm telling you, she's in on this." She'd been wrong about Greyson before and had let her guard down. Look what that had gotten her. She'd been taken in by Greyson's good looks and her charm and it had gotten her hurt. It wouldn't happen again.

Audrey sighed. "Time will tell. But the one thing I've learned in here is that nothing is what it appears to be. You can't afford to make any enemies."

Olivia frowned, considering everything she had learned. "So what about you? Does Ruby give you a hard time for being one of the Recruiter's girls?"

Audrey shifted her gaze to Ruby. "Not anymore. Samone and Amala and I are close. Ruby will never trust one of the Recruiter's girls, but she has accepted me. I've been here quite a while now. I thought he would have moved me back by now, but I think he's using me."

"Using you how?" Olivia asked.

"I think he knows I'm close to them. I think he uses me to control them. I'm like their pet. Sometimes I feel like I'm the cheese in a trap."

Olivia thought about this. "So Ruby thinks I'm a trap too?"

Audrey nodded. "Probably. She can be pretty rough when she gets something in her head. Watch yourself with her."

❖

Greyson spent the rest of the week watching and learning as much as she could. Olivia avoided her like the plague, and she was fine with that. The last thing she needed right now was more drama. Some of the girls were already treating her like she was the enemy, and she didn't need to keep the hornets stirred.

Greyson was quick to get in line when Uncle Dan arrived with the food cart. She wanted to see if she could get any information out of him about what was going to happen. She was shocked to see one side of his face swollen and bruised.

"What happened to you?" Greyson asked. When he didn't answer, Greyson pushed with a guess. "Looks like you and the bean counter went a round or two, and by the bruises, I'd say you lost."

At the mention of Marty, Uncle Dan's gaze shot to hers. Bingo—her guess had paid off. "What's up with you and that asshat? Someone needs to take him down a few notches."

The old man met her gaze with a fierce stare. "Those are big words, little girl. You won't even fight to save yourself."

Greyson flinched. "Yeah, well, what's the point in saving myself in a place like this. The way I see it, I'm already dead."

He looked at her with cold eyes like the gray hand of death. "You keep things up, and you'll be right."

"What's going to happen to me?" Greyson asked.

"That's up to you. But this is your shot to make an impression. You want to live, you've got to make yourself worth keeping."

"Keeping? Are they thinking of moving me or killing me?"

He looked away and reached for a bottle of water.

"Come on, Uncle Dan. Help me out here. How am I supposed to do what you want me to do, if I don't know what to expect?"

He pushed the tray and the water toward her. "They're going to draw a line in the sand and dare you to cross it."

"Damn it, what does that mean?" Greyson said, letting her frustration show.

He shook his head. "You're on your own, girl. It's time to prove your salt."

When Greyson moved away from the door, the room was silent and every eye was on her. Her stomach clenched. Great. She had just given everyone more evidence against her. She had run with the plan to try to play the men against each other, but at this point, the Recruiter was beating her at her own game.

Greyson sat at a table to eat alone. She studied the room, trying to figure out who she could trust.

Samone sat down next to her. "Good job, mole."

"I'm not a mole," Greyson growled.

"Then how do you explain your little chat with the old man?" Samone asked.

"I was trying to get information."

Samone raised one eyebrow. "I'm waiting."

Greyson sighed. "He just talks in riddles. He won't give me anything." She watched Ruby watching her across the room. Ruby placed a cookie into her mouth and smiled at Greyson. Something clicked in her brain.

"Did you get cookies with dinner?"

Samone laughed. "No. Of course not."

"Hmm. Me either. How do you suppose Ruby gets them?"

Samone frowned. "Be careful, Greyson."

"Come on. You can't tell me you haven't thought about it. Don't you think it's weird? I noticed she got them the night of the last fight too. Did you see if she passed anything to the old man?"

"No, I didn't. And I'm not looking. Ruby manages to keep us alive. We don't question how."

"Seriously? I come in here just trying to figure out what the hell's going on and you guys already have me strapped to the stake. But Ruby is passing information to these guys who are making money off your pain, and you don't ask any questions? No wonder you're still here."

A muscle jumped at the side of Samone's jaw. "I'm trying to give you the benefit of the doubt, but you're not making it very easy for anyone to trust you."

Greyson clenched her fists. "Well, after tonight, you might not have to worry about that anymore."

Samone nodded in agreement.

"So, does everyone go?" Greyson asked.

Samone shrugged. "Not usually. We won't know who's fighting until they come for us. They only take everyone for the big events."

Greyson looked at Samone. "Will you do me a favor?"

"What?"

"If they put me in there with you, will you take it easy on my ribs? I don't think I'm ready for that again."

Samone smiled. "We'll see."

Greyson played with her food, too nervous to eat. A line in the sand. What did that mean? What was the Recruiter up to? And what was she going to do about it?

Samone nudged her arm. "What are you planning?"

Greyson pushed her tray away. "Nothing. I keep trying to figure out a strategy, but how can I if I don't know what I'm up against?"

"And the girl?" Samone asked.

Greyson glanced toward Olivia. Greyson had been avoiding her, pretending she didn't exist, but she knew exactly where Olivia was in the room. It was as if she couldn't stop herself from wanting to protect her. She didn't want to be responsible for anyone. If she took on that cross, she would become their slave and she would never get free.

"She's not my problem," Greyson answered.

Samone's eyebrows shot up in surprise. "Really?"

Greyson shrugged. "I can't let him get to me."

Samone laughed. "You say that now, but wait till tonight, you'll see things differently. Everything changes in the pit." Samone slapped Greyson on the back and stood. "Eat. You may not be able to for a while."

Greyson's shoulders tensed at the thought of what she was about to face.

CHAPTER TEN

Guards came and removed all the women one by one, separating the group. No one knew who was being taken to cells and who was going to the pit. By the time it was Greyson's turn, she was relieved just to be moving. The fear, the anxiety bleeding off the other women was so strong she could smell it. The anticipation was driving her crazy. She had no idea what she was going to do but she was ready to get this show on the road.

Greyson was escorted by two men down a long, narrow hallway to a now familiar set of large doors. Her heart pounded and she clenched her fists. She drew in a deep breath to settle her nerves. Things were about to get real.

The guard to her left stepped forward and opened the door. To her surprise, the room was full of men and women she had never seen before. A small group of men in expensive-looking suits sat around the pit. The other men in the room appeared to be guarding these more important figures. Greyson chuckled to herself. It was like she was at some clandestine meeting of a cartel or the Mob.

"Guess I'm the entertainment tonight," Greyson mumbled.

The Recruiter rose from his chair and came to greet her. He leaned close to her ear and spoke as if they were the only two people in the room. "I hope you've thought about my little arrangement between you and Ms. Danner. But just in case you have any more questions, let me sweeten the deal." He glanced over his shoulder to the men in expensive suits. "My Employers have certain expectations, and it's your job to fulfill them. So I have something extra special for you tonight."

Greyson swallowed hard, trying to hold her tongue. She wanted him to keep talking. The more he talked, the more information she had to work with. The big doors opened and the gravity of the situation soured in her mouth as Olivia was escorted into the room and brought to stand in front of Greyson. Tears streaked Olivia's face and she looked like she could pass out at any moment.

"Here's my deal." The Recruiter motioned to a man at the back of the room. A second set of doors opened. Greyson's heart raced as Ruby was led into the room. "I'm sure you're familiar with the power and strength of your queen." The Recruiter laughed. "We call her the exterminator. She's very useful at getting rid of deadweight we sometimes acquire."

Greyson looked at him for the first time. "No way."

He smiled as if she had just said exactly what he had expected her to say. "Hmm. Then I guess Ms. Danner will do the honors tonight. Pity really, I liked her. She had such promise."

Olivia whimpered. Her entire body was shaking with fear.

Greyson clenched her fist until her nails bit into her skin. "You wouldn't."

He laughed. "Oh, but I would." He nodded to the men.

One of the men started to push Olivia toward the pit.

"Stop it. I'll do it." Greyson seethed.

The Recruiter smiled. "That's more like it." He started to leave but turned back to Greyson as if he'd forgotten something. "One last thing. If you throw this fight, I'll have Ruby take care of her anyway."

"Bastard," Greyson growled.

He smiled. "You have no idea."

Greyson met Olivia's gaze. Her eyes were wide with fear. Her chin trembled from sobs she could barely control. Greyson was certain she was condemned no matter what choices she made from here on, and she wasn't sure there was anything she could do to save Olivia, no matter what the Recruiter said. But there was one thing she could do.

"I'm sorry," Greyson said, never taking her eyes off Olivia.

Olivia shook her head wildly. Greyson looked to the tall, thin man to Olivia's left. Marty. The accountant seemed to pay Olivia a little too much attention. His grip clamped on to Olivia's flesh as if he owned her.

Greyson made up her mind. She thrust her fist into his face as hard as she could. The man rocked back on his heels and instantly covered his nose with his hands.

"That's for Uncle Dan," Greyson yelled as she was grabbed from behind.

"Stop," the Recruiter shouted a moment before the guards could retaliate. "Get her into the pit."

Greyson cursed the men as they dragged her into the pit. Her blood reached a boil when she saw the men drag Olivia to a wall and chain her arms above her head. They pulled her up until her toes barely touched the ground.

Olivia cried and begged them not to hurt her. The Recruiter walked up to Olivia and slid the blade of a knife beneath her shirt. He sliced the fabric free from her body, exposing the milky flesh and the ridges of her ribs as her chest heaved with each breath.

The Recruiter smiled at Greyson as he ran his finger across Olivia's breast. "We had a deal, Greyson."

Olivia screamed, "No."

The Recruiter made a motion with his hand, and three of his girls were brought into the room. Greyson knew they were his by the similarities in their features. Each one walked up to a chain on the wall and one by one they pulled. With each pull of the chain, ice-cold water poured from a grate in the ceiling. The water struck Olivia, drenching her. The water splattered across the floor, sprinkling Greyson with its ice-cold tendrils. Olivia screamed again, her chin quivering as tears streamed down her face.

Greyson turned to the pit. Ruby was waiting, her hands loose at her sides. Greyson swallowed. "How do you want to play this?" she said so no one else could hear.

Ruby smiled. "Easy. You will lose."

"Fine, but I have to make it look good or she's a goner."

Ruby's smile broadened. "I know."

The first blow came as a shock, knocking Greyson backward into the wall. Ruby was lightning fast and had the strength of a bull. This was nothing like what Greyson had seen Ruby do in training. Ruby was completely off script. She moved so fast, Greyson didn't even have time to throw a punch, or block one, let alone try to figure out Ruby's tell.

Greyson danced around the pit trying to avoid the punches. She heard the smack of something and a crack and heard Olivia cry out again. She looked up to see one of the women strike Olivia across the back with a long flexible rod that reminded her of the cane poles she used to fish with as a girl. The next strike rocked Greyson as Olivia's bloodcurdling scream ripped through her.

Ruby took advantage of Greyson's distraction. The blow caught her cheek. Pain exploded in Greyson's eye, and she stumbled. She caught herself on the wall, narrowly avoiding the next blow.

Out of desperation, Greyson charged Ruby, throwing punch after punch, hoping something would land. As luck would have it, Ruby seemed surprised by the attack and Greyson was able to earn a small reprieve as Ruby shoved her aside and backed away. Each time Ruby advanced, Greyson met the charge head-on and held her ground. She had to put up a good fight, or Ruby would kill Olivia. But if she somehow managed to beat Ruby, no one in the group would ever trust her again. *I guess this is that line in the sand.*

Greyson felt the air rush out of her body as Ruby spun, sending her left foot crashing into Greyson's chest. Greyson fell back against the wall before falling to her knees clutching her battered ribs, gasping for breath. Pain shot through her like a bullet ripping through her flesh in an explosion against her spine.

Ruby stood over her, her fist raised, her elbow rocketing toward Greyson like a guillotine. Greyson felt like she had been kicked by a horse. She struggled to breathe.

Ruby kicked her in the head. She heard Olivia's scream as the room went dark.

❖

Olivia shivered from the cold, but her heart thundered against her chest as if she was running. She was freezing, but that was nothing compared to the searing pain ripping through the flesh on her back. Despite the pain, she knew things could have been so much worse. She couldn't believe Greyson had saved her from fighting Ruby. Why? Olivia doubted anyone could survive a fight with Ruby.

She struggled against her restraints, trying to get a full breath and desperately trying to see what was happening in the pit. It was pretty clear Ruby had it in for her. Greyson could have let Ruby have her. Why hadn't she? She would have thought Greyson would have enjoyed watching Ruby annihilate her.

Olivia screamed as another blow cut across her back, but she forced herself to stay focused on the fight taking place in front of her. She flinched when Ruby hit Greyson so hard she stumbled. If this was part of Greyson's game, she had some sick ideas of fun.

Olivia's breath caught as Greyson exploded in a flurry of motion. Her punches were wild, as if she wasn't trying to hit anything in particular. She looked more like she was fighting off a swarm of bees than fighting a single person. This was the first time Olivia believed it possible that Greyson had been telling the truth. The look of desperation in her eyes was too real. Greyson was fighting for her life.

The Recruiter draped his arm around Olivia's waist. She recoiled at the contact.

"Good show, isn't it." He chuckled when Olivia tried to pull away. "Maybe I should have you fight after all, let you work out some of that feist on one of the girls."

Olivia froze. She had been saved once, but she doubted it would happen again.

"That's better. We wouldn't want to throw away all of Greyson's hard work, would we?"

Olivia glared at him, fighting back her tears. "You said I didn't have to fight if she fought Ruby."

He laughed. "I said you wouldn't have to fight Ruby, but I never said you wouldn't have to fight."

Olivia's heart sank.

Cheers erupted from the men around them. Olivia stared into the pit as Greyson fell to her hands and knees, clutching her side.

Ruby brought her entire body down on Greyson's back. She stared breathless as Greyson crumpled to the ground. Olivia screamed as Ruby kicked Greyson in the head. "Stop it, you're killing her." Olivia gasped for air. Was Greyson moving? Damn it, was she breathing? Olivia glared at Ruby. How could she?

This was all too much. There was no way Greyson was in on any of this. How could she be and allow herself to be beaten so badly? What was the gain?

The Recruiter nodded to someone across the pit. As the men around the room clapped at the display of Greyson defeated on the ground, two men moved into the pit, each taking Greyson by an arm and dragging her from the room.

Olivia was paying attention now. She cataloged the face of every man in the room in her memory. She hated every one of them.

The Recruiter shook hands with the men as if a business deal had just gone through. These were the men the Recruiter called his Employers. These were the men responsible for this barbaric game. One man stood out from the rest, as if he held a position of great importance. The Recruiter congratulated him as if his team had just won the playoffs. The man pointed to Greyson and made a gesture imitating the final blow that had been Greyson's undoing.

His fat face was ruddy from his excitement. He reminded Olivia of the pigs on the farm at feeding time. She couldn't imagine what could make a man feel he had the right to own and destroy another human being, but this man obviously took great pleasure from it.

Ruby was brought from the pit to stand before another much older man with silver hair combed back from his face. He looked to be in his seventies. He spoke softly to Ruby. Olivia couldn't hear what was said, but she jumped when Ruby spat in the man's face. She flinched as one of the guards struck Ruby across the back of her leg with some kind of stick. Ruby fell to her knees. The old man wiped his face with a handkerchief he pulled from his inside jacket pocket. He glared down at Ruby with a sinister sneer.

"You will pay for that," he said through gritted teeth.

Despite his anger, Olivia could see he was enjoying what he was doing to Ruby. Olivia didn't know what to think or feel anymore. A few moments ago, she'd been angry with Ruby too. Now she felt sorry for her.

Audrey had been right. They were all prisoners here. They were all just trying to survive. If someone as strong as Ruby or Greyson couldn't get out, what chance did she have?

Just when she thought things couldn't get any worse, the big doors opened again. Another group of women was escorted into the room. Each had the signature blond hair, pale skin, and slender features of the Recruiter's girls. They wore only black bikinis and stilettos. Each had a dog collar around her neck. Olivia had trouble keeping up with who was who as the women spread through the group of men. The similarity between the women was astounding. Olivia swallowed the bile rising in her throat as she realized this was what the Recruiter had in mind for her. She was to be one of his personal servants.

Olivia's stomach clenched as she watched the near replicas of herself take their places next to the Recruiter. His smile was a sickening gloat as two of the women stepped close and looped their arms through his as if he was their date to the ball.

"Gentlemen," he announced, drawing attention to himself, "I thought we would enjoy a bonus tonight. As you can see, I have brought in my own private collection for your viewing pleasure as I bring in a new initiate tonight. I would like you to meet my latest acquisition to my collective."

The men began to clap as strong hands took control of Olivia's arms, removing the chains that held her captive. Her heart raced as she was lifted and carried into the pit. No matter how hard she tried to fight against them, the bite of fingers into her flesh held her in place.

"I thought this would be a good time to remind our dear Ruby of her place as well," the Recruiter said with a hint of laughter in his voice.

"No," Ruby cried as the doors opened and another young girl was led into the room. Ruby screamed and fought against the men.

Olivia stared into the face of her opponent, a face almost a mirror image of her own. The woman was thin and looked as if she had seen a ghost. The fear in her eyes could only be a reflection of the terror Olivia felt. The woman looked wild, as if she stared into the eyes of the devil.

"Don't do this," Ruby yelled. Olivia looked up to see Ruby being dragged from the room. "Don't hurt her." Olivia wondered which one of them Ruby was talking about.

Someone shoved Olivia from behind, pushing her forward. In an instant, the other woman unleashed a barrage of blows, her fingernails tearing through Olivia's flesh like razors. Olivia did her best to block the flurry directed at her face. It seemed the girl wanted to erase every likeness between them.

Out of desperation Olivia grabbed the girl, pulled her against her, and buried her face in the girl's shoulder. It was the only way she could protect herself from the worst of the blows. Surely if she couldn't reach her, she couldn't hurt her.

Wrong. The woman pounded her fists against Olivia's back and twisted her body, managing to wrap her arm around Olivia's neck. The girl tossed herself sideways and slammed Olivia to the floor.

Olivia found herself face-to-face with the woman on top of her, punching wildly at her face and chest. Olivia pushed against the girl's shoulders, trying to get her off her.

The woman sat up, grabbed Olivia's hands, and opened her mouth in a scream. She let out a guttural noise that sounded like a dying animal.

Olivia peered into the woman's gaping mouth as the horror hit her. The woman had no tongue. Olivia's fear surged, giving her more strength than she knew she had. She lashed out with her hands and kicked her legs up, managing to wrap a leg across the girl's shoulder, kicking her away. Olivia managed to get free. Still on her back, she kicked wildly at the girl, as if trying to escape the wrath of a tiger. Her exposed wounds ground into the dirt, and the debris on the floor cut into her back. Unexpectedly her foot connected with the woman's jaw and she crumpled to the floor.

Olivia gasped in fear and relief when the girl didn't move. What the hell just happened?

❖

Rough hands held Olivia tight as she was tossed into a large room with several rows of beds. She fell to her hands and knees on the floor and gasped at the sight of Greyson lying crumpled on the floor. Olivia crawled to her, gently calling Greyson's name.

"Greyson? Greyson, can you hear me? Are you okay?"

Greyson seemed to try to move but moaned in pain as she did.

"It's okay. Just be still for now. I'll try to figure something out."

Olivia looked around the room. She needed to get Greyson off the floor, but how? Greyson outweighed her by at least thirty pounds.

"I need you to help me get you to a bed," she whispered to Greyson. She took Greyson's arm, but Greyson flinched in pain. "Damn it, I'm sorry. Is it your ribs?"

Greyson groaned again.

Olivia was frustrated. There was no way she could do this alone.

"I thought you two were mortal enemies," a cold voice said from the back of the room.

Shit. Ruby. The last person she wanted to see right now. What else could happen in one night? Olivia closed her eyes and hoped for a miracle.

Ruby stepped out of the shadows, her gaze focused on Olivia. Olivia could almost feel her gaze sliding over her face, taking in the claw marks and bruises on her skin.

"What happened to the girl?" Ruby asked coldly.

"I don't know."

Something flashed in Ruby's eyes, making her look as if she was on the brink of insanity.

"What did you do to her?" Ruby demanded.

Olivia shook her head. "I tried to stop her. She was on me,

clawing my face, hitting me. At some point, I kicked her. I think I knocked her out. She didn't get back up."

Olivia swallowed hard, trying not to think of the dark, empty cavern of the girl's mouth, her violence, her primal scream.

Ruby closed her eyes and sat down on a bunk. The color seeped from her face and Olivia detected a slight tremble in her hand as she reached for the bed frame for support.

"Who was she?" Olivia asked. "What happened to her?"

Ruby shook her head. "I don't know everything. These Employers have ways of punishing the girls if they don't obey or if they believe they've been betrayed."

"They cut out her tongue?" Olivia gasped.

Ruby's shoulders slumped. She rubbed her eyes as if trying to shut out the image.

Olivia waited, although she already knew the answer.

Greyson groaned and stirred next to Olivia. Olivia pushed the hair away from Greyson's face and trailed her fingers across her swollen cheek. She looked up at Ruby.

"Help me move her."

Ruby stared at her, unmoving.

"What's your problem?" Olivia snapped. "Are you enjoying her suffering? Haven't you already hurt her enough?"

Ruby flinched and Olivia saw the faint stab of guilt cross her face. Reluctantly Ruby helped Olivia lift Greyson from the floor and place her onto the cot.

Olivia covered Greyson with the wool blanket. She looked up at Ruby, more angry than afraid. "Why did you have to hurt her so badly? You knew she was injured and you used that to your advantage. How could you?"

Ruby's face turned red with anger. "They know of her injuries too. If I hadn't taken advantage of that weakness, we both would have paid the price. They want to see pain. And why do you care? I thought you hated her. She's the reason you're here, remember?"

Olivia shook her head. "That's what I thought. Now I don't know what to think."

"You might want to figure it out before you get her killed."

Olivia flinched at Ruby's cold, hard tone.

Ruby walked back to her bunk in the back of the room, as far away from Olivia as the room would allow. Olivia hated that Ruby was right. She had blamed Greyson unfairly. Greyson was trying to survive, just like all the others, and Olivia had made everyone doubt her. Whatever the connection between Greyson and this mess, she couldn't imagine Greyson would do anything to hurt anyone.

She seemed to have a pattern of blaming Greyson for things in her life. First it was the coffee, then this terrible nightmare. Greyson was just as much a victim in all of this as she was. She had been unfair. She had taken out her anger on the one person who was trying to help her. Guilt washed over her. She had been selfish. And despite all that, Greyson had defended her. Why? She had once compared Greyson to a superhero, but in this case she really had been her champion. Olivia sighed. She was determined she wouldn't let Greyson down again. She glanced over at Ruby. Greyson was hurt and vulnerable. The least she could do was watch over her. Olivia curled up on the cot across from Greyson. No one here was safe, but the least she could do was lessen Greyson's pain.

CHAPTER ELEVEN

Greyson cursed the root or rock that had buried itself against her rib cage. She heard birds singing and the undeniable smell of coffee. She rolled over and slipped from her sleeping bag. As expected the withered old woman sat on a log next to a fire.

"Lucile?"

The old woman held out a steaming cup of coffee to Greyson and smiled.

"What are you doing here?" Greyson asked, becoming aware that this must be a dream.

"Best I can tell, you've gone and gotten yourself lost," Lucile answered.

Greyson frowned. "I'm not lost."

"Hmm, even worse to be lost and not know it." The old woman winked.

Greyson's head hurt, and no matter how she shifted, she couldn't ease the pain in her side. Something was happening, but she couldn't sort through her thoughts and memories to put it together.

"I think I'm in trouble, Lucile."

Lucile nodded. "I'd say so." The old woman tossed the remains of her cup onto the fire and gathered up her things.

"Don't go. I don't know what to do. I need help."

Lucile stepped close to Greyson, her weathered skin like a roadmap to her life. Her gray eyes were like beacons shining through the mist.

"There is beauty in the rosebush, and a field of clover, but there's also beauty in the dandelion growing in the sidewalk."

Greyson frowned. "What does that mean?"

Lucile smiled, cupping Greyson's chin in her hand. "My sweet little flower, you're looking for the garden. What you need to find is the crack."

"But—" Greyson started to protest.

"Even the smallest pinpoint of light brings hope in the darkness. Follow the light." Lucile leaned in and kissed Greyson's forehead.

Greyson felt the tender lips brush across her skin, featherlight but solid as a promise. The tenderness was like the sun itself touching her skin.

"Don't leave me," Greyson murmured as the tender lips pulled away.

"I'm right here," a voice said.

Greyson frowned. This voice was different. She opened her eyes and met the gentle gaze of warm brown eyes. "Olivia?"

"Welcome back," Olivia replied, sitting up as she smoothed her hand down Greyson's arm.

Greyson was confused. "What's going on?"

"You were dreaming, I think, and talking in your sleep. I was checking to see if you have a fever. It's something my mother used to do when I was sick."

Greyson studied Olivia's face, taking in the fresh bruises and scratches that seemed so wrong against her otherwise smooth, creamy skin. Greyson reached up a hand to Olivia's face. "What happened to you?"

Olivia sucked in her breath as Greyson's fingertips grazed her cheek, tracing the line of a scratch across her face. She shivered as goose bumps ran down her arms and her skin warmed.

"Initiation. I had a fight of my own last night after you—well, you know. Thank you for that, by the way. I don't know what I would have done if I'd had to face Ruby." Olivia glanced over her shoulder to where Ruby sat slumped on her bed.

Greyson followed her gaze. "Is Ruby okay?"

Olivia shrugged. "Best I can tell. She isn't really talking to me."

"Why are you helping me?" Greyson asked. "I thought you hated me."

Olivia sighed. "Maybe you are the enemy and I've lost my mind, but I saw what she did to you in that pit. I know you're hurt, and right now you aren't as scary as she is."

Greyson smiled.

"But don't think that means I trust you," Olivia said quickly.

Greyson shook her head. "Of course not." She took a deep breath and took a mental assessment of her injuries. She ran her fingers along her side and winced.

"What is it?" Olivia asked, her eyes growing wide with concern.

"My chest hurts." Greyson pulled at her shirt.

Olivia grasped the edge of Greyson's shirt. "Here, let me help you." She gently lifted Greyson's shirt revealing the taut muscles along her stomach. Olivia's breath caught as her fingers grazed the smooth skin and hard muscle. She cleared her throat trying not to give in to the effect Greyson was having on her. Her heart raced. She licked her lips to pull back the moisture flooding her mouth.

The bruise to Greyson's side emerged, wiping the carnal thoughts from Olivia's mind and bringing reality back into sharp focus. "Oh God, that looks awful."

Greyson looked at her side and probed the area around the wound. "It was a lot worse last time. I guess Ruby went easy on me after all."

"Jesus. You're lucky your ribs aren't broken. She could have killed you."

"Exactly," Greyson agreed. "But she didn't."

Olivia scowled. "Now you're going soft on Ruby? Have you lost your mind?"

Greyson smiled. "No, just taking the advice of a friend."

Olivia frowned. "Well, you're crazy, and you're going to get yourself killed if you let her do that to you again."

There was movement in the hallway, and the sound of footsteps approaching. Someone was coming. They both sat staring at the cell door, waiting for the next monster to appear.

Uncle Dan stepped out of the shadows, his face still bruised and swollen. Greyson started to get up but sat back when Ruby ran to the door.

"What the hell happened up there? What did you do to her?" Ruby demanded.

"Back off, Ruby," the old man warned.

"Like hell I will. We had a deal. I've kept my end. I want to know what happened to her. Where is she?"

"Nothing happened to her. She's in lockdown."

Ruby's shoulders fell and she shuddered, letting her head fall against the metal bars. "You have to let me see her. She can't handle being locked away like that. She'll break down."

"That's not my problem. And what makes you think you can have any favors after that little stunt you pulled? Your owner could have had you put down for that, but I guess you're still worth the trouble. But not Nikki. No one needs Nikki."

"Don't hurt her. She can't help it," Ruby begged.

The old man held out his hand. "This is the best I can do for now."

Ruby slipped the piece of paper from his hand and clenched it in her fist.

The old man stepped closer to the bars. "The death match is coming. You need to be ready. There won't be any more fights until then. Everyone needs to be in good shape when the time comes."

Ruby shook her head. "No. I won't fight again. Not until I see her."

He glared at Ruby. "I'll see what I can do."

Ruby nodded and walked back to her bunk clutching the scrap of paper.

The old man turned his gaze to Greyson, then to Olivia, as if assessing them both. He nodded and tossed something to Greyson. She caught it with her good hand.

Greyson looked down at the small package of cookies, then back to the old man. Before she could respond, he turned and walked away.

"I'll be damned," Greyson muttered.

"What is it?" Olivia asked.

Greyson shrugged. "Progress, maybe."

"Progress?" Olivia asked, obviously confused by the interaction.

"It's a long story." Greyson nodded toward Ruby. "What do you think that was all about?"

Olivia shrugged. "Before you woke up, she asked me about the girl they put in the pit with me. I think that may be who she was asking about. The girl wasn't right. She seemed a little out of it, you know, like she was crazy or something. I think she's been tortured. Ruby said they did things to her to punish her."

Greyson frowned. "Torture? What kind of torture?"

Olivia shuddered. "She'd had her tongue cut out."

Greyson recoiled. "What the hell?"

"It was awful," Olivia said, closing her eyes to shut out the image.

Greyson's anger rose. "Jesus, these guys are sick."

The mist of newly formed tears shimmered in Olivia's eyes. "Do you think that will happen to me?"

Greyson clenched her jaw. She couldn't believe the depths of evil these men were capable of, but she couldn't let Olivia see her fear. She shook her head. "No."

Olivia searched Greyson's eyes, her gaze desperate for truth.

Greyson took Olivia's hand. "We won't let that happen."

"We?" Olivia's voice sounded weak and uncertain.

"Yeah, no one should be alone in here. We have to stick together. We have to look after each other until we can figure a way out."

Greyson felt Olivia's grip tighten around hers. Greyson offered a reassuring smile. She had to find a way out soon. She didn't want to think of what horrors were to come.

Greyson lay on her cot watching Olivia sleep on the bed across from her. Olivia wasn't exactly the fireball she had first met. She had an innocence about her that Greyson felt was slipping away with every day they were subjected to this prison. What had Olivia's life been like before everything went to hell? Greyson had believed her own life was complete, full of the adventures and accomplishments that drove her. But what about Olivia? What were her dreams? Where would she be right now if she hadn't run into Greyson on that fateful day?

Greyson imagined Olivia in a classroom surrounded by children looking up to her with innocent wonder. She imagined Olivia laughing with friends. She even considered the two of them together, picking up where they left off after that one special good-night kiss.

Greyson shuddered and tried not to think of her own unwitting part in the destruction of Olivia's life. She clenched her jaw in anger. She might have been careless, but she had nothing to do with getting them here. The Recruiter and his web of hellions were the reason, the evil behind all this.

Movement across the room drew Greyson's attention and she shifted her gaze to find Ruby watching her. She held her side protectively and slid out of bed.

Ruby watched her approach, her eyes solemn pools of despair.

"Mind if I sit?" Greyson asked.

Ruby nodded her head toward the cot across from her, offering permission.

Greyson eased down onto the bunk. "What's going on? You know more than you're saying. You were crazed in that pit the other night. Is this a game to you too?"

For the first time Ruby looked sad, maybe even regretful.

"You know I could have killed you, but I didn't. You are less injured than when you fought Amala, correct?"

Greyson nodded.

"When you have power, when they know you can break someone, that is what they expect."

Greyson frowned. "You expect me to believe all of it was an act?"

Ruby looked away. "Not all of it." She looked toward Olivia, still sleeping. "The more you care for her, the more they control you."

"The girl who fought Olivia…you and her?"

Ruby shook her head. "It's not what you think. She was little more than a child when they brought her here. She had already been captive elsewhere. She was rebellious, wild, reckless. They had been cruel to her. I have tried to protect her, but she doesn't understand. I'm afraid no one can reach her now."

"What's your problem with Olivia?"

"The Recruiter's girls are different from us. He plants them among us, penetrating our group, and they take information back to him."

"She wouldn't do that," Greyson said defensively.

Ruby chuckled. "Yes, she will, even if she doesn't want to."

Greyson sighed. "Help me find a way out. If we work together, we can do it."

Ruby leaned forward, piercing Greyson with her intense gaze. "This place used to be a maximum-security prison. No one gets out unless they are traded or dead."

"A real prison?" It made sense. The cells, the corridors, the thick walls, it all made sense. "Where?"

Ruby shook her head. "The rumor is that the building is surrounded by a stone mountain six stories high. Even if you get outside, you still can't break free. They will hunt you down like a dog. Then they will move on to our families. They will make us watch as they destroy them. You've already seen how far they will go to control the smallest part of our lives here. You haven't even touched the surface. Any plan to get out of here has to be perfect. We can't play around with your half-baked ideas. We have too much to lose."

Greyson racked her brain trying to put together the new clues.

Ruby interrupted her thoughts. "Have you met your Employer yet?"

"Who?"

"The man who owns you. The man who controls your fate."

Greyson shook her head. "I thought that was the Recruiter."

"No," Ruby explained. "He just supplies the women to the men who pay. The Recruiter only deals in the women like Olivia and Audrey and my Nikki. If your Employer wasn't here for the fight, he will be at the death match."

Greyson had a sinking feeling in the pit of her stomach. "What does that mean?"

Ruby shrugged. "I can't say for sure. But it usually means you're leaving here one way or another. If you survive, you'll likely be shipped to another group that your Employer controls."

"How do you know all this?" Greyson asked.

"I've seen it before. My Nikki came here from another group when the Recruiter bought or traded for her. Either you have an Employer already, or you'll be sold at the fight."

Greyson swallowed. When she gathered herself, she asked the question she had been chewing on all day. "Will you kill me the next time?"

Sadness crossed Ruby's face again. "We won't fight each other next time. I've already beaten you. I'll hold my place in the ranks. In the death match, we will both face opponents from other groups. We won't know who we are up against until we're in the pit."

Greyson's heart sank. "How many times have you done it? Killed someone, I mean."

Ruby looked away without answering.

Greyson studied her. She couldn't imagine what was coming. She couldn't imagine what it was like to kill someone. She couldn't just let herself die in the pit and leave Olivia here alone. But how would she ever find it in herself to kill anyone?

"How can you do it?" Greyson asked, needing to understand how she could possibly survive.

Ruby turned to her, her gaze distant and cold. "When someone is trying to kill you, something inside you takes over. The instinct for survival is stronger than you think. You will learn things about yourself, your limits, your strength, and more. The more you have to lose, the harder it is to give up."

Greyson looked to where Olivia lay sleeping. Ruby was right. Whether she liked it or not, she wasn't just fighting for herself anymore.

❖

"Ouch." Olivia winced as she tugged at the hem of her shirt.

"What is it?" Greyson asked, pulling the blanket down from her face.

"My shirt is stuck to my back."

Greyson frowned. She sat up facing Olivia. "Turn around and let me see."

Olivia shifted on her cot. Greyson could see dark blotches staining Olivia's shirt, each line marking the strike of the rod she had been hit with during the fight. Greyson grimaced at the thought of pulling the fabric loose from the wounds.

"The shirt has dried into the blood from your wounds. I'll need to soak it free. Is that okay?" Greyson asked, placing her hand on Olivia's shoulder. She mentally kicked herself for not thinking to ask about the wounds earlier.

Olivia glanced over her shoulder. "I'll be fine—it just pulls every time I move."

"Well, we need to get it cleaned up or it'll end up infected. Lie down on your stomach. This won't be fun."

Greyson wet a cloth in the sink and dabbed at Olivia's shirt until it was soaked through. Slowly she tugged the fabric free from the sticky, bloody mess oozing from Olivia's back.

"You should take off the shirt so we can get this cleaned up," Greyson instructed.

Olivia nodded, shifting to sit up. "Okay."

Greyson grasped the hem of Olivia's shirt and lifted it as Olivia raised her arms. Greyson gently slid the garment over Olivia's head. She sucked in her breath at the sight of the angry red marks streaking Olivia's back. Heavy black-and-blue bruises shadowed the wounds.

"Damn," Greyson said. "This is going to hurt."

Olivia was silent as Greyson cleaned the area. She kept the wet cloth as cold as she could to try to numb the pain.

Olivia sat with her arms crossed over her chest, covering her exposed breasts. She shivered as the cold water amplified the cool temperature of the room. Greyson pulled the blanket from her own bunk and wrapped it around Olivia, shielding her.

"Thank you," Olivia said, grasping the blanket in her fist and pulling it to her chin.

Greyson broke open one of the small packages of antibiotic ointment she had found on a shelf by the shower. She moved her fingers over the swollen wounds as gently as she could while working the ointment into the broken skin. With each touch Greyson felt the suffering Olivia had endured. The wounds were a stark contrast to the milky smooth skin of Olivia's back. Greyson absorbed the purity and innocence as if she was sitting in a field of wildflowers. The idea of anyone hurting Olivia was as offensive to Greyson as someone clear-cutting a forest. Some things were against nature.

Olivia moaned at Greyson's touch, the sting of the ointment making her flinch. She felt exposed and vulnerable as Greyson inspected her wounds. Each touch defined the lines that had been beaten into her body. Tears welled in Olivia's eyes despite her attempts to hide her pain. She was relieved not to have the fabric irritating her wounds, but the exposure had opened emotions she didn't want to face. As long as she had been the one tending to Greyson, she had been able to push away the memories and the fear, but now everything was flooding in at once.

She sniffed and rubbed her hand across her cheek, trying to hide the tears that had escaped. Greyson's fingers stilled, resting against Olivia's back.

"Are you okay?" Greyson asked.

Olivia nodded, not wanting Greyson to hear the tremor in her voice.

Greyson scooted closer to Olivia on the cot, moving beside her. Olivia could see the concern in her eyes.

"I'm sorry," Greyson said, her voice heavy with sadness. She leaned close to Olivia, wrapping her arm across Olivia's lap to rest her hand on Olivia's hip.

Olivia shook her head. She sniffed. "Are you done?"

Greyson handed Olivia a clean scrub shirt. "I think most of this needs to be left open to heal. The wounds aren't deep—they're just really swollen and bruised. Your back will be tender for a few days."

Olivia nodded. "Thank you." Greyson was so close, Olivia could feel the warmth of her body against her side. She felt goose bumps ripple across her skin as Greyson traced the line of a scratch on her face.

"We need to put some of this on these scratches too."

Olivia met Greyson's eyes. They were soft and tender with a hint of sadness. Olivia attempted a smile but felt her lip tremble instead as her tears began to flow.

Greyson wrapped her arms around Olivia, pulling her head to her shoulder. "Come here."

Olivia allowed Greyson to hold her. Greyson was strong yet tender and her touch was comforting. For a moment Olivia allowed herself to cry and release some of the hurt and fear that had been choking her since the moment the Recruiter had taken her. "I don't know if I can do this."

Greyson pulled back. "You have to stay strong. You can't let them win."

Olivia shook her head. "I'm so scared."

Greyson frowned and brushed the hair away from Olivia's face. "I know. I'm scared too, but this is not how I want my story to end. And I don't want it to be yours either."

Olivia nodded. "I hate him."

Greyson sighed. "Let that become your fuel. Whatever it takes, don't let him take your hope."

Olivia pressed her cheek against Greyson's shoulder, seeking the comfort of Greyson's embrace. "Keep reminding me."

She felt Greyson nod. "I will."

CHAPTER TWELVE

O livia, the boss wants to see you," a guard said as he stepped into the training room. Olivia's heart sank as the rush of fear made her head spin. She pushed her back against the wall and shook her head in resistance. The guard narrowed his eyes at her. "Don't play games with me, bitch. Get moving."

Olivia felt paralyzed. She couldn't get her feet to move. She jumped when someone gently touched her arm. She jerked her head around to see Audrey standing next to her. She hadn't realized Audrey was there.

"It's okay, sweetie. Take a deep breath," Audrey said softly.

Olivia nodded and tried to focus.

"Think of something besides him. Something that makes you feel safe. It won't help if you make him mad. Just go along with it. At least you know he won't make you do anything…you know."

Olivia nodded again. As she crossed the room, she could feel the women watching her. Her gaze landed on Greyson, who looked back at her with a clenched jaw and anger in her eyes. Greyson matched her steps, drawing closer as Olivia reached the guard.

The guard put his hand up toward Greyson. "That's far enough."

"Where are you taking her?" Greyson asked.

"Like I said, the boss wants to see her."

"Maybe she doesn't want to see him," Greyson said, stepping between Olivia and the guard.

A second guard stepped through the door. "Is there a problem?" He stared at Greyson. With a flick of his wrist a black metal bar extended in his hand. He grinned at Greyson, as if daring her to make him use it.

"Move," the first guard ordered.

Greyson stood her ground. Olivia watched the standoff. She didn't want to go, and despite Greyson's good intentions, she wasn't helping. Olivia knew the more trouble Greyson caused, the worse things would be for both of them.

"It's okay," she said, placing her hand on Greyson's arm. "It's better if I just go."

The guard reached for Olivia. Greyson hit his arm, knocking his hand away. Olivia gasped and jumped back when the guard swung around and pressed something to Greyson's chest. Greyson seized and fell to the floor gasping, her body jerking.

As Olivia went to help Greyson, the guard grabbed her arm and dragged her out of the room.

Olivia wiped tears from her face. "What did you do to her?"

"Just get moving—I don't have all day," the guard answered, his voice cold and angry.

Olivia was determined to keep her emotions in check. She didn't want to give him the satisfaction of knowing they were getting to her.

Olivia entered a large office and heard the door close softly behind her. The Recruiter sat on a sofa, his legs crossed, a glass of liquor in his hand.

"Olivia, sweetheart, come in. I've missed you." He talked to her as if she should be happy to see him.

Olivia took a deep breath and crossed the room.

He patted the sofa next to him. "Have a seat."

Olivia sat, pressing her body as far into the corner of the sofa as she could get to put distance between them.

He leaned toward her, reaching across the distance to brush his hand along her cheek. "You're upset. Why have you been crying?"

Olivia flinched but didn't pull away. She shook her head, afraid to speak.

"Don't worry. I'm taking care of everything. You really pleased me at your initiation. You fought well for your first time."

The mention of the fight brought back the memory of the unfortunate girl with no tongue. Olivia spoke before she could censor herself. "What happened to the girl? Is she okay?"

He smiled. "Nikki is fine. She's nothing for you to worry about."

"Is that what you're going to do to me, mutilate me and steal my voice? Are you going to keep me here until I go mad?" Tears stung her eyes as she gave voice to her fears.

"*Tsk, tsk, tsk.* No, my sweet. Nikki came to me that way. I saved her. Without me she would still be with her father. Even I see the way he treats his girls as cruel. I've given Nikki a home here. Didn't you see how hard she fought for me? She loves me. She understands, like you will understand in time."

Olivia swallowed. This man was insane. Did he really believe what he was doing was a good thing for the women here?

"I had a good life, a family who loves me, friends. How is this supposed to be good for me?"

He drained the amber liquid from his glass and stood to pour another drink. "Would you like one?"

Olivia shook her head.

"You mean a life with a mother who wouldn't accept you for who you are? How you struggled just to hold on to an empty life, no job, little money? I provide everything you need here. I can show you real love."

Olivia's mind raced. How did he know about her mother? What else did he know? What other part of her life had he touched with his poison? "Keeping us caged up like animals is not love. We are not your pets."

"Hmm, you're trying to make me angry again. I had hoped we were past some of this. Business, then." He turned to face Olivia, his expression casual, as if he was discussing plans for dinner. "The girls are training for the death match. A death match always shakes everyone up a bit, but it's a good way to weed out the weak ones. Who's your favorite so far?"

Olivia cringed. She had gotten to know most of the girls who would have to fight, and she hated the idea that some of them wouldn't live through it.

"I don't have a favorite. I hate all of this."

"Your friend Greyson seems to be coming along nicely. I was beginning to worry that she had been a bad choice, but you seem to be the motivation she needed to get with the program. Let's hope she delivers when it counts."

Olivia swallowed hard. "And if she doesn't?"

He let out a dramatic sigh. "I'm afraid your fate is tied to Greyson at this point. I have to keep my word. If she loses, you lose."

Olivia closed her eyes, letting the information sink in. "You're going to kill me?" she asked, her voice barely a whisper.

He smiled. "No. You haven't been listening. I don't want anything to happen to you. I love you. Greyson is the one you have to worry about. It's her carelessness that will kill you."

Unwanted tears stung Olivia's eyes again. "This isn't fair."

He leaned over Olivia and twirled her hair between his fingers. "Then I suggest you give Greyson a little motivation."

Olivia flinched. "What are you suggesting?"

He smiled and shrugged. "You're a smart girl. I'm sure you'll figure something out."

Greyson stopped what she was doing and the room fell silent as Olivia was let back into the training room. Olivia crawled onto her bunk, pushed her back against the wall, and pulled her knees up to her chin. By the looks of her, she was barely keeping it together.

Olivia brushed at a wet spot on her hand. She looked up as Greyson eased down on the bunk next to her.

"You okay?" Greyson asked.

Olivia sniffed and wiped her nose. "Not really."

"What happened?"

"Just more crazy mind games." Olivia looked up at Greyson. "Are you okay? What did that guy do to you?"

Greyson shrugged. "Taser. I didn't see that one coming." She rubbed her chest. "But I'm okay."

"He knew things about my life, my mother. How does he know?" Olivia said, her voice sounding desperate.

Greyson looked down at her hands. "I think he stalked us for a while before the kidnappings. It makes sense that he would find our weaknesses, the parts of our lives that made us vulnerable. He's been at this awhile. He always seems two steps ahead. Anything he can learn to get into your head gives him power."

Olivia shook her head. "I don't know how much more I can stand."

Greyson nodded. "I know what you mean." She rubbed her eyes with her palms. She was strong physically, but mentally she was fading. She couldn't remember the last time she saw the sun or had fresh air. She had lost track of the days and had no idea how long she had been there. She looked up at a small window in the wall about twelve feet off the ground. These small portals to the outside world were torturous reminders that her life was waiting just outside those monstrous walls.

The hours she had waited for Olivia to return had been like an eternity. Her mind had run rampant, creating horrific scenes of what the Recruiter might be doing to Olivia. Now that Olivia was back, Greyson was on edge. She needed to do something. She needed to feel like she was working toward something. Desperate, Greyson jumped up and began shoving the chairs around. "I've got to do something before I lose my mind."

She stacked the chairs on top of a table bolted to the wall, trying to build something high enough to reach the window. The chairs were molded aluminum and not very heavy, but they seemed sturdy enough to hold her. She guessed the guards used these chairs because they couldn't be broken down into weapons and were too lightweight on their own to do much damage.

"What are you doing?" Olivia said from behind her.

"I can't take it anymore. I have to see outside. I have to see the sun. I have to know the world still exists out there." Now that she had set her mind to a plan, Greyson was consumed by her need. She felt something brush the back of her arm and turned to find Olivia holding out another chair.

Olivia smiled up at her. "Can I help?"

Greyson smiled back, thankful Olivia hadn't tried to stop her. Everyone else always shut her down every time she did something out of bounds.

"You think I'm losing it, don't you?" Greyson asked.

Olivia shrugged. "I'd have to go back to thinking you were in on this if you weren't. I know I feel like this place is crawling under my skin. Sometimes I think I can hear him talking inside my head. Some sunshine would be good."

Greyson held out her hand. "Want to go first?"

Olivia smiled. "You sure?"

"Why not?" Greyson answered.

Olivia took Greyson's hand, allowing herself to be pulled up on the table. Greyson climbed onto the next level of a jumble of chairs. Olivia glanced around to see the others had started to gather around them.

Samone called out to Greyson, "Is this your big escape plan? Are you going to crawl through the window?"

The women laughed.

Greyson ignored them. "Don't listen to them. They gave up a long time ago." Greyson was able to reach the lip of the windowsill. She gripped the sill and braced her knees against the wall.

"Climb up. You can step on my legs and onto my shoulders."

Olivia held tightly to Greyson, certain they were about to fall.

"It's okay. I've got you," Greyson said confidently.

Olivia took a deep breath and did as Greyson said. Something in the sound of Greyson's voice, in her touch, made Olivia believe Greyson could do anything. Olivia pressed her knee into Greyson's shoulder and pulled herself up to peer out the window. She sighed at the sight before her.

"What is it? What do you see?" Greyson asked.

Olivia gasped. "I see the sun. I see a courtyard surrounded by a white building several stories tall. I see a giant rock and a mountain behind it. There are trees growing on the top." Olivia sucked in a breath of surprise. "Oh."

"What?" Greyson asked shakily.

"I need to get down." Olivia scurried down from her perch, clutching Greyson's arm. She glanced at the other women staring up at them. "I think I know where we are," she whispered.

Greyson opened her mouth to speak.

"Shh." Olivia gestured for Greyson to be quiet. "You look. We'll talk later."

Greyson gripped the edge of the window and pulled herself up. She could feel Olivia's hands against her sides, trying to help lift her. The scene was just as Olivia described. She had to find a way to get access to that courtyard. The more she could learn about this place, the better her chance of finding a way out.

Greyson lowered herself down, feeling Olivia's fingers slip beneath her T-shirt, grazing her sides. Goose bumps peppered Greyson's skin as a tingling sensation skimmed across her flesh. She met Olivia's gaze, not sure what to think of the feelings stirring inside. Greyson pushed the feelings aside. The excitement of learning something new must have her body on overdrive.

"Thanks," Greyson said breathlessly.

Olivia nodded and started her climb back down the makeshift tower.

Samone grabbed Greyson by the arm as her feet hit the floor. "Did you find the golden road you were looking for?"

Greyson laughed. "Hardly. But I did see something I want." She started to step away, but Samone's grip tightened around her arm.

"Be careful, Greyson."

"Why?" Greyson asked defiantly. "What have I got to lose that they haven't already taken? I'm already as good as dead." She pulled her arm away. "Relax. I just wanted some sunlight. I'm not Spider-Man."

Greyson was sure she could feel Samone's gaze on her back

as she walked away. She looked around to see Ruby watching. She nodded to Ruby. To her surprise, Ruby smiled and nodded back. Did Ruby know what was outside the window? Had she been outside? Was that how she knew about the prison, and the rock?

Greyson couldn't wait to talk to Olivia. If Olivia had figured out where they were, she might be able to figure a way out. But why had Olivia wanted her to keep it quiet? Greyson studied each woman in the room. Most had returned to the usual routine now that her stunt was over. Ruby didn't seem too worried, but she continued to watch Greyson. And what was up with Samone? Why had she warned her? It wasn't like there was any way she could get through the window, and if she could, it was a long way down, and there was nowhere to go.

Greyson went to Ruby. "We need to talk."

"About?" Ruby said, sounding bored.

"I need to know everything you can tell me about this building. As far as I can tell, you've been here longer than anyone. I need to know what you know. We're running out of time and you know it. One way or another this needs to end. We need a plan."

Ruby studied her, then trailed her gaze around the room, seeming to watch the other women. "You have to be careful. Not everyone here can be trusted. You aren't the only one who has made alliances, struck bargains, or made sacrifices."

Greyson nodded.

Ruby leaned over the table, her voice barely more than a whisper when she spoke. She told Greyson about the different areas of the prison, the strengths and weaknesses she had observed in each area.

Greyson's heart raced. She felt like she was finally getting somewhere. "Has anyone seen how the deliveries are made? Has anyone made any deals for contraband?"

Ruby glanced around them, as if to make sure no one could hear. "Yes. There are food deliveries, laundry services, and the van that moves the girls...and the bodies. Some of the women trade *favors* sometimes."

"Good, we need to know which guards we can manipulate the

most—who's easily distracted and who we can play against the other. How many guards are there? I've only seen a handful of men here. This may be a prison, but it isn't staffed like one. Outside, I didn't see anyone in the towers, and it's always the same faces that do the rounds and escort us around. I would bet there are times when they are working with only a few guards in key places. That's when we don't see them. They have to have a schedule. We need to figure out when they are most vulnerable."

Ruby shook her head. "I've never seen anyone in the towers. I only know of the men who come to get us and who we see at the fights. Audrey has told us of three others who stay with the Recruiter's girls."

Greyson thought for a moment. "There are other men in offices too. I saw the guard that held Olivia at the last fight coming out of an office when they took me to meet with the Recruiter. They must work out of the offices during the day as if this is some kind of business." Greyson thought hard, needing to know more if she was going to figure this out. "Is there any way to get to that courtyard? Have they ever let anyone out there?" Greyson asked, her excitement growing.

Ruby frowned. "No. We do not go outside. We might be seen. People might start asking questions."

Greyson thought about what she had learned. "The guards carry batons and Tasers, but I haven't seen any guns."

Ruby shook her head. "No, no guns that I've seen, but that doesn't mean they don't have them."

Greyson nodded. "It's a chance we'll have to take. We'll have to work together if anything is going to succeed," Greyson said pointedly. "If we're going to risk the lives of the others, they need to know."

Ruby shook her head again. "No. Trust me on this one, Greyson, if you tell them your plan, the Recruiter will know."

Greyson bit her lip, frustrated. "What if we don't tell them the true plan? What if they know parts of the plan but don't know everything? The Recruiter expects me to try something. He'll be more suspicious if things are too quiet. This is going to take everyone pulling every stunt in the book."

Ruby drummed her fingers on the table as if visually sorting through the idea in her mind. Finally, she looked up at Greyson. "That might work."

Greyson sighed. "Okay. Good. You get the girls to work on the guys. I want them distracted. The night of the fight there will be people crawling all over this place."

Ruby sat back in her chair. "You're going to get us killed."

Greyson leaned in, her gaze locked on Ruby's. "You and I both know if we don't do this, we're dead anyway."

Olivia couldn't sleep. She could hear the Recruiter's voice inside her head. The faces of all the women she had met, the violence she had witnessed and been victim of, played over and over in her mind. She closed her eyes to block out the images, but the Recruiter's voice remained, taunting her, reminding her that her fate was now tied to Greyson. She was afraid it was all going to drive her crazy. The worst was the fear, the not knowing what would happen next.

She and Greyson hadn't talked since looking out the window. Olivia needed to talk to Greyson—she needed to tell her about her suspicions about where they were being held.

Olivia slid out of bed, silently moving across the aisle to Greyson's bunk. She leaned down, gently touching Greyson's arm. "Greyson."

Greyson rolled over. "What is it?"

"I need to talk."

Greyson scooted over to the edge of the bed and pulled the cover back, making room for Olivia.

Olivia hesitated. She hadn't thought this through. Should she just crawl in bed with Greyson?

"Come on, I won't bite," Greyson urged.

Olivia rolled her eyes. Great. She slid into bed, fitting snugly against Greyson in the small cot.

Greyson pulled the blanket back up around them, wrapping her arms around Olivia. "See, this is cozy."

Olivia was glad Greyson couldn't see the redness she felt burning her cheeks. "Maybe this was a bad idea."

"No," Greyson said, tightening her hold around Olivia. "This is the only way we can talk that no one will be suspicious. Tell me what's going on. What did you see today? Where are we?"

Olivia wasn't sure why she had kept it a secret, but something told her this information was safer between her and Greyson. "I think this is an old prison that was shut down a few years ago, not far from where I grew up. I remember old stories about it, and my grandfather used to drive me by here when I was a kid on our way across the mountain to visit family. We used to hear of breakouts here when I was little. Everyone would be warned to lock their doors at night and not let in any strangers. So that means there has to be a way out of this place. The rock we saw today is an obvious dead end, but the road circles around it and crosses the mountain. That's the back side of what used to be maximum security, and if I'm right, that's the building we're in. But the front side is the much older prison and isn't as well built, and the structure is crumbling. It's one of the reasons they shut the place down. I'm guessing that's where the Recruiter keeps his girls and where the individual cells are that you were in when you first got here. I've been to the kitchen and the laundry there too. It's all pretty old. The stairs and railings are rusty and narrow, nothing like we have here."

Olivia told Greyson everything she knew about the area. "If we can get out, we won't have to get very far. There are houses nearby. If we could just get far enough to tell someone about what's happening here, we could shut the whole place down."

Olivia stopped talking as Greyson brushed the hair away from her face, her fingers lightly skimming across her skin. The touch was unexpected and took Olivia's breath. She was completely caught off guard by Greyson's tenderness. The warmth of Greyson's body pressed against her pushed through her skin into her heart, loosening the grip of fear.

"I have to tell you something." Olivia struggled with whether to tell Greyson about her talk with the Recruiter.

Greyson shifted, her thigh brushing between Olivia's legs. It was brief, and only an accident, but the sensation made Olivia's head spin and her heart race.

"What is it?" Greyson whispered close to her ear. Hot breath brushed Olivia's skin. Olivia shivered.

"Tell me," Greyson urged.

Olivia took a moment to gather herself. She wasn't sure why this was happening now, but something was changing. Olivia had come to Greyson expecting to talk about what she had learned, and possibly to tell Greyson about the Recruiter's message. But now that she was there, she couldn't bring herself to tell Greyson. She swallowed. "I'm worried about you. About the fight." She felt Greyson stiffen. "I'm sorry, I don't mean to upset you, but I know you're up to something. If you're planning something, I want in on it. I need to believe there's a way out of here."

"Don't worry." Greyson brushed her hand up and down Olivia's back. The contact was soothing and distracted her from the reality around her. Olivia felt nice against her. She shifted and thought she heard a hitch in Olivia's breathing.

"Greyson, I don't think I can make it here without you."

Greyson peered through the dark, trying to see the meaning behind Olivia's words. "I don't think you have to worry. I've been going along with the program. If anything happens to me, you're off the hook."

Olivia pinched her arm. "Don't say that. You know that's not true. I'm stuck here with or without you. I just...I really don't want anything to happen to you."

"Why?" Greyson asked. She could hear the urgency in Olivia's voice, feel the tension in her body, but she needed to know why.

"You're my last connection with the real world." Olivia's voice cracked when she spoke. "Even though running into you that day basically ruined my life, for that brief encounter, you were a part of my life, my real life. I had dreamed of seeing you again. I wanted to hear about your adventures on the trail. Even though we only had that one day, you became part of my future. You keep me tethered to that dream. I'm afraid if I lose you, I'll never have that again."

Greyson pulled Olivia's head to her shoulder and held her. She was surprised by Olivia's revelation. She knew Olivia was scared, and she half expected her to still blame her for the situation they were in, but she hadn't expected Olivia to want to have her in her life, even if it was a life of captivity and torture.

"You're going to have that life again. This isn't forever. We'll figure a way out of this," Greyson said, relishing the comfort of holding Olivia.

Olivia slid her arm around Greyson and sighed. Olivia's breath was warm against Greyson's neck. Greyson wanted to believe what she was telling Olivia was true. She wanted to believe there was a way home. For now, she would hold on to this moment of peace and comfort in the arms of a woman whose fate was in her hands.

Olivia sighed. "Did you get to go on the AT?"

Greyson stilled. "Yes. I was two weeks into my hike before he took me. Didn't you get the postcard I sent you?"

Olivia lifted her head to look at Greyson. "You sent me a postcard?"

Greyson nodded. "I did. I wanted you to know I was thinking about you. I thought about you a lot."

Olivia smiled. "Really?"

"Yeah. I was looking forward to seeing you again."

Olivia settled her head against Greyson's shoulder. "Tell me about the mountains."

Greyson stroked Olivia's hair. "It was peaceful. During the day the birds sang to me along the trail. Some days the heat and humidity made it feel like I was being baked in an oven, but then the night would cool so I had to burrow deep into my sleeping bag to stay warm. At night the birds grew quiet and the night sounds took over. Cicadas, frogs, owls, and even the occasional yip of a fox or a coyote were like a wild symphony. Nothing compares to the smell of the earth and forest after a soaking rain."

"It sounds like heaven," Olivia said as she gripped the seam of Greyson's shirt. "I'm glad you got to see it. I wish we were there now."

Greyson closed her eyes and breathed in the scent of Olivia's hair. "Me too." Greyson closed her eyes, losing herself in her memories. "I'll take you there someday when all of this is over. We'll sleep under the stars where there are no walls and you have the freedom to do whatever you want."

Olivia's breathing changed, signaling she had drifted off to sleep. Greyson smiled, allowing herself to rest. She had to believe the dream could be real, and they would be free again. Greyson fell asleep cradling Olivia in her arms.

CHAPTER THIRTEEN

Greyson gripped the cell bars in her fists. "Come on, Uncle Dan, you've got to help me out. I'm going nuts in here. Man, if you knew anything about me, you'd know I have to be outside. My whole life was about nature and sunshine and being outdoors. I feel like I'm going to lose it in here."

"No. No one goes out," the old man answered.

Greyson felt a hand clamp down on her shoulder, spinning her around. Ruby closed in on Greyson so fast she had no time to dodge the punch to her face. Greyson grabbed Ruby, wrapping her arms around her and lifting her off the ground. Greyson squeezed with all her strength as Ruby pounded on her head and shoulders.

"Traitor. I saw you talking to him. You'll be the death of us all," Ruby shouted.

Greyson heard the old man call for help. Moments later two guards rushed into the room, each grabbing hold of one of the women, pulling them apart.

Greyson yelled at Ruby as she fought against the guards to land another punch. "Are you out of your mind? You may think you're the queen around here, Ruby, but you don't tell me what to do."

The guards restrained them, but they continued to struggle to reach each other, kicking and lunging against the guards' hold.

"Take Ruby to the lower level," the old man ordered. "Maybe the girl can calm her down."

Greyson saw the flash of relief on Ruby's face. The plan had worked. Ruby would be able to see Nikki and tell her about the plan.

"What about this one?" the guard holding Greyson asked.

"Leave her."

The guards hauled Ruby out of the room. Her curses echoed down the hall, growing more distorted with the distance until they faded into silence.

Greyson chanced a glance at Olivia, hoping she was on to the charade.

"Cuff her," the old man ordered.

The old man watched as Greyson's arms were wrenched behind her back and cuffed with zip ties. "I'll take care of it now."

"Watch her," the other guard warned. "Everyone's getting twitchy about the fight. There's no telling what they're up to."

Greyson glared at the guard, imagining her fingers pressing into the spiderweb tattoo centering his throat. She wanted to cut off his words before the old man realized the truth.

The old man nodded. He clasped his hand around Greyson's arm, pulling her to her feet. "Come with me."

Greyson followed the old man out into the hall. She stood quietly as he closed and locked the door.

He took her arm again. "This way," he ordered.

"Where are we going?" Greyson asked.

"For a walk. What the hell is going on between you and Ruby?"

Greyson huffed. "Ruby has a big head. She thinks she gets to tell everyone what to do. We're all at our breaking point as it is—the last thing I need is her bitching at me. Hell, I know I can't win, but she just keeps pushing me."

The old man hesitated outside a heavy metal door that had rust showing around the edges. Greyson frowned. "What's this?"

The old man slid a key into the ancient-looking lock and opened the door. Greyson blinked, squinting her eyes against the brightness of the sun bursting from the room. As her eyes adjusted, she stepped through the door. She was surrounded by rows of tomato plants, peppers, and a host of other vegetables.

"What is this place?" she asked.

"It's a greenhouse. I can't let you outside, but I didn't think this would hurt."

Greyson turned to the old man, shocked. "Thank you," she said with genuine gratitude. She turned her face to the sun, letting the warm rays kiss her skin. She took a breath, feeling the air fill her lungs. It was the first real breath she had taken since arriving here. Her body tingled as if she was being energized by the plants around her.

Greyson leaned into the plants, letting the leaves brush her face as she breathed in the wild green scent. She gazed around the room, taking in every detail of its contents and construction. The walls were glass with giant fans at each end for ventilation. The only door she could see was the one they had entered.

"You won't get into trouble for bringing me here, will you?" Greyson asked.

"I'll take care of it," the old man answered.

"Why are you doing this?" Greyson asked, desperately wanting to rake her fingers through the loose soil. She twisted her arms against the ties binding her hands and felt the rigid plastic bite into her skin.

The old man looked at Greyson with something of a smile. "I need you to do well at the fight."

Greyson frowned. "Oh."

"And I guess I owe you one for the last fight," he added.

Greyson grinned and nodded. "How is the bean counter these days?"

The old man's smile widened. "He looks good with a broken nose."

Greyson had no idea she had managed that much damage.

The old man laughed. The sound was out of place and a bit sinister.

Greyson laughed too. She knew she had done the impossible. She had managed to win over the hardest old man she had ever met. She knew he didn't really care what happened to her, but if he thought he could use her, that was almost as good.

Greyson grabbed the opportunity to try to learn more about him. "How long have you been doing this?"

The old man stared at her, his eyes silently boring into her like lasers.

Greyson continued, "You don't seem like the others. You don't look at us like they do. What are you getting out of this?"

His mustache bristled as he worked his mouth, the way he always did when she made him think of something he didn't want to talk about.

"There are things you don't understand about this world. You think this is just about you and the girls. You think you're above all this. But the truth is, we are all slaves. You go to a job and complete a task for money. You use other people to advance in your career and get things done. We do the same. We've just found a different way to use our resources. This life has existed for centuries and it will go on long after you and I are forgotten."

"So this is just a business deal for you?" Greyson felt the cold grip of rage tighten around her heart as she imagined this man's worldview and complete disregard for human life.

"I like to study people. I like to see how you will adapt to the world you are thrown into. Women fascinate me because of their resilience, their willingness to sacrifice themselves for others. Even you. You were easy to break. All he had to do was make you responsible for another and you were willing to do his bidding. It's amazing, if you think about it."

"It's pretty disgusting, if you ask me."

He glared at her. "That's what makes you weak. You will never understand what it is to have power and control."

Greyson sighed. "I've heard of women being trafficked for sex, why the fights?"

"Sex is everywhere," he said with a dismissive look. "Pain is a special commodity that is much more gratifying. Anyone can overpower someone weaker than them, but it takes real power to get someone to hurt another person, to endure the physical pain, to do your will. Love is your weakness."

Greyson fell silent. Money and power, that was all these men cared about. This man would never care about what happened to her. His only concern was getting what he wanted and what he wanted was to feel like he could control her. She could use that.

"So what do I have to do to get to come back here, maybe without the cuffs?" Greyson asked. If she could make a deal with him, she would be able to turn his own game against him. Whether he knew it or not, she was playing his game.

His cold eyes studied her for a while before answering. "You're going to make sure someone doesn't make it through the fight."

Greyson swallowed hard against the lump of dread that suddenly developed in her throat. "You want me to kill one of the girls?" She shook her head. "That's not going to happen. I can't do that."

He shook his head. "No. When the time comes, I'll tell you exactly what I want."

"There has to be something in it for me." She turned so her hands were toward him. "The cuffs."

She felt the cold bite of steel against her wrist as the pliers were put into place. She heard the faint snap of the blade, and an instant later her hands were free.

Greyson rubbed her wrists and turned back to the old man.

His gaze was cold and hard. "We understand each other?" he asked.

Greyson nodded. She had the feeling she had just made a deal with the devil.

❖

Olivia sat on the sofa watching the Recruiter. He had sent for her almost every day for a week. Most of the time he didn't even speak to her. He just wanted her to sit in the room with him, get things for him, and clean up after him. Today he seemed out of sorts, as if he couldn't get a piece of a puzzle to fit the way he wanted. He rubbed his temples as if trying to grind his fingers through his skull. Stubble grew on his normally clean-shaven face and his hair was disheveled. More than once he yelled at his computer screen, cursing someone she couldn't see. His agitation made her nervous. Being with him was like sitting in a room with a ticking time bomb. She had been on the receiving end of his anger more than once and she never knew what might set him off.

Olivia was scared, but she knew she had to try to loosen the screws with this guy. Anything she could find out might help get her out of here. She swallowed her fear and gathered what courage she could muster.

"You seem upset today. Are you okay?" Olivia asked. Her voice sounded loud in the quiet of the room.

He looked up as if he had forgotten she was there. "No. But you wouldn't understand business."

Olivia nodded, ignoring the slight. "Is there anything I can do?"

He watched her as if trying to read her mind. She knew he didn't trust her, but she had to play the role he had assigned her. She had to pretend she was on his side.

"Can I get you another drink?"

He nodded. "Yeah. That would be good for a start."

Olivia felt her heart jump into her throat. What did he mean by that?

She poured the drink and stepped behind the desk next to him. He turned off the computer screen, preventing her from seeing what he had been working on.

"You look tense—that's probably what's causing that headache. Would you like me to rub your shoulders for you?"

He took the drink and sat back in his chair as Olivia moved behind him and began massaging his shoulders. She tried to control her hands from shaking as she stared at his neck, wondering if she had the strength to strangle him. She peered over his shoulders as she worked.

"You really carry a lot of stress in your neck." She moved her hands to the muscles on either side of his spine. She imagined wrapping her hands around his neck and choking him to death, but she knew she wasn't strong enough to do it. She glanced around for something she could use as a weapon. It was easy to imagine killing him, but finding a way to do it was proving much harder.

"How does that feel?" she asked, trying to keep him calm and distracted as she searched for anything that could be used against him.

"Nice," he answered.

Olivia took a steadying breath. The ledger on the desk was full of figures she didn't understand, but she caught sight of a few names to the side of each row. She frowned as understanding dawned on her. They were the names of cities. Just based on what she could see, she would guess they covered half a dozen or more states. Were these accounts? Were they places like this one where more women were being held? She couldn't imagine that so many places could exist and no one know about them. She read through as much as she could, trying to absorb the information in front of her. Three columns seemed to be specific to three cities that stood out to her, Nashville, Columbus, and Louisville. If she had to bet, those were the sites of the big fights and most likely more trafficking cells. Distracted by what she had learned, she absently let her hand still.

He grabbed her hand and pulled her around the chair to face him. "That's enough."

Olivia gasped and flinched away, expecting to be struck.

His expression softened. "I'm sorry. I'm not very good company today." He closed his hand around Olivia's neck, rubbing his thumb up and down her throat. "So soft." His eyes glazed over as if he was in a dream, making Olivia even more afraid of what he might do. He leaned in and sniffed her hair.

The pressure of his thumb against her throat grew rough until Olivia whimpered from the pain. She shivered as fear and revulsion crawled across her skin like freezing fog. Something told her he would enjoy killing her. "Please stop," she whispered.

He pulled back, staring at her as if he was seeing her for the first time. His brow furrowed. "I've scared you again. I'm sorry."

He pushed a button on his desk phone. There was a knock at the door, and a second later the door opened.

"Sir?"

He never took his eyes off Olivia. "Take Ms. Danner back to the others."

"Yes, sir."

He kissed her cheek. "Tomorrow will be better. I'll make everything up to you, I promise."

Olivia fought the urge to claw at her skin as she walked down the hall. She wanted a shower. She wanted to scrub every trace of him off her. The only thing holding her together was the anticipation of telling Greyson what she had found.

Greyson had become her cornerstone. She was there for her every night, talking her through her fear after long days with the Recruiter. Greyson never showed her own fear of what was coming. She was determined to find a way out before then. But Olivia was skeptical it could happen. She didn't want to think of what it would mean for both of them when Greyson faced the death match.

❖

Greyson rolled onto her side and slid back the covers the moment Olivia moved to her cot. Olivia was quiet. Some nights were like that, when Olivia had had an especially difficult time with the Recruiter. Greyson wrapped her arms around Olivia protectively, hoping to give her comfort for at least a little while.

"Do you want to talk about it?" she whispered into Olivia's ear.

She felt Olivia sigh. "He disgusts me. He's absolutely raving nuts."

Greyson waited, stroking her hand along Olivia's back.

"I think this is much bigger than we thought. I saw a ledger today that had the names of cities in different states with figures next to them. I've been trying to figure out what it means, but I can't fit it together. I think some of them may have been dates—the rest, I'm not sure. But if I'm right, there have to be hundreds of women like us held in places all over the US. It looked like there are some pretty big things going on."

"Damn," Greyson muttered. "That's huge."

"Yeah." Olivia cuddled closer, curling her arms between them, against Greyson's chest.

Greyson heard Olivia sniff and knew she was crying. "What's wrong?"

Olivia sighed. "I've been thinking about my parents. I can't imagine what this has been like for them. The last time I saw my momma, we had a fight. I may not ever get to tell her I'm sorry."

"You will," Greyson reassured.

"You always say that."

Greyson chuckled. "It's true."

Olivia was silent for a long time, but Greyson knew she wasn't asleep. She could feel her troubled emotions as if their hearts shared feelings they didn't give words to.

"What's your favorite flower?" Greyson asked.

"Don't," Olivia protested.

"Come on, tell me. What is it?"

Olivia sighed. "You'll laugh."

"No, I won't. What can be funny about a flower?"

"A thistle," Olivia said, her voice soft as if she was whispering a secret.

Greyson frowned. "Really? You know that's a weed, right?"

Olivia tapped her hand against Greyson's chest. "See, you're making fun."

"I'm sorry. You're right." Greyson thought about Olivia's answer. She'd expected her to say roses, or buttercups, or daisies, but not a thistle. "What do you like about the thistle?"

"Well, they're wild and gnarly, and they grow tall and thorny. I like that they aren't perfect, but despite the rough edges they have such a beautiful flower. It helps that I like purple."

Greyson smiled and her heart warmed. "Is there anyone else missing you? Besides your parents, I mean?"

Olivia pulled her head back and looked at Greyson through the dim light. She smiled at the memory flooding her mind. "My friend James. He's got to be absolutely mad crazy by now. He's like the brother I never had. I tell him everything." Olivia chuckled. "He's so funny. I love to hear his stories about the guys he goes out with. He's funny, charming, handsome, and a complete dating disaster."

Greyson smiled. It was nice to hear a hint of happiness in Olivia's voice. She wished she could keep that happiness there between them forever.

"He sounds like a great friend."

Olivia was quiet for a long moment. "He is. I've never been closer to anyone before—until now."

Greyson pulled Olivia closer. "My buddy Dawn probably has the National Guard out scouring the Smoky Mountains looking for me. I hope she hasn't gone out there herself."

"Why?" Olivia asked.

Greyson laughed. "Dawn has city blood. She breaks out in hives if someone in a ten-mile radius of her cuts the grass."

Olivia laughed.

"She wanted to go with me on the AT. She was convinced something bad was going to happen. I guess I should have listened."

Olivia drew circles against Greyson's chest with her fingers. "No one could have known this was going to happen."

"No," Greyson agreed. "And who knows what that freak might have done to her if she had gotten in the way." She sighed. "I don't even know for sure how long I've been here now. The days all run together. Even if they haven't called off the search for me, they'll be looking in the wrong place."

"I know what you mean," Olivia answered. "I just got out of my car and went with him like an idiot. It was storming and I was waiting it out on the shoulder. He stopped to help, said my car had a flat. I knew better, but I still trusted him. I keep hoping someone saw us, that maybe there was some clue left behind that can help. But why would anyone even think to look here? There are so many other explanations that make more sense than the truth."

Greyson pressed her cheek against the top of Olivia's head, trying to reassure them both. "We're going to get out of here. You can't give up. You have to keep believing, even if the fight doesn't go well. You have to keep trying."

Olivia gasped. It was the first time she had heard doubt in Greyson's voice. "Who's the one giving up now?"

"I'm not," Greyson argued. "But we both know I'm not cut out for this. I'm no fighter, let alone a killer. I can't just go into that pit and take someone's life, especially someone that's in the same situation I am. They aren't the enemy."

Olivia was surprised to hear Greyson talk so honestly about the fight, but she wasn't surprised by the revelation. She knew in her heart what Greyson said was true.

"So what's the plan? You must have some ideas in that big brain of yours."

"I don't really have one. I have bits and pieces in the works, but the truth is, nothing will matter if I can't find a way to get us outside. Nothing has worked so far. I'm sorry I don't have better news."

Olivia's heart sank. If Greyson didn't have a plan, there was no hope left.

Greyson tightened her arms around Olivia. "Don't count us out yet. I won't give up until the last breath leaves me. I will get us out, or I'll die trying."

Olivia bit back her tears. Her heart was breaking. She knew Greyson would do exactly what she said. She just wasn't ready to let Greyson go. She felt like they were sitting on death row, just waiting for the executioner to call their names. She tried to press closer to Greyson, needing that closeness to chase away her fear. The time they spent together suspended between day and night was the only time she felt hope. After everything they'd been through together, she couldn't believe she had been so determined to hate Greyson. It had been so easy to put the blame on the first person presented.

Greyson wasn't anything like she had believed. If she was honest with herself, she had judged Greyson harshly from the first moment fate had brought them together. She couldn't have been more wrong. She wished she could turn back time and go back to that first day. She would have been nice, for starters, she would have invited Greyson into her apartment, she would have talked through the night, learning everything about Greyson, and she would never have believed the horrible things the Recruiter said about Greyson.

Olivia closed her eyes against the memory. She had thought

that job interview was the most important thing in her life. How many more opportunities had she missed because of her narrow view of what was important?

"What are you thinking?" Greyson asked, pulling her back to the moment.

Olivia smiled. "I was thinking about the first day we met."

"What about it?" Greyson asked.

"I'm sorry I was so awful to you. I'm glad you gave me a second chance. I wonder where things would have gone if you hadn't left the next day and we would have had more time together. If I ever get out of here, I'm going to be different."

"What do you mean?"

"I was so determined to have things my way, I missed out on so many possibilities. I don't think I could ever take things for granted like that again. It took me years to come to terms with my sexuality, and I just expected my momma to get it in an instant, even though it went against everything she'd been taught to believe. I never considered how difficult it was for her. If I ever see her again, I'll be more patient."

Greyson ran her hands up and down Olivia's back. "Don't be so hard on yourself. I'm sure she knows you love her. That's what really matters."

Olivia nodded. "I just wish I could tell her."

"I know."

Greyson pressed her lips to Olivia's forehead. Olivia knew it was meant to comfort her, but it stirred something much deeper. She dreamed of what it would be like to kiss Greyson for real. Not a kiss to soothe fear, but a kiss to test the feelings she felt growing between them. They had one kiss, one real kiss, and it had been enough to spark hope and dreams of more. So much had happened between them now. What would she feel after all they had been through? She could only dream.

Chapter Fourteen

G reyson followed Uncle Dan to the greenhouse. She looked forward to her time here. It was the only time she didn't feel the walls closing in on her. Over the last few days he had started locking her in the room a few hours at a time alone. It was as close to outside as she was ever going to get.

To her surprise he didn't leave today. He shut the door behind them and turned to her. "The fight is in two days. You leave tomorrow and you won't be coming back here."

Greyson swallowed. There it was. Her time was up. She looked around the room as if needing to say good-bye. "The fight isn't here?"

He shook his head. He continued, seemingly unaware of her discomfort. "This death match will be different than any other. It isn't about one fight. Think of it like a tournament. You win the first fight, you advance to the next round. You'll have to fight until one of you can't go on or there's a knockout. The final match is like the championship game. That's the only fight that has to result in death. The Employers decided there was no point in losing that many investments in one night."

Greyson thought about this new information. "What happens if I lose early?"

"You're fighting to prove your value. Girls who lose in the early rounds are seen as scraps. We find other uses for them. Someone's always looking for something."

Greyson cringed. She didn't want to imagine what those things might be.

"The higher up the tier you climb, the more your value. Bets will be made on each fight. The Employers have a lot riding on their girls. They don't like to lose."

"Do I have an Employer, or am I selling myself?"

He narrowed his eyes. Greyson guessed this wasn't something he expected her to know.

"You were a special order. Your Employer will be there."

"And where is there?" Greyson asked.

"That's not important," he answered.

Greyson's heart sank. As much as she hated this place, she didn't want to leave Olivia, and from what the others told her, this was the better place to be. One thing was certain, she would choose death before she would allow any of these sick assholes to touch her.

Greyson shifted on her feet, getting a sense of where this was going. "Why are you telling me this?"

"I have my investments in this too."

Greyson frowned. "You want me to fix the fights?"

"I want you to win," the old man growled.

"Why?"

"I have my reasons."

Greyson studied him. She still had no idea what he was up to, but for some reason he thought she had value. "Will you be betting for or against me?"

He smiled. "Maybe both, depending on the fight."

"Then why tell me this?"

He pierced her with a hard stare. "Because I want to make sure someone else doesn't win."

Greyson frowned. "The bean counter?"

His smile let her know she was on the right track.

"You won't want him to win either." His voice was flat and cold and sent a shiver up Greyson's spine.

"Why's that?"

The old man drew a long deep breath. "Let's just say he's ready to start counting his own beans, and he's got his eye on a girl."

Greyson's heart twisted. "Who?" she asked, certain she already knew the answer.

"You played a dangerous game with us. You embarrassed him in front of the men. He's going to want to see you hurt in more ways than one."

"Dammit." Greyson kicked herself. Every move she made was the wrong one. She might have gained an alliance, but she had set Olivia up again. Why did everything she do keep hurting the one person she wanted to protect? "Can you protect her?"

He twisted his mouth, making his bushy mustache bristle like a giant caterpillar. "You make sure I get what I want, and I'll make sure you get yours."

"I can't make any promises when I don't even know what I'm up against."

He smiled. "That's why it's called gambling. I don't know what cards you thought you were holding, but right now, you're all in. Win, lose, or die, the girl is the prize."

Greyson ground her teeth together until she was certain they would break. She had seen how that man looked at Olivia. She had no doubt that if he managed to gain control of Olivia, the hands-off policy would be out the window. Bile rose in her throat at the thought of anyone touching Olivia. Her mind raced, but she just couldn't see a way out. They were out of time. Disappointment crashed down on her like an avalanche. She knew in her heart that no matter what she did, win or lose, Olivia would never be safe. Even if she managed to win the fight, what would be next? What would be the next evil plot to use them against each other?

"This is never going to end, is it?" Greyson said bitterly.

The old man shook his head. "You are part of the game. You decide how well you want to play, but the game goes on with or without you."

❖

Olivia paced the floor waiting for Greyson to return. It was almost time for the Recruiter to send for her, and she was growing more and more afraid she would be separated from the group, and from Greyson. It would be just like the Recruiter to mess with her head by taking Greyson away now. They all knew the fight was close. Everyone grew more anxious and moody with each passing day.

Olivia ran to Greyson the moment she was let back into the room. Greyson took her hand and squeezed. Olivia could feel the tension vibrate off Greyson's skin the instant she took her hand.

"We need to talk," Greyson said with a note of caution in her voice.

Olivia was shaking with anticipation as Greyson led her away from the other girls. Something big was coming. "What's going on?"

Greyson turned to her abruptly. "We're out of time. The fight's in two days. We leave tomorrow."

"Leave? How do you know?" Olivia asked.

"The old man told me. It's some kind of tournament."

Shifting feet drew their attention and they turned to see the other girls had started to gather around them.

"What's going on, Greyson? We know you know something. You have to tell us. You can't just leave us in the dark," Raquel said. The rest of the group nodded as murmurs spread around the room.

Olivia touched Greyson's arm. "They're right. There's no point in keeping it a secret. Everyone deserves to know."

Greyson nodded. She cleared her throat and turned to face the group. "We ship out tomorrow. I don't know where we're going. The fight is in two days. Instead of worrying about one fight, we have to keep fighting over and over again in a tournament. The winner of each round is determined by who can still stand."

Olivia clasped her hand over her mouth as she gasped. "Oh my God. I've seen what one fight does. How can they expect anyone to keep that up?"

Greyson closed her eyes a moment before meeting Olivia's gaze. "I think that's the point. They want to see how much we can suffer and still come back for more. At least this way we have a chance to survive. Anyone who loses early in the match is considered expendable. I don't know what exactly that means. The final two women who face off will fight to the death."

The room was a buzz of noise as the women began to process the information. Greyson raised her hands and shrugged. "That's all I know."

Greyson led Olivia to an empty table where they could have a little space. "There's something else."

Olivia pierced Greyson with her gaze, her eyes dark pools of worry. "What?"

"There's this guy I punched at the last fight. He's out to get me now. He's going to be betting on the fights to try to buy one of the girls."

The fear she saw in Olivia's eyes cut through her like a knife.

"Who?" Olivia whispered.

Greyson let out a defeated breath. "You."

Olivia whimpered. Greyson held on to Olivia's arm, afraid she might faint. A moment later, Olivia straightened, a look of resolve settling on her face. She clenched her jaw.

"That's it then. I lose no matter what."

Greyson wanted to reassure Olivia, but she knew her words would just be empty promises even she didn't believe.

Olivia added, "The Recruiter is going to punish me no matter what you do. Then I have to face some sick bastard who wants to use me as a live voodoo doll to get back at you. Great."

Greyson sighed. "I'm sorry. Every move I make comes back to hurt you."

Olivia shook her head. "There's no point assigning blame for any of this. What's your plan now?"

Greyson swallowed. She hated not being able to put this right. "I don't have one."

Olivia nodded.

"There's more," Greyson said, watching the muscle at the side of Olivia's jaw jump. "No matter what happens at the fight, I won't be coming back here. Whoever paid to put me in this hell will be moving me somewhere else."

Tears welled in Olivia's eyes.

"I'm so sorry for all this, Olivia. I'm going to do whatever I can to…" Do what? What could she do? She felt like she was juggling grenades.

"It's okay, Greyson. This really isn't your fault. It isn't fair to keep making you feel responsible for me. From the beginning they've used me against you, and I let them. I don't want that to happen anymore. It's time that you do what's right for you."

Greyson shook her head. "It's more than that. We're in this together. I'm not doing this because I have to, I'm doing it because…" Greyson wasn't sure what she wanted to say.

"Because?" Olivia asked.

"Because…because…" Greyson stammered. "Because I want to know what you like for breakfast."

Olivia frowned. "I don't know what that means."

"It means this." Greyson placed her hand behind Olivia's head and kissed her. She pressed her lips hard against Olivia's mouth with urgency. Weeks of building attraction were expressed in that one kiss. She was out of time, and she didn't want another moment to escape without knowing the taste and feel of Olivia's mouth.

The instant their lips met, Olivia responded with her own need for connection. Her mouth parted, allowing Greyson entry. Her lips were sweet, her mouth hot against Greyson's. Greyson explored Olivia's mouth with her tongue, searching for time they didn't have. In the moment of their connection, Greyson felt life and hope fill her again. Everything she had lost was right there in Olivia's touch.

Olivia slowed the kiss. Her breath was heavy, and she had her arms wrapped tightly around Greyson's shoulders.

Greyson broke the kiss, pulling away to look at Olivia. She was surprised to see tears in Olivia's eyes. Her heart sank. "What's wrong?" Greyson asked, afraid she had just screwed up.

"Why'd you have to do that now, with everything that's going on?"

Greyson smiled. "I didn't want to wait until it was too late. I'd always regret it if I'd never tried."

"This will just make it harder to let go."

Greyson kissed Olivia lightly, letting the tenderness of Olivia's lips warm her soul. "I don't want to let go."

Olivia shook her head. "You won't have a choice."

Greyson sighed. "Pretending there isn't anything between us won't make this less real."

Olivia swiped at a tear trailing down her cheek. She glanced over Greyson's shoulder. "Everyone's watching," Olivia whispered.

"So let them watch. You're the only thing I care about right now. We're all listening to the clock tick, grasping for something worth fighting for." She brushed her fingers across Olivia's lips. "This is worth it to me."

❖

The room was eerily quiet as the women sat contemplating their fates. Greyson looked around her at the defeated expressions, the grief, the despair that was so overwhelming it hung over the room like the outstretched hand of death. She knew they were thinking of home, the families they might never see again. She knew because that was what she'd been thinking too.

Raquel came and sat next to her, her shoulders slumped. "You know I used to like to read. Well, I guess I still like to read, but you know what I mean. I read a quote once that said something about having to give up the ideas we have about our life in order to accept the life before us." She picked at a string on her sleeve as if she had gotten lost in her thought.

"Are you saying we have to accept this?" Greyson asked.

Raquel shook her head. "No. The despair we are feeling is because we are holding on to old hope. I'm suggesting we start using our training to our advantage."

Greyson looked at her, giving her all of her attention. "I'm listening."

"Some of us have been taking orders, training, and fighting for years. We are consumed by the fight and our expectation of what that might mean for our lives. But what if we don't make it to the fight? What if we take matters into our own hands before then?"

"You mean a riot?"

Raquel shrugged. "I'm saying if there is an opportunity to act, we should take it."

Greyson looked around the room. "What about the others? Will they take a stand?"

Raquel grinned. "Vinny and I are in. From what I saw a few days ago, Ruby will be too. If Ruby stands, we all stand."

Greyson nodded. "Okay. I might have a plan, but it's going to depend on how we're moved tomorrow. If this place is as big a secret as everyone believes, they'll have to be discreet. We need to find a way to be seen, set off an alarm of sorts. Count the guards, know who's with you at all times. If this is anything like what we usually see around here, we have a chance. Just look for the crack in the sidewalk."

Raquel nodded. "If one makes a move, we all move."

"Exactly," Greyson agreed.

Raquel stood. "Let's get started." She patted Greyson on the back as she walked away.

Hope had taken root in Greyson's mind. This was the first time the others had been willing to take a chance. She got up and made her way to Olivia and a couple of others gathered around a table. It was time to rally the troops.

Murmurs of excitement began to spread as more and more women agreed to the scrap of a plan. It was working.

A hush fell over the room as the sound of the guards echoed down the hall. It was as if everyone inhaled at once, sucking all the air out of the room.

"Mail," the guard said, his tone harsh, as if barking an order.

One by one he called the names of the women. One by one they went to the door to retrieve a single yellow envelope. Neither Olivia nor Greyson was called.

Greyson watched, curious about this change in protocol. They never got mail.

Raquel opened her envelope. With trembling fingers, she pulled a photograph from the envelope. She gasped, instantly clasping her hand over her mouth. One by one the others began to react with similar levels of shock.

"What's going on?" Olivia asked, stepping close to Greyson.

Greyson shook her head. "I have no idea, but I'm going to find out. Come on." She took Olivia's hand and led her across the room.

"Raquel?" Greyson said.

Raquel looked up at them with tears in her eyes.

"What is it?" Olivia asked.

Raquel held out the photograph of two young women at a graduation ceremony. "My girls. They're all grown up."

Greyson closed her eyes as realization dawned on her. The Recruiter had bested her again. Just when she thought she had everyone on board to revolt, he gave them a reminder of what they had been fighting for all along.

Greyson fell to her knees in front of Raquel. "Listen to me. You can't let him inside your head. He sent this to you so you'll behave. He's trying to control you through fear. Your girls need their mother back."

Raquel sniffed, wiping at the tears flowing freely down her face. She pulled the photograph to her chest as if holding her girls in her arms. She rocked slowly back and forth, singing a children's song under her breath.

Olivia looked at Greyson, clearly confused. "Would you please explain this to me?"

"They all got pictures of their families. It's a threat. He's implying if they don't do their jobs, their families will be harmed. He's using their families against them, the same way he uses you against me."

"Oh." Olivia looked around, her heart breaking for them. She missed her own family and couldn't imagine anyone hurting them. She knew she would do anything to prevent that. Slowly she began to understand these women and how they had survived under such cruelty. The realization made her ashamed of her own selfishness. All this time, she had only been thinking of herself.

"Why didn't they call my name?" Olivia asked.

Greyson frowned. "I'm not sure. Maybe it's because you won't be the one fighting."

"I hate this," Olivia whispered.

Greyson wrapped her arms around Olivia. "Come here." Olivia cradled her head against Greyson's shoulder, embracing her around her waist.

They swayed together as if listening to a faraway tune. "I want my life back," Olivia said into Greyson's neck. "But if I can't have that, can I just freeze this one moment forever? I don't want to have to imagine tomorrow."

Greyson was quiet. Too quiet.

"What are you thinking?" Olivia asked.

Greyson chuckled, her laugh vibrating through her chest like distant thunder. "I was wondering if things were different, if you would let me take you out on a second date."

Olivia laughed. "You've lost your mind."

Greyson laughed again. "No. I just don't want my time to be chewed up with fear and dread. I want to dream. When I dream, that's what I dream about. I dream about taking you to dinner, holding hands, dancing, and finding out all your secrets."

"I had no idea you were such a romantic," Olivia teased.

Greyson stopped and looked down at Olivia. "Would you? Would you go out with me after all that's happened?"

Olivia smiled. "I would love nothing better."

Greyson smiled and pulled Olivia close again as if the answer satisfied something inside her. But Olivia wasn't like Greyson. She couldn't pretend things were going to be okay. She couldn't stand to dream about a life she couldn't have. She closed her eyes and pressed her cheek to Greyson's chest, comforted by the solid beat of Greyson's heart.

Tomorrow her life would change again. She would lose Greyson, the one real thing left in her world. Olivia thought of Liz and her devotion to the Recruiter. She would never let that happen to her. A vision of Nikki flashed in her mind and she flinched.

"You okay?" Greyson asked.

"Yeah. I'm fine." She pulled Greyson closer, not wanting to

talk about the fears ravaging her mind. She had no control over her future, but she wouldn't allow the Recruiter and his prison to steal her last moments with Greyson.

She closed her eyes against the irony of the situation. She had been fighting so hard to build the perfect life. She had dreamed of finding someone she could share her life with. How was it that she'd lost everything, only to find what she had been looking for all along? She wondered if the two lives could exist together. Would she and Greyson have this connection without their terror binding them?

It didn't matter. Olivia smiled, brushing a kiss against Greyson's cheek. She knew the old life, those old dreams, had changed. Even if they did get a miracle, she couldn't go back to the way things were before. She had been blind to the world. That innocence was gone now.

CHAPTER FIFTEEN

Greyson slipped the small spear of plastic from her shoe. She had found it in the greenhouse on one of the days she'd been left on her own. She had managed to sharpen the end into a point by rubbing it against the concrete floor, a trick she had learned on some prison documentary she had watched once. She twisted the small shaft in her hand, trying to find the perfect hold. It wasn't much of a weapon, but she hoped it would be enough. She had passed the idea on to Raquel and Olivia, encouraging them to find similar weapons of their own. Greyson had been surprised to find that several of the other women had weapons hidden already.

Olivia had managed a small spear fashioned from the end of a toothbrush, while Raquel had long been weaving a makeshift rope out of threads she had pulled from towels and garments, hiding the loose strands in her mouth until she could add them to the rope. She had even woven in strands of her own hair for added strength and a personal binding. The process had taken months, and she'd managed to conceal it by tying the work in progress inside the loose scrub pants they all wore. The women had been quite creative in the individual design of their weapons and procuring the materials without being discovered. But truthfully, she held little hope in their rudimentary tools. It would take a miracle for them to pull off an escape, but what choice did they have?

They stirred as the sound of the guards' footsteps echoed in the corridor. Greyson glanced from woman to woman as they silently nodded their agreement, their commitment to the plan. She slipped the weapon back into her shoe. They were ready.

"Raquel and Samone, let's go," the guard with the spider tattoo barked.

As expected, the usual guards. So far, so good.

Raquel and Samone were handcuffed together and pulled into the hall to wait.

"Vinny and Audrey."

The guard continued to call them in pairs until all those attending the fight were assembled in line in the corridor, each pair handcuffed together. The last pair called was Greyson and Olivia.

Greyson took Olivia's hand. "It's okay. We can do this."

Olivia nodded and walked with Greyson to the guard.

The guard smiled knowingly at Greyson. "I hope you've learned a thing or two in the past few weeks," he sneered.

Greyson glared. "Where's your boss? Maybe you and I can put on a little show right now."

The guard smiled. "Boss isn't here. He's already gone ahead to get things ready. But what he doesn't know won't hurt him."

"Let's go then," Greyson dared him.

"Don't," Olivia warned.

The guard laughed. "That's right, hero. Listen to the little girl. Every step you make has her name on it." He ran his finger across Olivia's cheek. "I'd hate to mess up that pretty little face before the boss has a chance to show her off."

Greyson glanced at Olivia. Olivia shook her head in warning.

The guard secured the cuffs around Greyson's wrists and laughed as he walked to the front of the line.

"I can't wait to get that guy," Greyson growled under her breath.

"I know," Olivia agreed. "But not yet."

Greyson nodded. "I have to mess with them a bit or they'll think I'm up to something."

Olivia looped her pinkie finger around Greyson's. "You are up to something."

Greyson grinned. She counted three guards. One at the front, one at the back, and the guy with the keys who opened the doors. Greyson studied the keys, memorizing his habit of looping the large ring around his wrist while he held the key in his hand, making it harder to grab the keys from him. She hoped Raquel had noticed the same thing. If she made a move, the girls at the front would have to take out two guards, leaving Greyson to handle the one at the back. They had agreed to wait until they were outside to move, but the farther they went, the more she could feel the tension building. If anyone jumped too early, they'd be in trouble. They would not only have to deal with the guards, but they would still have to find their way out before others arrived.

Greyson's heart sank as they were led into a large open room set up for deliveries. Two large service vans had been driven into the room. The bay doors were shut. "Dammit."

They had hoped to be able to make a move on the outside. Now they would have to wait until they were in the vans. It was more risky, but maybe getting outside the gate was better.

Raquel looked to Greyson for the signal. Greyson shook her head. The time had to be just right.

"What do we do now?" Olivia asked.

Greyson heard the anxiety in Olivia's voice, but she couldn't risk talking now. "Just trust me."

Greyson ground her teeth, trying to find a weakness in the system. The men had covered their tracks well. The women were being loaded into cargo vans with no windows. The logo painted on the side was for a generic plumbing and electrical service. From the outside, it would look like just another service call. No one would suspect they were trafficking women in these vans. Greyson looked past the women in front of her, to peer inside the van. There was a metal wall dividing the back and the front, with only a small door with a window for access between the two compartments. There would be no way they could get to the driver. Again, this was nothing out of the ordinary for a service vehicle. They had similar vans at work for some of the maintenance staff. Two benches lined either side of the cargo area, where the women would sit, but the walls had been padded, likely to quiet any noise they might make from the inside.

Greyson groaned when Raquel was loaded into the first van along with Samone and Amala and seven others. One more strike against them. They were supposed to work together as a team. It would be much harder in separate groups. Raquel peered at Greyson from the cargo van. Greyson could feel her eyes on her, trying to read her mind. Greyson began to sway back and forth from side to side in an exaggerated fashion. She looked pointedly at Raquel hoping she would somehow interpret her movement.

Greyson flinched as one of the guards slammed the door shut, cutting her off from Raquel.

"Looks like we're next," Olivia whispered.

"Yeah." Greyson leaned closer to Olivia. "What's the road out of here like? Is it straight, narrow, curvy, flat, anything you remember?"

Olivia took a deep breath. "I remember a narrow road, lots of curves, with some houses on either side for a while. Some of the road is just trees and mountain."

Greyson nodded. "Good."

The best she could tell, there were three guards for each van, a driver and a second guard in the front and a third in the back. Who knew if more would be following them. Greyson pulled at the plastic cuffs around her wrists as they were led into the second van. She peered through the glass in the small door blocking them from the cabin, then around at the blank padded walls encasing them. They would be trapped like fish in a barrel.

Greyson sucked in her breath as the last two women were brought to the van. Ruby clutched the hand of a young woman who reminded Greyson of a feral version of Olivia. Her hair was matted and dirty, her eyes wild. Ruby's touch seemed to be the only thing holding this woman in her skin. Ruby allowed them to be led into the van. She murmured reassuringly to the young girl.

Ruby met Greyson's gaze. A muscle twitched at the side of her jaw. Ruby nodded to Greyson almost imperceptibly.

Greyson nodded in return, the agreement made. Ruby would stand with them. She looked to the other women. "Does anyone have anything sharp?" she whispered. "Anything we can use to cut through these damn plastic cuffs?"

Vinny leaned forward, working at the lace of her shoe with her one free hand. She slid a long screw out of her shoe. "It isn't sharp, but we can use the threads like a file to wear through the plastic."

"Good. Get started, but don't let them see you." Greyson smiled. "If anyone else has anything useful, now is the time to use it."

The guard, a short man with a receding hairline that made his head look like someone took a bite out of an eraser, stepped in and slammed the door, locking them inside. The van shifted as the front doors opened and the driver and another guard got into the cab.

Greyson fidgeted on her seat. There was little room to move with ten women and a guard packed in the small space. She knocked a knuckle against the metal bench covering the wheel well. "Hold on to your butt cheeks, girls—this is going to be a bumpy ride."

❖

The group was quiet as they waited. It seemed everyone was holding their breath. Nikki whimpered when the engine started and the large cargo doors opened. Light streamed in through the small window, a blinding glow of hope.

Olivia squeezed Greyson's hand. "I'd pray right now if I thought it would help."

Greyson sighed. "God is not in this place."

The women grumbled as they struggled to stay seated when the van began to move, tipping forward as they descended a ramp. Every eye was on the window and this rare glimpse at the outside world.

The moment the van turned onto the road, Greyson shifted her attention to the guard. "I haven't seen you around before. How did you get so lucky today?"

The guard glared at her.

"Guess you must have done something special to earn a ticket to the show."

"Shut up. They said you would be a pain in the ass." He pushed past Greyson to the small window, tapping the glass with his fist. "Step on it, will you."

Greyson pulled the small spear from her shoe. She nodded to Ruby. As the guard turned, Ruby lunged, throwing her free arm around his neck and pulling him down on top of her. Greyson and Olivia stood, blocking the view from the window. The guard raised his arm in defense, but Nikki grabbed his hand before he could use the Taser. Vinny pried the baton from his belt. He pushed and struggled against Ruby, but he had no balance and she was too strong. He yelled out for the other guards, but his cries were muffled by the crushing power of Ruby's arm around his throat. The struggle was short, but when he stopped moving, Greyson thought her heart would stop too.

Ruby let the lifeless body slide to the floor. Her eyes were wild with rage and satisfaction when she looked up at Greyson.

Greyson nodded. She turned to the bonds tying her to Olivia and began prying at the clasp of the zip ties. It took some work, but she managed to maneuver the plastic enough to loosen the grip of the plastic teeth. As soon as she was free, she moved to Ruby and Nikki while Vinny worked on the others.

"We don't know how much time we have," Greyson cautioned. "We have to make a move before we get to our destination. This is the only chance we'll have."

Ruby nodded.

"That's it, we've done it," Vinny said with pride showing her freed hands. "What's next?"

Greyson peered through the glass trying to see as much of the road as possible. She shifted so she could see ahead of them, trying not to draw the attention of the guard. She could tell by the movement of the van that the road was very curvy. They were moving pretty fast for such a narrow road. She could see the occasional house along the road as they passed.

She looked back at the others. "You're not going to like this, but it's all we've got. Let's hope Raquel can see us and figures it out too."

"What will you have us do?" Ruby asked.

"If we all stand up and rock our weight from one side of the van to the other at the right time, we might be able to make the driver lose control."

Olivia gasped. "You're going to make us crash? We could all die."

Greyson nodded. "It's a risk. I told you, you wouldn't like it."

"There has to be another way," Vinny protested.

"No. There isn't. We have to do this. We have to make sure none of us ever have to go back into the pit. This is our last fight. If we wait till we get to the destination, there will be too many guards and we won't have a way out."

The women erupted in argument, some for and some against the plan.

"We don't have time for this," Greyson argued.

"Enough," Ruby said with finality.

They fell silent.

Ruby looked to Greyson. "Tell us what to do. We will do it."

"I'll watch the road. The next big curve, we all slide to one side. When we make the turn, I'll give the signal, and we'll all rush to the other side and push against the wall to try to flip the van."

Ruby let out a long breath. "You're crazy."

"Maybe," Greyson agreed. She looked to Olivia. "But we have to try."

Olivia nodded. "I know."

Greyson kissed her tenderly on the lips. "Trust me."

Olivia attempted a smile. "I do."

Greyson turned back to the window. The guard was playing on his phone, not bothering to watch the back. The driver was changing the radio station. The road had no shoulder and there was barely room for two cars to pass on the narrow road. They were fast approaching the next bend.

"Everyone shift to the right side," Greyson said, moving

quickly to the other side of the van. The women were crowded together, pressed against one another.

"Now," Greyson yelled as the van entered the turn.

Everyone rushed to the other side of the van, hitting the wall with the force of their weight and momentum. The van rocked to the side, then jerked as the driver tried to correct for the shift. The van swerved.

"Again," Greyson ordered.

The shift this time was enough to send the van out of control. The back wheel slid off the pavement, hitting gravel, then sliding off an embankment.

Olivia screamed, her voice mingling with the terrified cries of the women around her. They were being thrown around like rag dolls as the van rolled and crashed through the brush. The van was on its side, the women piled on top of one another like flying debris. They jolted to a stop as the front of the van crashed into a tree.

Olivia tried to get up, but someone was on top of her. "Greyson? Are you okay?"

The women started to shift, helping each other out of the pile.

Olivia gasped when she saw Greyson's face. Blood trailed from a gash above her eye. "You're bleeding."

Greyson pressed her hand to the cut. "It isn't too bad. I'm okay." She called out to each of the women. "Is everyone okay?"

Olivia pushed herself up, wincing at the pain in her wrist.

Ruby was holding Nikki. Nikki held her arm to her chest, and blood streamed from a gash on her hand.

"No," Vinny cried. Greyson helped a couple of the women shift and sit up, pulling them out of the pile of twisted bodies. Audrey wasn't moving. Greyson cradled the girl's head and felt for a pulse. The woman's head was twisted at an odd angle and her eyes stared blankly at nothing.

The women were crying and screaming, beating against the walls trying to hammer their way out with their bare hands.

Greyson peered through the cracked glass into the cab. The guard had been thrown on top of the driver. She could see blood on the side of his face. He wasn't moving. The front of the van was a mangled mess that looked like it had been eaten by a tree. They wouldn't be able to get out that way.

She climbed over the others, pushing her way to the back of the van, stumbling over the bodies of two other women. "We have to get out of here. The other van had to be right behind us. They'll be on us in a minute. As soon as these doors open, run. Split up the best you can, but stay in pairs. They can't chase us all. Get to the houses and call the police. Tell them about the prison and the girls. Make them understand."

Greyson grabbed the arm of one of the women she had rarely heard speak in their time together. Her English was not great, but Greyson had to convince her she had to try. "You can't be afraid to tell them who you are. You have to speak up or we can't stop this from happening to more women like us. What if they come for your children next?"

The woman nodded.

Greyson slipped her hand inside a small access panel on the back door, praying this was like the vans at work. She wrapped her fingers around a flat metal bar. "Get ready." She pulled, and to her relief the door popped opened. She pushed the door up enough to release the other door. The instant she pushed through the opening, she was struck from the side. She fell, rolling to her back, ready to defend herself.

Ruby was the second one through the door and was on the guard before he could hit Greyson with the baton he held over her head.

Olivia scrambled from the wreckage, falling to her knees at Greyson's side. Greyson pushed her away. "Run. You have to get out of here. Run!" Greyson yelled.

Olivia looked stunned but jumped to her feet and bolted away. Greyson saw her look back over her shoulder as she ran. *Good. She'll be safe.*

Greyson stumbled to the front of the van, reaching inside for anything she could find that might help them. She pulled out a cell phone, and dialed 911. Something struck her in the back and her muscles seized before she could speak. She fell to the ground in a fetal position, unable to move her arms or legs. The instant the pulse stopped, she gasped for a breath, letting go of the pain. She was dazed and had difficulty focusing. She yelled out in pain as someone kicked her hard in the back. She rolled to her side.

"You're going to pay for this, bitch," the guard said as he raised his foot again, this time aiming for her head.

Greyson stared at the tattoo on his throat. She should have taken a shot at this guy when she had a chance. Just as his foot was about to crash down on her face, someone hit him in the head. He stumbled, falling to the ground with a crash. Greyson blinked against the blinding sun and the lingering pain. Olivia stood over her holding a tree branch.

"You were supposed to run away," Greyson croaked.

"Good thing I didn't. We're in this together, remember?" Olivia said reaching for Greyson.

Sirens sounded in the distance. Greyson wasn't sure if they were police or medics, but they were music to her ears. The guards that were left must have heard them too. They let go of the women they'd been fighting and ran.

"We can't let them get back to the other van. We have to save the others," Greyson said stumbling to her feet. She tried to run but still couldn't get her legs to work correctly.

The van on the road suddenly roared to life. The horn blared as the van took off at a dangerous speed, leaving the guards stranded. A black car was on fire by the side of the road. She guessed there had been more guards following them in that car. An arm waved from the window of the van as it sped away.

Greyson fell to her knees in relief. The others were safe. "Way to go, Vinny," she yelled.

She crawled over to Ruby, who continued to beat the life out of the guard caught in her wrath. Nikki lay on the ground near them, not moving, blood pooled from a wound to her head.

"Stop, Ruby, stop," Greyson said pulling Ruby off the guard. "He's dead, Ruby. You can let go."

Olivia went to Nikki. Olivia choked back a sob, clasping her hand over her mouth.

Greyson swallowed hard. The wild girl was gone.

Ruby slumped back against Greyson, the fight leaving her as she stared at the girl she had most wanted to protect.

"You did your best," Greyson said, not knowing the words that could possibly comfort Ruby.

"No, she did. He would have had me if she hadn't been there. She saved me."

"They can't hurt her anymore," Greyson said as reassuringly as she could.

Ruby nodded. She slipped from Greyson's arms, crawling on the ground to Nikki's side. She laid her hand on the girl's chest, speaking words in a language Greyson didn't understand.

Olivia kneeled next to Greyson and wrapped her arms around her, pulling Greyson's head against her chest. "You did it."

Greyson sighed. "We did it." She looked up as two police cars raced toward them. "Come on, this isn't over yet."

They walked toward the officers with their hands held over their heads. Greyson explained what had happened and told the officers about the prison. The officers called for assistance. In no time it looked like the whole police force had arrived.

Greyson hoped it wasn't too late for the women they had left behind.

CHAPTER SIXTEEN

Olivia paced the room. They'd been waiting for hours. She understood what a mess the authorities had on their hands to sort out, but she hadn't seen Greyson in so long she was beginning to feel like they were back in the prison. She half expected the Recruiter to walk through the door at any time. She could imagine his smug expression and shivered at the thought of how he would punish her.

Had the police gone to the prison yet? Had they saved the other girls there? Would they ever find the Recruiter? Olivia grew more agitated at the thought of him still being out there. Even if they shut down the prison, wouldn't he just start up again somewhere else? If that ledger she had seen was any indication, there were dozens of places he could go. Had the police found the ledger? Would they figure it out and get to those women in time?

Her head hurt. It was too much to think about, and she didn't have any control over any of it. She needed to see Greyson. She wanted to call her family and let them know she was okay. She needed a connection with someone she trusted.

The door opened and Olivia jumped, turning quickly. "Greyson," she called the moment Greyson stepped into the room. "Oh, thank goodness you're okay." She wrapped her arms around Greyson, stopping to brush her fingers across the bandage above Greyson's eye. "Is it bad?"

Greyson shook her head. "A few stitches, no big deal. They checked me out pretty good. I had a few X-rays and they even took photos of the bruises and Taser burns."

"How are the others?" Olivia asked.

"Ruby and a few of the other girls were at the hospital. The police were asking a lot of questions and the FBI showed up. Vinny and Raquel and the others are okay too. I saw them come in on my way back here."

"That's good news. I'm glad one of us knows something. The most I can get out of these guys is that they know we are who we say we are." Olivia sighed. "Why won't they let me call home?"

Greyson shrugged. "Maybe they don't want any of this to get out too soon. Maybe it'll buy them time to get these guys before they can get away."

"Yeah, I guess," Olivia agreed.

"I'm sure they'll let our families know soon," Greyson said, brushing back the hair from Olivia's face.

A man entered the room. He cleared his throat the moment he saw them. "I'm sorry to interrupt, but would you ladies like something to eat? We ordered pizza—it's the best we could do for now."

Olivia let out a relieved sigh. "Yeah, we'd like that."

All of them murmured excitedly as the food was brought in. The smell filled the room, making Olivia's mouth water. In that moment her freedom felt real.

A few moments later Vinny and the rest were brought into the room. Vinny grabbed Greyson in a hug. "We did it. We pulled it off. I thought for sure I'd die in that place. But we did it."

Greyson patted Vinny on the back. They went around the room exchanging hugs. The room buzzed with their barely contained joy.

Olivia's heart swelled. It was the first time she had seen most of these women smile. The distrust and fear that had hardened their features had lessened and she could see the shimmer of hope begin to grow in their eyes.

Olivia nodded toward Raquel, who was seated at the end of the table clutching the photo of her children. "You should go talk to her," she said to Greyson.

Greyson nodded. "Yeah." She stepped away from the group, taking a seat across from Raquel.

"You okay?" Greyson asked.

Raquel shook her head. "I don't know what will happen to them. I don't know where they live. The authorities said they will do their best to find them and keep them safe, but what if the Recruiter gets to them first?"

Greyson wrapped her fingers around Raquel's hand. "That won't happen. If he knows what we did he'll be in save-his-ass mode. They have some of the guards too, remember. Maybe one of them will know where your family is, or where they can find the Recruiter. This is a long way from over."

Raquel nodded.

"You did the right thing," Greyson continued. "He's a lying bastard. You know your girls were never safe as long as he had anything to do with their lives. There was never any promise he wouldn't hurt them. This way you can do everything you can to stop him."

Raquel brushed aside a tear with a swipe of her hand. She straightened. She squeezed Greyson's hand. "I hope they get him."

Greyson nodded. "Me too."

"Ms. Danner," an officer called.

Greyson met Olivia's gaze. Her eyes were wide with fear.

"Come with me, please." The officer gestured for Olivia to follow. Olivia turned to Greyson, her eyes pleading. Greyson's heart broke at the sight of fear once again marring Olivia's face. She hated every moment Olivia had endured in that hell, but at the same time she was thankful for her. Without Olivia, she might have given up—she might have given up on all of them.

Olivia reached for Greyson's hand. "Can she come with me?" Olivia asked.

"Of course," he answered.

❖

They were led down the hall to another small room. "We sent someone for your parents. They should be arriving any moment now."

Relief almost took Olivia's breath away. "Oh, thank God. Thank you," Olivia said with tears welling in her eyes.

"Is there anything else you need?" the officer asked.

Olivia shook her head.

"I'll be just outside if you think of anything," he said as he turned to leave.

"Wait," Olivia called, just as the door started to close. "Could you leave the door open, please."

He nodded, his lips pursed in understanding. "Sure."

Olivia turned to Greyson. Greyson smiled. "Thank you," Olivia said burying her face against Greyson's shoulder.

"For what?" Greyson asked.

"Everything."

There was a gentle knock at the door. Olivia looked up to see her mother standing in the doorway, her father behind her, his hands on her mother's shoulders.

"Momma." Olivia ran to her mother, almost knocking her over with the force of her embrace. Her father wrapped them both in his arms and they cried. "I'm so sorry, Momma. I was afraid I'd never see you again."

Her mother's hands trembled as she held her. "Thank God. I knew he would bring you back to me. I just knew."

Greyson watched Olivia and her parents, a bit uncomfortable with being an outsider in the room. Olivia's mother looked up at Greyson. "Who's this?"

Olivia swiped at the tears flowing down her cheeks. She stepped back, turning to Greyson. "This is Greyson Cooper. She was in that…place with me. She saved us."

Greyson wanted to argue that last point but was overwhelmed

when Olivia's mother crossed the room and wrapped her arms around her in a hug. "Thank you. Thank you for bringing her back to us."

Greyson lightly wrapped her arms around her, allowing her to cry against her chest. Greyson looked up at Olivia's father, who was also crying. He smiled at Greyson and nodded.

Greyson understood Olivia's parents in that moment. Whatever conflict had been between them in the past was swept away. They might still have differences, but their love for each other would endure anything.

Greyson stepped aside. "I'll be down the hall if you need me."

"You don't have to go," Olivia said, grasping her hand.

"It's okay. You need a little time together. I'm not going anywhere."

Olivia smiled. She kissed Greyson lightly on the lips. "I'll see you later."

Greyson smiled. "I'm counting on it."

Greyson left Olivia to visit with her family, happy to know Olivia had her life back. She knew they all had a long road ahead of them, but she didn't care. They were free. She had a life worth living again.

❖

Greyson was met in the hall by a tall man in a black suit. "Hello, Ms. Cooper. I'm Special Agent Piper. I need a word with you, if you don't mind."

Greyson nodded and followed the agent into a small office. She had the feeling she wasn't going to like what he had to say.

"I'm sorry to have to do this. I can't imagine what you've been through, but we have a development and we need your help."

"What kind of development?" Greyson asked.

Agent Piper cleared his throat. "We raided the prison. We have several men in custody and we were able to uncover a lot of information that is going to take a while to process. As I'm sure you understand, this is a time sensitive matter. We need the location of this death match you told us about if we're going to be able to intercept the other cells."

Greyson sat down in a leather chair, fatigue settling over her, making her feel weak. Her head hurt and her other injuries were becoming harder to ignore. "How can I help you with that? I've told you everything I know."

Agent Piper nodded. "One of the men we apprehended has proposed a deal."

Greyson frowned. "What kind of deal?"

"In exchange for leniency, he says he can give us the information we need, if he can talk to you first."

Greyson leaned forward. "Who?"

"We've identified him as Adam Polk Sr. He said you'd know him as Uncle Dan."

Greyson blew out her breath. "What does he want?"

The agent clenched his jaw. "No idea. I know this is unusual, and normally I wouldn't allow it, but there are lives at stake."

Greyson nodded. "I get it."

"An agent will be in the room with you at all times. It's up to you, Ms. Cooper."

Greyson swallowed. She didn't really have a choice. If there was any chance she might be able to save others and put a stop to this sick underground world, she would have to do it. She blew out her breath. "Okay, I'll do it."

Greyson was led into another small room. Uncle Dan sat at a table. His hands were cuffed and shackled to a ring in the floor. Greyson had a moment of satisfaction at the turn of fate. But there was no joy in any of this.

She sat in a chair across from the old man. He stared at her, appraising her the way he did that first day she'd come to in that dark cell. She rested her hands on her thighs, surprised by her own calm. "You asked for me?"

He shifted his head to the side, still assessing her. "I knew you were different from the start. I tried to tell him he had made a mistake with you."

Greyson lifted her eyebrows, surprised. "How so?"

"You were more than he bargained for. I've been waiting for you for a long time."

Greyson frowned, confused. "I don't understand."

His mustache bristled the way it did when he was about to tell her something important. "I knew a day would come when someone would challenge him, when someone would make it stop."

This made no sense at all. "But you were a part of it. You could have stopped it yourself. You even bet on the fights."

He nodded. "You were my special order. I had doubts about you, but you've turned out to be the fighter I was looking for after all."

Anger rose in Greyson making her skin burn as if her clothes were on fire. "You? You were the one? You were the Employer?"

He nodded. "He doesn't know that, of course. I couldn't let him know."

"Why?" Greyson's head was spinning from this news. She wasn't sure what she expected, but he had taken her by surprise. She had known he was playing her, just like she was playing him, but not this. She hadn't seen this one coming.

"After his mother...left us, I taught him everything I knew. Once he got a taste, he wanted bigger things. He wasn't happy with keeping the fights small—he had to have more. It started with an obsession with Elizabeth. They'd always been close, and her devotion to him was infectious. He wanted to replicate that with other women. He wanted to extend his family. He started collecting, and it became a game to him to play the women against one another. The power he felt from controlling others became his drug. I tolerated his games because he brought in good money."

Greyson leaned forward. "Are you saying the Recruiter is your son and Liz is your daughter? You started all this?"

He nodded. "Of course, I had no idea how far he would take it. His obsessions have corrupted everything."

"Where is he?" Greyson asked.

The old man smiled. "The last I saw him he was on his way to Nashville to finalize plans for the death match."

The old man gave Greyson and the agents all the information he had on the fight, where to find the Recruiter, and where the other cells were hidden. He never hesitated in answering any of their questions.

After what felt like hours of listening to him, Greyson was overwhelmed. "Why are you telling us all of this?"

"Things changed. Some of the men Adam involved have corrupted the mission."

"The bean counter?" Greyson guessed.

He nodded again. "I'm getting old. I'm a sick man. You were my last bet."

Greyson sighed. "You're crazy."

He leaned forward. "Maybe. Judge all you want. I got what I needed. They thought they could push me out because I'm old. We'll see who's in charge now."

Greyson shook her head and leaned back in her chair. She'd had enough. "Can I go now?" Greyson asked the agent next to her.

He nodded.

Greyson stood to leave. She had heard more than she would ever be able to process.

"You won't catch him," the old man said as Greyson reached for the door.

Greyson turned to face him. "What?"

"Adam is already gone. You won't find him until he's ready to find you."

Greyson's stomach twisted. The idea of the Recruiter being out there stalking her was more than she could handle. She threw the door open and pushed her way out of the room. Down the hall she turned on the agent.

"Is he right? Have you found him? Are we ever going to be safe?" she asked, her voice rising.

The agent met her gaze. "We're going to do everything we can to bring him in. We won't give up until we have him."

Greyson took a steadying breath. "This is never going to be over as long as he's out there. What are we supposed to do until you find him—hide away, lock ourselves in another prison?"

The agent looked uncomfortable. "He gave us a lot of information. We already have agents moving on it. We'll do everything we can."

"Well, I hope you're good at your job," Greyson said, feeling her freedom slipping through her fingers.

❖

Olivia took Greyson's hand, needing the comfort of her touch to handle the news. "What are we supposed to do now? It could take days or weeks before they catch him."

Greyson rested her hand against Olivia's thigh, gripping Olivia's hand in hers. "I don't know."

"I can't stand the thought of being locked up in some safe house or even my parents' house for weeks or even months, but I'm scared," Olivia admitted. "I'm afraid he'll be back. What if he hurts my family?"

Greyson sighed. Olivia could hear the frustration being pushed from her lungs. She knew Greyson didn't have the answers, but she had gotten used to turning to Greyson for strength.

"I'm sorry. I know this is hard for you too."

"Yeah. It's hard. It's hard not knowing what's going to happen next. It's hard not knowing how to keep you safe. It's hard feeling like he's still controlling my life," Greyson said, her voice a low growl. "He won't let this go. He'll be pissed that I messed everything up for him, and he's sick enough to think he owns you. How do you defend yourself against someone like that?"

Olivia shivered at the thought of the Recruiter. "Well, we know who he is now. It isn't like before when we didn't even know people like him existed. The police are looking for him and the guards have given up a lot of information. A lot of the places he would hide have been exposed."

Greyson nodded. "I know I need to give it time. You know, before all of this I never could have imagined taking someone's life. I fought that idea the whole time we were locked in that place. Now I find myself imagining what it would be like to kill him."

"Oh, Greyson."

"I'm serious. What does that say about me? Have I become exactly what he wanted?"

Olivia turned to Greyson. "You are nothing like him. Everything you have done has been to survive. You never chose any of this. It's normal to think things like that in this situation. I've even thought about it myself."

Greyson looked surprised. "Really?"

"Really," Olivia answered. "There were times when I was alone with him that I spent hours trying to figure out a way to do it. I have to believe that given a choice between his life and mine, I'd take his in a second."

Greyson frowned. "Do you think we'll feel any different when they catch him?"

Olivia shrugged. "I don't know. I think there are some things that are going to be changed forever. But I've seen you survive things I never could have imagined. I know you'll get through this too."

Greyson squeezed Olivia's hand. "I think it's good you'll have some time with your parents. They love you very much."

Olivia smiled. "Yeah, it's strange, but before all this, I hated the thought of staying there. I felt trapped by my mother's judgment and need to control my life. Now I know what real control is like. She never really meant me harm. We were so busy fighting, we weren't listening. I need to show her that I'm okay. I think once she knows I can be happy, she'll be happy too."

"Don't be surprised if she still holds on to those old ideas. It won't be easy for her."

Olivia nodded. "I know. I'll be patient." She smiled. "And persistent."

Greyson laughed.

A knock at the door made them both jump.

Greyson sighed. "I guess it's time to go." She pulled Olivia into a hug. "Remember, when this is over, you promised me a date."

Olivia smiled. "Don't forget me, Greyson Cooper."

"Never." Greyson kissed her, lingering against her lips,

savoring the closeness between them. Things were about to change, and she wasn't sure where they would land on the other side. "We'll talk soon."

Olivia nodded. "Okay. Stay safe."

Greyson nodded. She held Olivia's hand and walked her out. She watched as Olivia climbed into the back of the car and disappeared around the corner. Greyson felt like she had run out of air.

A horn blared and she looked up to see her Scrambler speeding through the parking lot. She smiled as the Jeep came to a stop and Dawn jumped out, running toward her.

Dawn threw her arms around Greyson in a bear hug. "Man, you are a sight for sore eyes."

Greyson returned the hug. "Sorry I worried you."

Dawn stepped back, looking Greyson over. "Damn, what happened to you? You look like you've gone a few rounds with Mike Tyson."

Greyson shrugged. "Something like that. Come on, I'll try to explain. How's my boat?"

Greyson was thankful when Dawn wrapped her arm around her shoulders. The contact was a comfort and helped settle some of the uncertainty clouding her life. She had people who loved her. She would get through this.

CHAPTER SEVENTEEN

The rhythmic sway of the houseboat soothed Greyson's nerves as she attempted to tame the persistent cowlick at the back of her hair. "Dammit!" She was going to be late.

Dawn laughed. "I never thought I'd see the day when Greyson Cooper would be nervous about a date."

Greyson scowled at her. "You're not helping."

Dawn shrugged. "That's what you get for not letting me tag along."

Greyson shook her head. "It's a date. I don't need a chaperone—I'm not twelve."

"You know what I mean," Dawn said as she slid down off the counter she had been perched on. "It still makes me nervous."

Greyson turned to her friend. She did understand. Dawn had done everything to try and find Greyson. She blamed herself for not being there with her. She still believed if she had been there, the Recruiter wouldn't have gotten to her. No matter how many times Greyson reassured her or explained how deranged the guy was, Dawn just couldn't believe it. Dawn had barely left Greyson's side since she returned home.

"You don't have to worry anymore. They got him. There are no more shadows to hide from. I'm safe." Greyson knew that just because the Recruiter was behind bars didn't mean the ordeal was over, but she could at least take a breath without fearing it would be her last.

Dawn sighed. "Thank God they got him. I don't think I've slept a single night since you disappeared. This has been one hell of a nightmare."

Greyson clasped her hand over Dawn's shoulder. "Thank you for staying with me. I know this hasn't been easy. I don't know what I would have done without you."

Dawn blushed. "So why don't you just let me drive you to town. I can hang out while you're on your date. You won't even know I'm there."

Greyson smiled. Dawn was a good friend. She was just trying to look out for her. "I promise to check in as soon as I arrive. You already know where I'll be. And I won't be alone—Olivia will be with me."

"Fine. But you better call me if you decide not to come home tonight. I swear I'll call the police if you don't."

Greyson laughed. "I promise." She checked her watch. "Shit, I'm going to be late." She gave her hair one last stroke of the comb, then gave up and bolted out the door. "Don't worry," she called to Dawn.

She hoped luck would be in her favor and traffic wouldn't be too bad on the way back into town. The sun was already low in the sky and a blazing sunset cast an orange glow across the water. She stopped on the dock and looked out across the lake, letting the warmth and the beauty kiss her skin and warm her heart. She blinked against the bright glare of the sun on the water and lifted her hand to shield her eyes. The open water made her feel safe, buffering her from the evil in the world.

Her phone buzzed, pulling her out of her spell, and she jerked it from her pocket. The message on her screen had her moving again.

Running late. I'll be at the restaurant in thirty minutes. Sorry.

Greyson picked up the pace. She would be lucky to get downtown in thirty minutes, let alone make it to the restaurant. She moved her fingers deftly over the keyboard and sent a reply.

She slammed the door to her Jeep and started the engine. She was halfway across the parking lot before remembering her seat belt. She ran her hand across her forehead to capture the sweat that trickled across her brow. She hadn't been this nervous about a date in years. Greyson laughed. She and Olivia had survived the unimaginable together. Why was she so nervous now?

She sighed. She knew the answer. They were about to test their connection in the real world. She had missed Olivia since they'd parted. It was as if her body ached on a cellular level to be reconnected with Olivia in some primal, instinctual way.

Greyson shook her head and scolded herself. She sounded like a lovesick teenager, but she didn't care. She had never been one to waste a moment of her life on doubt and insecurity. When she wanted something, she went for it with her whole heart and soul. That kind of intensity was sometimes too much for people, but she wasn't about to sacrifice her passion for conformity. She would rather be alone than temper the passion that fueled her life. She had been away from Olivia too long already.

Greyson jogged around the corner into Market Square and scanned the crowd. Not Watson's had its usual crowd and she could see a few people gathering outside on the patio. She slipped into the restaurant and made her way to the bar.

Olivia was nowhere in sight. Greyson's stomach tightened as the thread of doubt began to wind its way through her gut. Maybe Olivia had changed her mind. Greyson pulled out her phone to check the time. She was only a couple of minutes late and there were no new messages. She took a deep breath. This didn't look good.

She pushed aside the pang of disappointment and took a seat at the bar. There was no need to panic. Olivia had said she was running late. There was still time.

The bartender nodded to Greyson. "What will it be?"

"How about a dirty martini?"

The bartender cocked her head and appraised Greyson as she wiped invisible spots off a wineglass. "Let me guess, shaken, not stirred."

Greyson smiled. "Always."

The bartender winked. "Coming right up."

Greyson didn't miss the flirtation in the bartender's voice and she had to admit the woman was beautiful. She wore faded jeans and a black suit vest over a white T-shirt that hugged her biceps. Her black boots were shined to a mirror finish and a leather band adorned her left wrist, while an intricate tattoo of ground ivy snaked up her right forearm. At any other time this woman would have Greyson's undivided attention, but tonight her thoughts were elsewhere.

She drummed her fingers on the bar top and scanned the room, keeping an eye on the door. Her trepidation grew with each passing moment.

The bartender set a napkin on the bar in front of Greyson with *007* written in the corner. Moments later a frosty martini graced its center. She tapped the napkin with her index finger. "My name is Ashley. Let me know if I can get you anything else."

Greyson dipped her head in a nod of acknowledgment and smiled. "Thanks."

She lifted the glass to her lips and sipped, allowing the cold bite of vodka to fill her mouth as the salty bitter taste of olive brought her taste buds to life.

Greyson licked her lips savoring the flavor when someone slipped a hand along her back and around her waist.

"Looking for someone?" Olivia's soft voice whispered close to her ear.

Greyson lowered her head and peeked over her shoulder. Olivia smiled playfully back at her. The sense of relief and excitement that filled Greyson in that moment was more intoxicating than the drink in her hand. She turned slowly to face Olivia, dancing her gaze across Olivia's face, memorizing the glint of mischief in her glowing brown eyes, the fullness of her teasing lips, and the tantalizing curve of a faint line at the corner of her mouth.

"I was afraid you weren't coming," Greyson admitted.

Olivia's lips curved into a crooked grin as she played her fingers along Greyson's thigh. "I couldn't stay away. But I have to admit I indulged in a little voyeurism and watched you from across the room for a while."

Greyson was intrigued. "Really? Why?"

"I wanted to have a little distance between us so I could see who you really are when you don't know someone's watching, and when I'm not so flustered by you I can't think."

"Do I fluster you?" Greyson asked.

Olivia smiled. "Let's just say I'm not sure I've been thinking very clearly since we met."

Greyson stood and motioned for Olivia to take her chair. As Olivia settled into the seat, Greyson tucked a strand of hair behind Olivia's ear. The pixie cut was a lot shorter than Olivia had worn it before. "You cut your hair."

Olivia smiled. "I decided I needed something new. Do you like it?"

"You look beautiful. It suits you." Greyson said. "I like how it frames your face. Your eyes even seem brighter."

Olivia blushed. "Thank you."

Greyson sipped her drink. "So what did you learn while you were spying on me?"

Olivia pursed her lips in a playful smirk. "Hmm. I think I'll keep that to myself for now. Let's just say it left no question where I want to be right now."

Greyson tried to stay calm, but the hungry look in Olivia's eyes, the closeness of her body, and her willingness to admit what she was feeling were driving Greyson crazy. Her pulse danced in her neck as her heart raced, and her palms began to sweat.

"I'm glad you feel that way," Greyson said, taking another sip of her martini to cool herself down.

Olivia slid her fingers around the stem of Greyson's glass and slipped it from her hand. She watched Greyson over the rim of the glass as she sipped the drink.

"Would you like more?" Greyson asked, taking the now empty glass from Olivia's hand and placing it on the bar.

"Oh yes, I would like that very much," Olivia teased.

Greyson smiled and licked her lips as she stared at Olivia's mouth, imagining the taste of her lips. She turned and nodded to the bartender, raising two fingers. The bartender smiled and gave a knowing nod.

❖

Olivia snaked her hand up and down Greyson's arm. Greyson was an intriguing woman. With her body and good looks, she could clearly have anyone in the room if she desired. But Greyson didn't come off like someone who played on the vulnerability of others, or someone who used her looks to seduce women. Greyson was a woman totally and completely comfortable with who she was, and her confidence made her alluring without an air of arrogance.

Olivia looked around the room and found more than one woman eyeing Greyson's every move. She could see their appreciative stares and hungry gazes undress and devour Greyson in fantasies that danced in their eyes. She understood that hunger. She had filled her days sequestered at her parents' farm thinking of Greyson, imagining the two of them together.

The bartender set two fresh martinis on the bar in front of Greyson and winked.

"Thanks," Greyson said without the slightest acknowledgment of the flirtation.

Olivia took the glass Greyson offered her. She watched as Greyson's lips closed around the rim of her glass and sucked in the tart liquor. Olivia shuddered as her body responded as if Greyson's lips had graced her skin. She liked the way Greyson seemed to caress her with her eyes and how she could see the rhythm of Greyson's heartbeat in the artery in her neck.

"Do you have any idea the effect you're having on the women in this room right now?" Olivia asked.

Greyson looked momentarily confused and glanced curiously around her. When she returned her gaze to Olivia, she was calm and seemingly unaffected, but her eyes bored into Olivia, penetrating the last barriers between them.

Greyson leaned close, allowing her lips to brush Olivia's ear. "Right now, I'm only interested in you, and how I make *you* feel."

Olivia felt the heat rise in her cheeks. "Good answer."

Greyson smiled. "If you like, we could go somewhere else."

Olivia had the sudden image of them back at her apartment only a block away and quickly decided it was time to slow things down. "Uh, I'm okay here, for now."

Greyson took Olivia's hand and gave it a little squeeze. "I meant we could get a table or go for a walk, or find another place that isn't so crowded."

"Oh." Olivia was embarrassed by her presumption and the fact that Greyson had called her on it. But she was also touched that Greyson was concerned about her feelings. "This is fine, really. I like it here. Besides, we'll never get a table with this wait." Olivia laced her fingers through Greyson's. "I kind of like the way this is working out."

A pager on the bar lit up and began vibrating, and the couple next to Greyson left to find their table. Greyson took the seat next to Olivia. She slid her arm around the back of Olivia's chair and leaned close. She could smell Olivia's perfume winding its tantalizing fragrance around her senses like a mountain breeze. Orange blossoms and mint teased her until she was only inches away from brushing her lips over Olivia's hair.

"You smell wonderful."

Olivia turned her head, and her cheek brushed Greyson's lips before she could pull away. Greyson wanted to taste those lips. She wanted to fall into the warm promise of Olivia's smile and claim her mouth.

"Hey, how about another drink?" the bartender asked.

Greyson pulled away and turned back to the bar. "Maybe we could see a menu, and how about some water? Thanks, Ashley." Greyson was grateful for the interruption and a chance to get herself together. She had been about to kiss Olivia, and she wasn't so sure it was the time or the place. Olivia was special. Greyson didn't want to disrespect her by coming off like she was trying to get her into bed.

"Are you hungry?" Greyson asked.

Olivia bit her lip and stared into Greyson's eyes. She smiled mischievously. "Starved."

Greyson swallowed, trying to keep her pounding heart from beating its way out of her chest. Olivia's flirtations had her wishing for a little more privacy.

❖

Olivia couldn't remember the last time she'd had so much fun. She had spent weeks with Greyson in captivity and thought she knew the woman to whom she owed her life. But Greyson continued to surprise her. She was attentive and playful, not at all the brooding, defiant woman Olivia had thought she had known.

Greyson opened the door and waited for Olivia to pass through. Olivia wasn't used to being treated this way. Greyson wasn't like the women she usually dated, who were more like herself—slightly feminine, independent, and unassuming in a way that didn't play to gender roles. But Greyson was the perfect butch. The change was refreshing and exciting.

Olivia slipped her hand into the bend of Greyson's arm as they walked through Crutch Park. "I know this park isn't much, but I love walking through here at night. There's something magical about how it's tucked away right in the middle of everything. The twinkle lights are my favorite part."

Greyson pulled her arm against her side, trapping Olivia's hand against her body. "I mostly come through here during the day. I used to have lunch here most days that I was in the office. But I can't ever recall being here at night."

Olivia sighed. "It's hard to believe we were so close to meeting so many times, and when we finally did—"

"You hated me," Greyson interrupted, keeping Olivia from bringing up the Recruiter.

Olivia laughed. "Hate may be a little strong."

Greyson raised her eyebrows showing her doubt.

"Well, I was stressed," Olivia countered.

"It turned out to be my lucky day. Until tonight it was my favorite first date," Greyson said fondly.

Olivia closed her other hand around Greyson's arm leaning against her. "Maybe tonight's your lucky night."

Greyson smiled. "I think it already is."

Olivia felt heat rise in her cheeks and was thankful for the fading light.

Greyson stopped by a park bench and motioned for Olivia to sit before taking her own seat.

"How are your parents?" Greyson asked.

Olivia smiled. "Good. I wasn't sure they were ever going to let me out of their sight again. It was good to have time with them. I couldn't explain everything. I couldn't put them through it. I imagine they'll hear enough at the trial, if there ever is one."

Greyson rubbed her fingers across Olivia's hand. "Maybe they need to know. It'll help them understand you better."

Olivia looked up at the stars. "I told them all about you."

"Really?" Greyson said, surprised.

"Of course." Olivia looked back at Greyson. "How could I not? You seem to be woven into every moment I was there."

Greyson nodded. "Yeah, I know." She sighed. "It's been weird being home. Sometimes I feel like it was all a bad dream. Like my brain is trying to reject it all."

"I don't want to forget," Olivia said. "What happened to us was unimaginable, but we know it happens all the time. How many others are there out there? Everything's different now. I'm different."

Greyson looked sad.

"Don't worry, I'm okay," Olivia reassured her. "I always felt like my life had purpose and I had good goals, ideas about what I wanted my life to be like. But now, that doesn't seem like enough."

Greyson nodded. "What are you going to do?"

Olivia shrugged. "I may go to law school."

Greyson smiled. "That's great."

Olivia studied Greyson, unable to read her emotions. "I'm sorry I keep talking about it. Here you are, telling me you just want to forget everything, and I keep bringing it up."

"I don't want to forget," Greyson corrected. "I'm just having some trouble compartmentalizing everything. I don't know how to step back into my daily life. I don't want people to be afraid to talk to me. I don't want their looks of sympathy."

"Then don't show them the victim, show them the survivor," Olivia countered. "How have your friends been since you've been back?"

Greyson smiled. "Dawn is still staying at my place. I think she's afraid I'll disappear again if she lets me out of her sight. I didn't think she was going to let me come alone tonight."

Olivia laughed. "She loves you."

Greyson nodded. "She's a good friend. She was really scared. This whole thing has done a number on her too."

"Yeah, I know what you mean. I'm surprised James hasn't called already. He even came to my parents' house to see me, and I thought nothing could make him do that."

Greyson brushed her fingers along Olivia's cheek. "I've missed you."

Olivia took Greyson's hand in hers and held it in her lap. "Me too." She leaned forward and touched her lips lightly against Greyson's. "I have a feeling there isn't enough time left in the world for me to get enough of you."

"I hope that's true." Greyson pressed a kiss to Olivia's cheek. Her skin was buttery smooth against Greyson's lips. Greyson wanted to memorize everything about Olivia's face so she could picture her in her mind every day.

Greyson slipped her arm around Olivia, pulling her closer until she could feel Olivia's breath on her skin. She kissed her. She kissed her with tender touches of her lips, like the sun coaxing open a flower. She kept her touch gentle, but with each passing moment she wanted more. She wanted her, all of her. That one kiss was enough to confirm everything she had already known. Olivia was someone she could surrender to. Someone she could dare to love.

Greyson broke the kiss, her breath shattered and her heart thundering.

Olivia's cheeks were pink under the glow of the streetlamp and her lips were full and swollen from the kiss. Greyson wanted to claim them again and lose herself in the sweet heat of Olivia's mouth.

Olivia placed her hand on Greyson's chest and pushed, creating space between them.

"You're getting pretty hot for a first date," Olivia said with a hint of uncertainty in her voice.

Greyson smiled. "I don't want to waste any time."

"How do you know this is real between us," Olivia asked, voicing the fear Greyson had been pondering too. "I'm afraid when we manage to get our lives back together you'll realize we don't really fit."

"We fit," Greyson insisted. "I feel it every time I look at you. I felt it every night I held you in my arms to keep you safe. I felt it every time anyone threatened you. I felt it the moment I realized I was willing to give my life for you."

"Greyson," Olivia whispered.

Greyson pressed her lips to Olivia's cheek. "Why did you come back for me? Why didn't you just run?"

Olivia sucked in her breath. "I couldn't leave you."

"Why?" Greyson persisted.

Olivia closed her eyes and pulled away. She looked around the park, her eyes unfocused as if she didn't really see what was in front of her. She sighed and stood.

Greyson watched the subtle changes in Olivia's face as she struggled with her feelings.

"Olivia?" Greyson coaxed, drawing Olivia back to her.

Olivia looked at Greyson and smiled as if she'd just made up her mind. She held out her hand to Greyson. "Walk me home."

Greyson took her hand.

They walked in silence for a while.

Olivia said, "What now? How do we put the pieces of our lives back together again?"

Greyson squeezed Olivia's hand. "I think I need to go back to where I left off. I started something and I need to finish it. I can't let him take that from me."

"You're going back to the trail?"

Greyson nodded. "I was free there. There's nothing like laying your head down at night and looking up at the stars, listening to the pure night. The air is fresh and rich with the earthy scent of the forest. There are no walls and no locks to cage me."

"Your descriptions of the mountains got me through a lot of nights. I can see why you want to go back. It sounds beautiful."

"It is." Greyson paused. "There's just one thing I need to do different this time."

Olivia looked at her, the question visible in her eyes. "What?"

"You. I want you to come with me."

Olivia gasped. "Are you serious?"

Greyson nodded. "Whatever I do, wherever I go, I can't imagine any of it without you."

Olivia pulled them to a stop outside her door. "This is me. Will you come in?"

"If that's what you want." Greyson smiled.

Olivia entered the code into the keypad on the wall. They heard the *snick* of the lock and Greyson opened the door, allowing Olivia to lead the way. Another keypad awaited outside Olivia's door. Greyson waited as Olivia's fingers danced deftly over the surface.

The room was white, with a blue sofa set in the middle of the room facing the window. The space was simple and clean. It suited Olivia.

Olivia turned to Greyson, wrapping her arms around her neck. She kissed her, trailing her lips down Greyson's neck. She brushed her fingers down the front of Greyson's shirt and slowly began to undo the buttons. She tugged the shirt loose from Greyson's trousers, pulling the fabric open, exposing Greyson's chest. She brushed a kiss against Greyson's chest as she guided Greyson to the sofa, pushing her into the soft cushions. Olivia kicked off her shoes and climbed onto Greyson's lap, straddling her.

Greyson's hands were soft as she ran her fingers up Olivia's back. Olivia almost whimpered at the warm touch of Greyson's skin. She had dreamed of Greyson for weeks. She had endured night after night of lying in Greyson's arms, unable to really touch her. She didn't want to wait any longer.

The kisses grew fevered until Olivia was certain her skin would erupt in flames, her desire rising to an all-consuming need.

Greyson slid her hand beneath Olivia's blouse, cupping her breast in her hand. She groaned as Olivia claimed her mouth with passionate sweeps of her tongue. She rocked forward trying to press more of her body against Olivia, needing more of her. The energy between them reaching the point of no return.

"I need you," Olivia whispered.

Greyson took Olivia's hand. "Take me to your bedroom."

Olivia slid off Greyson's lap, grasping her hand.

Greyson followed Olivia, silently watching the sway of her body as she moved.

Next to the bed, Greyson stepped close, slipping her hands beneath the hem of Olivia's shirt. She pulled the blouse up, over Olivia's head, letting it fall to the floor. She brushed her fingers down the ridges of barely healed scars along Olivia's back.

Olivia shuddered under her touch.

She turned Olivia to face her, wrapping her fingers around the fragile lace covering Olivia's breasts, brushing a hard nipple with her thumb. She touched a kiss against Olivia's lips before moving to claim her breast in her mouth.

Olivia arched her back, her breath coming in short gasps. Greyson wrapped her arms around Olivia, lifting her onto the bed.

Olivia pushed at Greyson's shirt until Greyson sat up and pulled it off, throwing it across the room. Greyson smiled down at her as she crossed her arms and pulled the undershirt over her head, exposing her small round breasts. Olivia smiled, reveling in the sight of taut muscles shrouded in soft, delicate skin.

Olivia wrapped her fingers around Greyson's belt, pulling the leather free before moving to undo the button of her jeans. She ran her hands across Greyson's stomach, feeling the muscles bunch beneath her hands. Greyson slid off the bed, shedding her jeans. She wasn't wearing underwear.

Olivia was certain she would orgasm the moment Greyson touched her. She couldn't wait. "Come here," she whispered.

Greyson smiled as she slid Olivia's pants over her hips, adding them to the growing pile on the floor. Greyson kissed her way up Olivia's body, letting her tongue linger on her breasts, before returning to claim her mouth.

Olivia whimpered as Greyson lowered her body against her, allowing their skin to touch for the first time. Olivia felt like she had never been touched before and was discovering things about her own needs she had never known.

They moved their bodies in unison as they rocked against each other, hands exploring, grasping, mouths tasting, sucking.

Olivia gasped as Greyson slid her hand between her legs, the brush of her fingers pushing her dangerously close to the edge. She groaned. "*Yes.*"

Greyson filled her with one stroke of her hand, then another, and another until Olivia was soaring. Her body hummed with pleasure rippling through her like electricity coursing through a wire. She was on the edge, but Greyson kept taking her higher until she could hold on no more. She arched her back, groaning in pleasure. The instant she fell back against the bed, Greyson's mouth was on her, sucking her back to oblivion.

Olivia couldn't stop. She couldn't get enough of Greyson. She reached for Greyson, pulling her up to taste her lips. She slid her hand between Greyson's thighs until she parted her wet folds. Olivia looked up into Greyson's eyes. Greyson peered down at her, her body tense and trembling beneath Olivia's touch. Olivia felt the bond grow between them with each stroke of her fingers, each shudder in Greyson's breath.

"Olivia." Greyson's voice was both pleading and open.

Olivia pulled Greyson's lips to hers and kissed her, filling her mouth and her body. Greyson shuddered against her as her orgasm exploded, waves of energy crashing through her like waves upon the shore. Greyson lay against Olivia, her breath warm against her breast. Olivia drew her fingers through Greyson's hair, cradling her head in her hand, thankful to have her in her arms.

❖

Greyson lay next to Olivia, studying the way her eyelashes curled against her cheeks as she slept. They had made love through the night, desperately holding on to one another. Greyson had given herself to Olivia completely, holding nothing back. That time in her life was over. She would never deny herself what Olivia offered.

Sunlight began to filter into the room, filling it with a warm glow. Greyson watched a beam of light filter through the window to shine on Olivia's milky white skin, making her look almost ethereal. Olivia twitched in her sleep, and Greyson wondered what she was dreaming. She had held Olivia night after night in that dark place, shielding her from the evil around them. She knew the safety she had offered wasn't real, but the comfort they'd found in each other had made their hell more bearable.

Holding Olivia now was different. She felt as if a part of her soul had been restored. The soft, even rise and fall of Olivia's chest with each breath was testament to her resilience, her innocent belief in the good in the world. Greyson needed that reminder so she wouldn't become lost in the horrors of her fear.

Olivia shifted, opening her eyes to find Greyson watching her. She smiled. "Who's spying now?" she teased.

Greyson smiled. "Good morning."

"Good morning," Olivia replied. "How long have you been awake?"

Greyson smoothed her fingers over Olivia's lips. "A while. I've enjoyed watching you sleep."

"Did you get any rest at all?" Olivia asked, worry beginning to crease her brow. "It was really late when we finally went to sleep."

Greyson kissed her lightly on the lips. "I'm fine."

Olivia smiled. "Okay. I'll stop dithering." She slid closer to Greyson, laying her head on Greyson's shoulder. She sighed as Greyson wrapped her comforting arms around her.

"Can I ask you a question?" Olivia asked, thinking of their conversation the night before.

"Of course," Greyson answered.

"Why do you need to go back? What do you think you'll find on the trail?"

Greyson hesitated. "Like I said, I want to finish what I started."

"But there's more, isn't there?" Olivia coaxed.

Greyson nodded. "When we were in that place, I kept having these dreams of being on the trail. There was this old woman, Lucile, who kept visiting me. She gave me warnings, advice. I felt like she was watching over me. I guess I want to go see if she's out there."

Olivia frowned. "Have you dreamed about her since we got out?"

Greyson nodded. "Once. I feel like she wants me to come. I know that sounds weird, but it's just something I need to do." She peered down at Olivia. "Will you come with me?"

Olivia pulled Greyson tighter against her and brushed a kiss against her cheek. "I would follow you anywhere, Greyson Cooper."

Greyson smiled. "Can I tell you something?"

Olivia looked up at her. "Anything."

Greyson stared at her a moment, gathering her courage. "I love you."

Olivia's eyes widened.

Greyson swallowed. "I know that's a bit heavy for the second first date and everything, but I didn't want another day to slip by without telling you. I hope that doesn't change your mind."

Olivia smiled. "I'll never change my mind about you." She pulled Greyson's head down and kissed her. "I was so afraid of losing you in that place that I was afraid to allow myself to feel, but the truth is, I've loved you for a while now. So much, I haven't been able to think or talk about anything else since I got home."

"Really?" Greyson asked, trying to hide her smile.

Olivia nodded. "Yes, really. I love you." She kissed Greyson again.

Greyson groaned against her mouth.

Olivia sat up, pulling the covers around herself. "What would you like to do today? Or do you need to get back to your place?"

"Well, I thought we could go to my place together. I'd like you to see my boat."

"Hmm," Olivia purred. "I'd like that."

"Good, but first I would like to take you to breakfast."

"Breakfast, huh?"

Greyson shrugged. "It sounds like the perfect beginning, don't you think?"

Olivia smiled. "Perfect."

About the Author

Donna K. Ford is a Licensed Professional Counselor who spends her professional time assisting people in their recovery from substance addictions. She holds an associate's degree in criminal justice, a BS in psychology, and an MS in community agency counseling. When not trying to save the world, she spends her time in the mountains of East Tennessee enjoying the lakes, rivers, and hiking trails near her home.

Reading, writing, and enjoying conversation with good friends are the gifts that keep her grounded. Her book *Love's Redemption* was a 2016 Foreword INDIES finalist.

Books Available From Bold Strokes Books

Captive by Donna K. Ford. To escape a human trafficking ring, Greyson Cooper and Olivia Danner become players in a game of deceit and violence. Will their love stand a chance? (978-1-63555-215-7)

Crossing the Line by CF Frizzell. The Mob discovers a nemesis within its ranks, and in the ultimate retaliation, draws Stick McLaughlin from anonymity by threatening everything she holds dear. (978-1-63555-161-7)

Love's Verdict by Carsen Taite. Attorneys Landon Holt and Carly Pachett want the exact same thing: the only open partnership spot at their prestigious criminal defense firm. But will they compromise their careers for love? (978-1-63555-042-9)

Precipice of Doubt by Mardi Alexander & Laurie Eichler. Can Cole Jameson resist her attraction to her boss, veterinarian Jodi Bowman, or will she risk a workplace romance and her heart? (978-1-63555-128-0)

Savage Horizons by CJ Birch. Captain Jordan Kellow's feelings for Lt. Ali Ash have her past and future colliding, setting in motion a series of events that strands her crew in an unknown galaxy thousands of light years from home. (978-1-63555-250-8)

Secrets of the Last Castle by A. Rose Mathieu. When Elizabeth Campbell represents a young man accused of murdering an elderly woman, her investigation leads to an abandoned plantation that reveals many dark Southern secrets. (978-1-63555-240-9)

Take Your Time by VK Powell. A neurotic parrot brings police officer Grace Booker and temporary veterinarian Dr. Dani Wingate together in the tiny town of Pine Cone, but their unexpected attraction keeps the sparks flying. (978-1-63555-130-3)

The Last Seduction by Ronica Black. When you allow true love to elude you once and you desperately regret it, are you brave enough to grab it when it comes around again? (978-1-63555-211-9)

The Shape of You by Georgia Beers. Rebecca McCall doesn't play it safe, but when sexy Spencer Thompson joins her workout class, their nonstop sparring forces her to face her ultimate challenge—a chance at love. (978-1-63555-217-1)

Exposed by MJ Williamz. The closet is no place to live if you want to find true love. (978-1-62639-989-1)

Force of Fire: Toujours a Vous by Ali Vali. Immortals Kendal and Piper welcome their new child and celebrate the defeat of an old enemy, but another ancient evil is about to awaken deep in the jungles of Costa Rica. (978-1-63555-047-4)

Landing Zone by Erin Dutton. Can a career veteran finally discover a love stronger than even her pride? (978-1-63555-199-0)

Love at Last Call by M. Ullrich. Is balancing business, friendship, and love more than any willing woman can handle? (978-1-63555-197-6)

Pleasure Cruise by Yolanda Wallace. Spencer Collins and Amy Donovan have few things in common, but a Caribbean cruise offers both women an unexpected chance to face one of their greatest fears: falling in love. (978-1-63555-219-5)

Running Off Radar by MB Austin. Maji's plans to win Rose back are interrupted when work intrudes, and duty calls her to help a SEAL team stop a Russian mobster from harvesting gold from the bottom of Sitka Sound. (978-1-63555-152-5)

Shadow of the Phoenix by Rebecca Harwell. In the final battle for the fate of Storm's Quarry, even Nadya's and Shay's powers may not be enough. (978-1-63555-181-5)

Take a Chance by D. Jackson Leigh. There's hardly a woman within fifty miles of Pine Cone that veterinarian Trip Beaumont can't charm, except for the irritating new cop, Jamie Grant, who keeps leaving parking tickets on her truck. (978-1-63555-118-1)

Death in Time by Robyn Nyx. Working in the past is hell on your future. (978-1-63555-053-5)

The Outcasts by Alexa Black. Spacebus driver Sue Jones is running from her past. When she crash-lands on a faraway world, the Outcast Kara might be her chance for redemption. (978-1-63555-242-3)

Alias by Cari Hunter. A car crash leaves a woman with no memory and no identity. Together with Detective Bronwen Pryce, she fights to uncover a truth that might just kill them both. (978-1-63555-221-8)

Hers to Protect by Nicole Disney. Ex–high school sweethearts Kaia and Adrienne will have to see past their differences and survive the vengeance of a brutal gang if they want to be together. (978-1-63555-229-4)

Perfect Little Worlds by Clifford Mae Henderson. Lucy can't hold the secret any longer. Twenty-six years ago, her sister did the unthinkable. (978-1-63555-164-8)

Room Service by Fiona Riley. Interior designer Olivia likes stability, but when work brings footloose Savannah into her world and into a new city every month, Olivia must decide if what makes her comfortable is what makes her happy. (978-1-63555-120-4)

Sparks Like Ours by Melissa Brayden. Professional surfers Gia Malone and Elle Britton can't deny their chemistry on and off the beach. But only one can win… (978-1-63555-016-0)

Take My Hand by Missouri Vaun. River Hemsworth arrives in Georgia intent on escaping quickly, but when she crashes her Mercedes into the Clip 'n Curl, sexy Clay Cahill ends up rescuing more than her car. (978-1-63555-104-4)

The Last Time I Saw Her by Kathleen Knowles. Lane Hudson only has twelve days to win back Alison's heart. That is, if she can gather the courage to try. (978-1-63555-067-2)

Wayworn Lovers by Gun Brooke. Will agoraphobic composer Giselle Bonnaire and Tierney Edwards, a wandering soul who can't remain in one place for long, trust in the passionate love destiny hands them? (978-1-62639-995-2)